BY THE AUTHOR OF
CHESS RUMBLE

SURF MULES

SURF MULES

G. NERI

G. P. PUTNAM'S SONS

G. P. PUTNAM'S SONS
A division of Penguin Young Readers Group.
Published by The Penguin Group.
Penguin Group (USA) Inc., 375 Hudson Street, New York, NY 10014, U.S.A.
Penguin Group (Canada), 90 Eglinton Avenue East, Suite 700, Toronto, Ontario M4P 2Y3, Canada
(a division of Pearson Penguin Canada Inc.).
Penguin Books Ltd, 80 Strand, London WC2R 0RL, England.
Penguin Ireland, 25 St. Stephen's Green, Dublin 2, Ireland (a division of Penguin Books Ltd.).
Penguin Group (Australia), 250 Camberwell Road, Camberwell, Victoria 3124, Australia
(a division of Pearson Australia Group Pty Ltd).
Penguin Books India Pvt Ltd, 11 Community Centre, Panchsheel Park,
New Delhi - 110 017, India.
Penguin Group (NZ), 67 Apollo Drive, Rosedale, North Shore 0632, New Zealand
(a division of Pearson New Zealand Ltd).
Penguin Books (South Africa) (Pty) Ltd, 24 Sturdee Avenue, Rosebank,
Johannesburg 2196, South Africa.
Penguin Books Ltd, Registered Offices: 80 Strand, London WC2R 0RL, England.

Published simultaneously in Canada.
Printed in the United States of America.
Design by Marikka Tamura.
Text set in Janson.
Library of Congress Cataloging-in-Publication Data
Neri, Greg. Surf mules / by Greg Neri. p. cm.
Summary: When a tragic accident and sudden financial woes cause recent high school graduate
Logan to question plans for his future, he agrees to make a road trip with his best friend and surfing
buddy, Z-boy, transporting marijuana from southern California to Orlando, Florida.
[1. Coming of age—Fiction. 2. Surfing—Fiction. 3. Automobile travel—Fiction.
4. Drug couriers—Fiction. 5. Death—Fiction. 6. Friendship—Fiction.] I. Title.
PZ7.N4377478Sur 2009 [Fic]—dc22 2008026144
ISBN 978-0-399-25086-6
1 3 5 7 9 10 8 6 4 2

D.

Thanks for taking me along for the ride.

"If you find the perfect wave, you can ride it forever."
—Buddy "Shredder" Hamilton,
Hermosa Beach surf legend

"You can't go home again, even if you live there."
—Logan Tom's mom

"**DUDE, CHECK IT** out. *Surfers!*" Z-boy shouted as they sped down Interstate 10. Logan glanced over at the beat-up Jeep top-loaded with surfboards. They were a motley crew of shirtless sunburnt cowboys—Ray-Bans and hillbilly tattoos. Logan wondered what they were doing out here in the middle of Nowhere, Texas. Then he noticed the bumper sticker: SURF NAZIS KICK ASS.

Logan pressed on the gas and sped up a bit. "Let's keep going."

"Come on, man. When are we ever gonna get to talk to Texas surfers? That's kind of like . . . running into Bigfoot or something. Hey, they're even wearing cowboy hats!" Z-boy said. "Yeehaw!"

Z-boy leaned out the window, his blond crew cut ruffling in the wind. He flashed the back of his fist with his thumb and pinkie finger extended—the universal surfer hand gesture. "Shock 'em, brah!"

The driver of the Jeep, a big chiseled ape of a guy, looked over, baffled. He nudged his squirrelly tattooed friend next to him, who pointed at Z-boy and laughed.

Logan would have laughed too if he had seen what they saw: two clean-cut high school students a thousand miles from home, dressed like Republicans in suits and ties, for Christ's sake.

"They're laughing at us, Z," Logan said.

Z-boy howled, "We're surfers too. Hermosa Beach *rules!*"

The driver flipped off Z-boy. Z stuck his head back in the car. "What's up with that?" he asked Logan.

Logan glanced at Z-boy's polyester suit and close-cropped hair. "Uh, you don't really look like a surfer anymore, Z."

Z-boy looked down at his clothes. "We're on business!" he shouted out the window. He rolled up his sleeve and pointed at the SURF OR DIE tattoo on his arm. "Dude!"

"Posers!" the chiseled guy spit, as the Jeep veered off to an empty exit ramp.

It should have ended right there, Logan thought later. They could have gone on their way, stayed on schedule, made the drop-off point. But stupid Z-boy couldn't handle the rejection and reached over and grabbed the steering wheel, swerving the car toward the off-ramp.

"Are you crazy!?" Logan yelled. "We're supposed to be pros, remember?"

"We're not gonna be dissed by some Texas yahoos . . ."

But as soon as they hit the off-ramp, Logan knew there was going to be trouble. The Jeep had stopped in the middle of the exit, blocking the road. The Surf Nazis hopped out and quickly surrounded the car.

The engine was still running. Logan could have made a break for it—but the squirrelly guy reached through Logan's open window and pulled out the ignition key. "Don't get any ideas, boy. You in Texas now." He put the key in the pocket of his thrift-store shirt, which sported a name tag that read BRAD.

Logan started to sweat. "Maybe we can work something out here."

A white light blinded Logan. His face felt numb from the punch. Then he tasted the blood on his lip.

"What the fuck?!" Logan yelled.

Z-boy was riled up. "Nobody hits my friend . . . ," he hissed.

Brad got in the backseat and held out the keys. "I just did. Now move over and drive this heap under the bridge over there."

Logan held his nose. His hand had blood on it. "What the fuck do you want?!"

Brad sneered, "What do we want? Everything you got. What're you gonna do, call the cops?"

Logan could see Z-boy figuring the odds in his brain. There were three of them, so Z-boy was in no position to play hero. Even if losing the car meant they'd have a price on their heads.

Z-boy sighed and got out. Logan slid painfully over into the passenger seat, his bloody nose throbbing with every move.

Z-boy got into the driver's side and just sat there. "You're violating the code."

Brad sat up. "The code? What code is that?!" he asked.

"The surfer's code."

The dude was getting pissed. "There is no freakin' surfer code!" he yelled.

Logan glanced at Z-boy out of the corner of his eye and saw Z-boy mouth *Hold on*. When Z-boy put on his seat belt, Logan did too.

Z-boy gunned it, the car peeling out past the Nazis' parked Jeep. Brad flew against the backseat. "What the hell're you doing?!" he screamed.

Logan checked the speedometer. They were heading past ninety. Then he checked the side-view mirror as they shot back onto the interstate. The Jeep was right on their tail. "Shit. They're chasing us!"

Logan watched hopelessly as the Jeep made up lost ground and suddenly, they were right next to him, casting glares that meant they were dead meat.

Logan turned away. If he was going to die, he didn't want to see it coming.

Instead, he saw something else. A sign for a rest stop one mile ahead. A highway patrol car parked next to it with a speed gun.

And Z-boy speeding *up*.

"Z, what're you doing?!" Logan yelled.

"Getting us out of this mess," he said, ratcheting up the speed past one hundred.

The highway patrol's red and yellow lights flashed behind them, the siren blared in Logan's ears, and Brad was yelling like a madman. Logan slunk down in his seat and shut his eyes tight.

He wondered how, two days after graduating high school with honors, he was being chased by cops and a group of redneck Surf Nazis, in a car that wasn't theirs, loaded to the gills with one hundred pounds of pot. *How the hell had that happened?*

All he could remember was this: it had all started with the Perfect Monster Wave.

1

THE WAVE CAME crashing down, a giant wall of white water barreling toward Logan Tom. He sucked in his breath, pushing down hard on the front of his board with all his weight. He dove deep beneath the white water seconds before it swallowed him whole.

As the currents fought to rip Logan from his board, a strange calm settled his pounding heart. Surrounded by the whiteness of the churning surf overhead, he wondered what it'd be like if he could stay down there forever. He could forget about graduation. Forget about leaving the only life he'd ever known behind. Forget his deadbeat dad, his mom working two shifts, the fight with Fin at the prom. He could just chill out in the deep murky green of the Pacific with some mermaid honeys, getting high on killer seaweed bud. Z-boy could supply him with a steady stream of pepperoni mini-pizzas, and at night, they could surf the glassy waves by the light of the moon. That would be the life . . .

He shot up to the top, blasting out into a roar of unruly surf. Then he remembered why he was out there. He needed to feel alive again. He needed to ride a Perfect Monster Wave.

"*Goddamn!* That's what I'm talking about!" he shouted, wiping the dark, tangled mane away from his eyes. Logan grinned at the set of massive waves lining up before them. They were way bigger than they'd ever surfed before, that's for sure. And they kept coming, one after another.

Z-boy flung back his bleached-blond dreads as he forged ahead. "Perfect Monster Waves, brah! Just what the doctor ordered!" His real name was Zane, but he called himself Z-boy after that crazy Dogtown Zephyr Boys surf team, which he totally idolized. Now he was trying to live up to that gonzo reputation.

"Hell, yeah. Bring it on!" Logan laughed as he headed into the surf. These were real beasts, two to three times his height, thick and explosive. He'd heard that when the fearless big wave rider Manoa Drollet rode his Perfect Monster Wave, his whole life crystallized before him and he suddenly realized his purpose in life. Playing with death will do that to you, he thought as he shot up over the top of the final mammoth wave of the set.

Logan and Z-boy fought their way through a rolling sea of thick snapping foam to the lineup, where maybe fifteen hardcore locals were waiting for the next waves. He had only a minute to catch his breath before he felt the water slowly pulling him out to sea.

"Goddamn, check it out, Z . . . ," Logan said in awe as a massive wave rose from the deep waters of the bay, blocking out the horizon. It was so far out that it would've been impossible for them to catch it.

Z-boy pointed to the small figure shooting across the face of the monster. "Shit, Fin got it," said Z-boy.

Riding the beast was Fin Hamilton, the hott[...] old surfer in Southern California. Wearing his tr[...] trunks and his newly shaved head, Fin fearlessly [...] monster curl, riding it like a true big wave rider. He di[...] deep into the tube that surrounded him as the other [...] whooped and hollered at his triumph.

But suddenly, they went silent when the wave closed out o[...] Fin with a huge *THWOMP!* Logan was the only one grinning. He hoped that one hurt.

"Bastard. See, karma pays." He knew that wave would hold Fin down for a while. At least that was some form of payback.

Logan and the others scrambled and dove under the wave's oncoming white water. When they emerged on the other side, Z-boy shook his head at Logan. "Dude, you can't hold a grudge forever."

"It's only been a month. Can't I hate the guy at least that long?" Logan huffed. He gazed at the horizon, anticipating the next wave.

Z-boy paddled past him. "I think you're jealous."

Logan shot a look at Z-boy. "Of Fin Hamilton?"

"Yeah, because Fin got a sponsor and is going on tour and has a 'famous' surfer dad."

Logan rolled his eyes. "So?"

"So?? Okay, how 'bout this: you can't stand that he has all that *and* he beat your ass."

Logan glanced toward the shore to see if Fin was paddling back. He couldn't see him. "One punch is not a beating. And it wouldn't have happened if he hadn't stolen my date."

"Dude, you didn't even like that girl."

Logan paddled farther out, waiting for a rise in the water. He knew Z-boy was right, of course. He had taken that girl just so he

est seventeen-year-
demark orange
attacked the
appeared
surfers

n alone. Then Logan got drunk and
front of everybody. Maybe he was
ying to show Fin up, but their long
ight when things got out of hand.

is eyes. "Why are you taking his
ride!"

t you some more free wax at

Fin's dad, the legendary Buddy "Shredder" Hamilton, ran the biggest surf shop in Southern California. When Logan was eight and started to surf, Buddy was already in his fifties, and too busy to teach his own son. So he gave Logan free board wax to surf with Fin and the rest was history. That was, until their *friendship* became history.

Logan felt the ocean rumble. He and Z-boy looked up to see another giant wave rising from the water.

"Let's show Fin who's hot shit," Logan said. "We got this one!"

The wave shot up quickly as he whipped his board around and paddled into position.

The sheer size of it freaked Z-boy. "You sure?" he shouted, staring down the wave's face.

"Let's go, man! It's now or never!" Logan paddled frantically into the wave, rising to his feet as he imagined the photographers on shore capturing this moment for all eternity—him and his amigo, riding side by side on the biggest swell to ever hit these shores—

Out of the corner of his eye, he saw Z-boy pull out of the wave at the last second. When Logan saw the drop in front of him, he suddenly knew why. It was like diving off a cliff.

Logan quickly found his board almost vertical. His arms flailed about, trying to keep his body upright as he plunged straight down the face of the wave. He only regained his balance by ripping a freakish turn, and suddenly he was shooting across the wave faster than he'd ever gone before—

Then, Logan saw a flash of orange and was airborne.

As he floated through the air, time seemed to stand still. Logan felt his leash snap and he hit the water, skidding down the wave on his back. All he could do was wait for the towering beast to smash him to smithereens.

Logan took the deepest breath of his life. He thought it might be his last.

He forced his body into a tight ball, fighting to keep his limbs intact as the wave barreled down on top of him. Thrown about like a rag doll in a washing machine, Logan bounced off the ocean floor, skinning his legs and arms as he rolled head over heels in the turmoil.

Logan finally found the ground and pushed off with enough force to shoot his way up through the mayhem. But as soon as he broke through to the surface, a second wave pummeled him, slamming him back down again.

It was in this chaos that Logan, dizzy and confused, caught a glimpse of a lifeless body in orange trunks tumbling about in the murky surf.

Fin.

Before he knew it, Logan felt a hand hauling him up by the neck of his wet suit. He had no strength left. The last thing he saw was Fin being sucked into a blizzard of white water.

When Logan finally came up, he hacked and swallowed huge gulps of air. He held on tight to the arm that was around him, looking up out of the corner of his eye to see who it was.

"Z-boy . . . ," he sputtered.

"Don't fight me," said his amigo, exhausted. "I'm trying to save you!" They battled against the raging current to stay afloat, but quickly got sucked under again.

Logan held on to him, dragging Z-boy farther down as they fought in opposite directions. Now Z-boy was in trouble. When Logan's foot finally touched the ground, he pushed off, bringing Z-boy back up with him. They struggled against the current until the tide receded enough to where they could stand again.

Logan gasped for breath. The ground had never felt so good. The water receded to chest level, but the surf still echoed in his head. Logan labored hard to breathe, his body hurt like someone had sucker punched him right in the heart.

Then Logan remembered.

"Fin," he said in a daze. "I-I thought I saw Fin down there—"

Z-boy tried to grab him. "Whoa, hold up, will ya? What'dya mean you saw Fin out there? He was surfing like the rest of us—"

"No! In the water! In the water!" Logan screamed. "*In* the water—"

Then Logan saw him. A body in orange trunks floating facedown.

"Fin!" He grabbed Z-boy and pointed frantically.

Z-boy's eyes went wide, and they both scrambled over. A few other surfers saw the commotion, then the body, and rushed over to help.

But Logan got there first. He forgot about nearly drowning. He grabbed Fin's body, fighting to flip his former friend over.

"Fin!" yelled Logan. He held Fin's head up out of the water. There was a big gash in his forehead, blood seeping out into the sea. "We gotta get him outta here!"

Logan and Z-boy dragged him back to shore, leaving a

brownish-red trail of blood in the murky water. A crowd gathered as they brought his lifeless body onto the sand. A lifeguard rushed over to perform CPR, but as Logan gazed down into Fin's vacant eyes, he knew that it was too late. He felt sick to his stomach. Just a few minutes ago, he'd wished the worst for his ex-friend. Now Fin was . . .

He couldn't think it. Logan lay down on the wet sand away from the madness, the mud cooling his feverish head. His mind drifted back to when they were eight. He, Z-boy and Fin used to lie on their backs in the wet sand to play chicken. They were always trying to outdo each other as the tide rushed in, swallowing them whole. They would hold their breath till the water slowly receded. The first one to move would lose.

Logan took a deep breath and held on.

2

LOGAN GLANCED AT his alarm
clock: 5:15 A.M. It was still dark out, but sleep was not going to
happen. He felt a pull to go back down to the shore to sort things
out in his head. The ocean air always cleared his mind.

He couldn't stop thinking about yesterday, about Fin lying
dead in the sand. He'd laughed at Fin as he bit it on that wave . . .
the wave that ended up being his last. Logan felt like an ass.
Maybe he would've made up with Fin by the end of summer,
tying up loose ends before he split for college. But now, that
would never happen . . .

Logan sneaked out of the house, careful not to wake his mom.
She'd freaked out pretty good when he'd told her about Fin's
death. She hadn't liked surfing to begin with, mostly because his
dad was such a bad example of what happened to surfers who
never grew up. But Fin's accident was the final straw. She made

Logan promise to stop surfing. He agreed just to calm her down. He knew he would never keep that promise.

He hopped on his old beat-up Vespa and headed down the alley toward the pier. The air was damp with mist, the streets quiet except for the hammering surf in the distance. He took the same route he always did to the beach—past the million-dollar homes that lined the hill overlooking South Bay, down one of the tiny walkways that populated old Hermosa, and out onto the concrete boardwalk that lined the entire beachfront, the Strand.

But all Logan could think of was Fin's vacant gray eyes.

How could Fin Hamilton be dead? He'd been riding big waves since he was fourteen. He remembered the night Fin showed up and told him that superstar Malik Joyeux had died on an unspectacular ride at the Pipeline even though he had been one of the best big-wave riders in the world. That night, they spent hours watching YouTube videos of Malik conquering all kinds of monsters in Teahupoo. But the only thing Fin kept saying was how much it sucked that a giant wave rider died on such a small wave. Logan wondered if the wave Fin had died on would've been big enough for his satisfaction.

Logan found himself riding toward Fin's house, one of the last original beach houses left over from the 1920s—brown shingled front, big windows and a faded green concrete patio. The waist-high concrete wall that bordered the Strand, usually lined with locals watching the chickitas roller blading by, was empty at this hour.

Logan pulled up in front of the house. How many times had he headed the dawn patrol, throwing pebbles at Fin's window to wake his sorry ass so they could hit the waves? A lot, until one morning a year ago, when he had showed up to find Fin already gone, surfing as he did from then on only with the other pros from Shredder's surf team.

Logan parked his scooter, kicked off his slaps and started walking toward the water. The coolness of the sand chilled his feet. It was low tide, but the surf was relentless.

In the moonlight, Logan could make out a series of shapes lining the shore. When he moved closer, he saw the metal warning signs the lifeguards had posted.

DANGER!
HIGH SURF CAN CAUSE SERIOUS INJURIES
OR DROWNING.
IF IN DOUBT, JUST STAY OUT!

Where were you yesterday? He smacked the sign with his fist.

He stood on the sand at the edge of the water, rubbing his hand. The waves were really cranking now, the roar filling the early morning air. The spray shimmered in the waning moonlight, forming a shroud and casting an eerie haze over the ocean.

Up until a year ago, surfing was all he, Z-boy and Fin had ever done and all they'd talked about. They'd get up at dawn, grab their boards and head down to the shore, waiting to see if the waves were breaking, then hitting the surf if it was worth hitting, or smoking some of Z's weed if it wasn't. Then they went to school, where they checked the surf reports throughout the day from their cell phones or hung out with the other Pier Avenue crew. When the sixth-period bell rang, Fin would be leading the charge as they raced down to the beach for the afternoon sets with the high school surf team. At night, they'd watch surf videos at Fin's, or scouer the Web for reports of approaching storms and swells. They'd dream up how they'd be immortalized in a full-page spread in *Surfing* magazine, barreling through a honkin' tube of some perfectly smooth, glassy monster of a wave. A video of the ride would end up on YouTube, of course.

It had been the good life. Heck, it was perfect. Logan had a free place to stay (even if it was with his mom), plenty of waves and two amigos to surf with from dawn to dusk.

But then, with his senior year, things started to sour. First Fin stopped hanging with them, then there was the fight at the senior prom, and now Fin was dead. What the fuck was going on? If this was what lay ahead for him after graduation, he might as well freeze his brain now and never grow up—

"I'm gonna save you."

Logan heard the voice. He looked around, but didn't see anyone. The voice drifted in and out of the roar from the surf, and the wind made it hard to hear.

"Hold on, just hang on . . ."

Logan squinted into the darkness. He saw a dark shape on the sand about fifteen yards away. The voice, muffled and deep, came from the direction of the mound. Logan started walking toward it.

"He's gone, he's a goner."

Then he saw the lump was a sleeping bag. It was Z-boy.

Logan stood over him. "Z, what're you doing down here?"

Z-boy's eyes were halfway open. He was muttering to himself. "Did you see that? Did you see it?"

Z-boy talked in his sleep. A lot. Usually when he was stressing about something. When they used to do sleepovers, Z would hold bizarre conversations with Logan and Fin while still out cold.

"Hey. Z-boy." Logan nudged him with his foot. Z-boy's face changed from serious to goofy, like he was channeling through different dream states.

"The penguin gave it to me." Z-boy talked about the weirdest things in his sleep.

Logan couldn't resist. "The penguin? Where is he?"

"The penguin, over by the bar."

"Oh yeah." Logan looked over at the nonexistent bar. "Hey, why's he wearing a football helmet?"

Z-boy giggled. "Helmet? Dude, penguins don't wear helmets."

Logan knelt down next to him. Whatever party Z-boy was at, Logan wished he was there too. He grabbed Z-boy's shoulders and shook him. Z giggled and kept muttering to himself. He could sleep through anything.

Logan nodded. "Okay, you asked for it . . ." Logan stood up, then with all the force of an 8.0 tremor, pounced, yelling, "EARTHQUAKE!!"

Z-boy leapt up, grabbed Logan's arm and flipped him onto his back. He straddled Logan's chest, breathing heavily, staring down with foggy eyes. "We gotta save the penguin, man . . ."

"Z! Wake up! It's me, Logan!"

Z-boy sniffed and didn't say anything. His matted, sandy locks stood up on end, like a comic fright wig.

"Zane!"

Z-boy finally opened his eyes all the way. There was about a five-second lag where Logan could see him processing the situation. Suddenly, his eyes came into focus.

"Logan. Why are you—" When Z-boy realized he was sitting on top of Logan, he scrambled off quickly. "Dude, what, what're you doing?!"

"You were talking in your sleep again," Logan said. "Z, what are you doing down here?"

Z-boy looked around the empty beach, his face becoming somber. He got up and brushed the sand off his legs.

"Z?"

Z-boy stopped brushing. "My parents kicked me out."

"What? Kicked you out? Why?"

Z-boy gazed up at the stars. "Everything's fucked up, man. They don't care that Fin died . . ."

"Z. Why . . . would they kick you out?"

Z-boy sniffed. "They found out I'm not gonna graduate."

Logan froze. "What d'ya mean? We're graduating this weekend."

Z-boy looked down at the sand. "You will. I failed the exit exam."

Logan was at a loss for words. "What're you talking about? We aced that thing last year—"

"*You* aced it. I just said I did."

Logan scrambled. "But you get like, *four chances*—you can take it again!"

"I know. I mean, I did. Four times." Z-boy laughed nervously. "You know what they say, four strikes and you're out . . ."

"No way . . ." Logan studied Z-boy's face. "Are you *serious*? I fucking chased you around for like a month to get you to study for that thing! I can't friggin' believe this, Z . . . Did you even study on your own? Why did I waste my time doing flash cards and all that shit?"

Z-boy tugged on his hair. "I wanted to . . . study, I mean. I guess I didn't say anything after 'cause I didn't want you to think that I was . . . some kinda fuckup."

Logan knew Z couldn't help being distracted by everything

around him—waves, girls, pot. So there was no point in going there. Nothing he said now would change anything.

He threw up his hands, dumbfounded. "Shit! What's going on? It's like God's out to get us or something . . ."

They sat there together in silence, listening to the waves. Finally, Z-boy said, "Why'd you and Fin have to go and ruin a good thing? Everything was great until you couldn't handle him getting all the attention . . ."

"What, now it's my fault? That's why you didn't pass? Listen, he was the one who—" Logan cut himself off. What could he say about someone who was dead? Logan hit the sand with his fist. He felt like such a bastard—what good was he to anyone?

"You got any weed?" Logan asked.

"Nah, smoked it all. I still owe Broza for my last batch. And a few others . . ." His voice trailed off as he dug his feet into the sand, resting his head on his knees. "I was kinda freaking about Fin and I didn't even have anything to smoke. That was fucked up."

Logan imagined Z-boy sitting out there all night with Fin's ghost. "Your parents really booted you out?"

"Yeah. Some BS about supporting myself so I could see what it's like in the *real world.*"

Logan considered Z's sleeping bag. "You're not gonna stay on the beach, Z-boy . . ."

"Why not? It's free, they have showers, a nice view . . ." He looked around. "Actually, it's kinda nice down here. No more checking the wave cam to see if there are any waves." He pointed at the ocean. "*This* is the wave cam!"

Logan gazed out into the darkness. That was the only thing that sucked about living so close to L.A. You couldn't see the stars. It was just a big, black void.

"So what're you gonna do?" Logan asked.

"Dunno. But I sure as hell ain't gonna work the night shift at Taco Bell. And I'm not gonna go back to your uncle's seafood restaurant."

Logan cracked up. "What, you don't like wearing a fish on your head?"

"I ain't wearing that shark hat again. That shit was humiliating."

Logan nodded. "It was pretty bad . . ."

Z-boy wrapped his sleeping bag around himself and stared out to sea. "I heard from Neelyman that Buddy's gonna have Fin cremated. They're gonna have a ceremony or something, in a few days, to spread his ashes out there in the water. Then he's gonna have a big party at his house. Just like back in the day. You gonna go?"

"Of course I'm gonna go. Why wouldn't I?" He remembered Buddy calling him, Z-boy and Fin the Three Musketeers. They had had some great parties at Buddy's, real ragers. The first time they got drunk was at Buddy's. The first time they smoked pot together too. Fin used to sneak some herb from his dad's stash and they'd lie on his roof and watch the clouds float by. Good times. Now it was down to the two of them.

Z-boy picked up some sand and let it dribble through his fingers. "Maybe it's not the perfect wave we're searching for. Maybe it's just an adventure. You know, to shake things up, get us over this hump."

"Shit, Z, I've had enough adventure lately . . ."

"No, no, not like that. I mean . . . I need to figure out what I'm gonna do from now on . . . and maybe . . . I was thinking maybe we could do something together. You know, for old times' sake?"

"What, you mean like get summer jobs together?"

Z-boy shrugged, then looked away. "I don't know . . . maybe . . ."

Logan waited. "Got something in mind, Z?"

Z-boy shook his head. "I'm just saying something might come up. You never know . . ."

Logan let it go. He did need a summer job. Things were tight at home and so far, his uncle's restaurant was the only option waiting for him. But Z had no options now. They each needed to figure out what they were going to do with the rest of their lives.

Logan nudged his friend. "Hey, I'm sure you can stay with us, Z. I got a nice floor waiting for ya. We'll see what happens after that."

Z-boy looked disappointed. "What, I can't share your bed?"

Logan laughed. "I ain't your hag, bitch."

Z-boy smiled. "Thanks, brah. You're always there when I need ya."

But soon, Logan would be gone too. Then what?

3

IT WAS RAINING paper. Logan staggered through the crowded hallway of Hermosa High, as old notes, useless printouts and months of old trash flew out of students' lockers high into the air, like confetti at a New Year's Eve party. It was Seniors Day, the last day of school, three days after Fin's last day on earth. Logan made his way to his locker on autopilot and, like he'd done a thousand and one times before, dialed his combination, popped open his locker door and stared in.

Inside were all his notebooks and textbooks, his gym clothes, which hadn't been washed in two weeks, and a stash of peanut butter crackers and Mountain Dew (his favorites), surrounded by pictures of beautiful surfer babes and gnarly wave action.

He reached in and grabbed his trig notebook, flipped it open and scanned the pages. All that work, just to get into college. Would he even use it in real life? Up until recently, his only goal had been surfing and hanging out with his buds. But then, his mom kept saying he was in danger of ending up like his dad if he didn't get serious about school. He didn't want to end up like his dad, always looking for a free ride through life.

He popped the binder rings and ripped the pages out into the air. He'd studied hard for his mom's sake, but deep down, he knew he wasn't really college material. He barely got into one, Sacramento State, California's second-tier university. But when he got the acceptance letter, all he could do was stare at it. *What if he couldn't hack it? What if he really was like his dad, a deadbeat surfer with no options in life? Then what, crawl back home and be like Z?*

He ripped all the papers out of his English folder and let it all fly, then tossed everything else: chem, world history, English lit . . . all the notes, the gym clothes, the stale crackers. He dug around, rooting for something, something that would tell him what to do, where he was supposed to go, what he was supposed to become. Suddenly the locker was empty and he had no answer. He leaned his head against the cold locker door.

"Are you okay?"

He felt a hand on his shoulder. When he turned, there was Emmie. Emmie Slater, the blond-haired, blue-eyed, freckle-faced surfer girl who would challenge Logan to any contest—surfing, volleyball, even drinking—just to prove herself. He hadn't talked to her since Fin passed. He'd always secretly liked her, but backed off when she became one of the Pier Avenue surf chicks because he thought it wasn't cool to date within the ranks.

But then he found out she'd dated Fin on the sly for a few months, though they'd never shown it in public. When Fin didn't ask her to the prom, that was the end of that. Logan felt bad when no one else asked her. He'd wanted to, but he didn't want people to think he was picking at Fin's leftovers. Now they had both been rebuked by Fin.

He swallowed hard. "Are you okay?"

She looked at him, and he couldn't tell if it was with pity or understanding. She sighed and gazed down at the ground. He changed the subject.

"Do you want me to sign that?" He pointed to the yearbook she was clutching to her chest.

She nodded. "I can sign yours too, if you want," she added softly.

"I didn't order one." He flipped through the pages, carefully scanning the pictures for anything that meant something to him.

Football players, cheerleaders, after-game dances, marching band, student council, fashion parade, the talent show, the Happiness Ball . . . God, this was not his life. He was nowhere to be seen . . .

Finally, on pages 122–123 there was a spread called Tubular Swells and Good Times. On one side was a whole page about Fin—Most Likely to Become Famous. There was a picture from earlier in the year with Fin and Logan goofing it up at a local surf meet. Fin had won it, of course, but Logan placed fourth. That seemed so long ago, like it was ancient history or something. Emmie had scrawled *R.I.P.* and the date Fin had died under the picture.

He thought of Fin, and suddenly felt that the life that meant something to him— the days of riding skate ramps and waves, of partying and craziness, of being with other surfers who lived for the ocean—was quickly slipping away. His eyes suddenly misted up, but Logan fought it, wiping them with his sleeve and trying to act as if nothing was happening.

Emmie put her hand on his arm and he looked up at her, embarrassed. He wiped his face and turned his attention to the other page. There were the rest of the Pier Avenue Rats: Z-boy, Cutter,

Neelyman, Mateo and Cheeba. And of course Emmie, shooting through the pylons under the pier like a maniac. That made him smile again.

"Now, that's a cover shot, girl! I never saw you do that!" said Logan, surprised.

She smiled too, probably glad to see the old Logan again. "You never cared, unless I was stealing your wave," she countered. "That one of you is pretty nice too."

The photo of Logan showed him cranking a nice backside slide maneuver along the top of a wave, his hair whipping a halo of water around his head. He nodded at the picture, satisfied. Next to it was Z-boy, ripping down the face of a six footer, grinning like a madman.

That's what I'm talking about. Even *pictures* of surfing calmed him and took away all his doubts for a moment.

"You don't have to sign anything special if you don't want to . . . ," Emmie said.

"Hold on, I'm getting to it . . ." He saw a choice spot next to her photo and held the book up, so she couldn't see what he was scribbling.

> EMMIE, WAY TO RIP IT UP! YOU'RE THE BEST
> BROCHICK I KNOW. HOPE TO SEE YOU DOWN
> THERE THIS SUMMER!
>> YOUR PAL, LOGAN

That seemed kind of generic, like what he would have written before the accident. He knew she had to be a little messed up in the head—it must be weird knowing you'd made it with a dead guy.

He added:

PS: CALL ME IF YOU WANT TO TALK.

He wanted to say, *Maybe we could get together sometime?* but thought it might creep her out.

He slapped the book shut and handed it back to her. He really hoped she would call him. They stood there awkwardly for a moment.

She glanced around at the mayhem of seniors throwing away their work with total abandon. "They make such a big deal of everything you learn here, then it all just ends up in a pile of trash for the janitor to clean up. Figures, huh? I can't wait till graduation . . ."

Logan made a face.

Emmie looked disappointed. "What? You're going to miss this dump?"

Logan scanned the ancient linoleum hallway, which smelled of disinfectant and afternoon sweat. "Hell, no . . . but everything else . . ."

Emmie studied Logan's tanned face for a minute. "You'll do fine, Logan. You were always the smartest. Go away and become somebody. Don't let any doubts in that head of yours stop you."

"What about you? You have the grades. Why aren't you leaving?"

She shrugged. "My parents need me to stay right now. I'll do community college for a couple years, then see what's up. Besides, I'm too much of a local girl. I mean, we go back four generations."

"Yeah, well. You gotta do what you gotta do. I'm just not sure what I'm supposed to do . . ."

"You'll figure it out." She leaned over and gave him a hug. "And if you don't, you'll just fuck up the rest of your life . . ."

Logan held on to her. She felt good, smelled good too. He remembered when she had started surfing. He had called her a wannabe, but Emmie never gave up. Soon she wasn't the one backing off a wave.

When she turned fifteen, her tomboy looks disappeared. She started looking pretty fine, especially in a bikini, when she would fly up and down the face of the wave, like some surfing pixie leading him on.

"Is that . . . perfume you're wearing?" asked Logan.

Emmie blushed. "Maybe. What's it to you?"

Logan laughed out loud. "You don't have to get all defensive. I just didn't figure you for the perfume type . . ."

"You mean, like a girl?" she asked with a mischievous look on her face.

He stared into her big blue eyes and wondered if he might have a shot with her. He wondered what it'd be like to kiss her. Logan blushed.

"I should go," he said. He turned to close his locker, then realized that it didn't matter anymore.

They both smiled. "I guess I'll see you at graduation practice tomorrow . . . ," said Emmie.

Logan strapped on his empty backpack. "Yeah, I'm not sure if I'm going. But I'll see you at Fin's . . . thing on Friday, right?"

Emmie nodded halfheartedly.

Fin's thing sounded so lame, but what else do you call it when you spread a friend's ashes at sea?

4

IT HAD BEEN sunny up until the day Fin died. Then the fog rolled in and *June gloom* engulfed everything, as it did at the start of every summer. Kids heading into summer break were always bummed after seeing the sun in May, only to get to June, when it was too cold to lie out on the sand.

It was in this gloom that Logan and Z-boy waited on the beach for Fin's ashes to show. They'd gotten there early because sitting around the house was just too damn depressing.

Logan almost freaked when he first saw the water. The sea looked the color of the blood he had seen in the water that day. Only now it seemed to cover the whole ocean.

"Red tide's coming in," Z-boy said.

Red tide happened when algae turned the water a warm brownish red. At night, it caused the waves to glow fluorescent when the white water stirred them up.

Logan saw that the waves were small but fine—smooth and glassy, with excellent angles breaking both ways. Logan thought it was a nice day to remember Fin. They stood there on the shore letting the moment soak in.

"Well, might as well get out there. The others will be coming soon," Logan said.

"You think Fin would want us to surf?" asked Z-boy.

Logan thought about it and smiled. "Hell, yeah. What better way to honor him?"

Since it was early afternoon and cold out, they had the spot pretty much to themselves. Logan caught wave after wave, nonstop for half an hour. Nothing spectacular, but enough to lighten his mood and make him feel like a kid again.

He, Z-boy and Fin had surfed this spot a thousand times before, but today was different— the surfing had meaning. With each wave he took, he thought of Fin and imagined what his last second on earth was like. Did that perfect wave give him his moment of clarity? Did Fin know he was going to die?

He and Z-boy took one last ride as they snaked their way across the wave, milking it for all it was worth until it just petered out in the shallows. They stood smiling, satisfied with their take for the day. They noticed a smattering of friends and locals on the shore, somber and quiet. Neelyman, Mateo, Cutter, Cheeba, and all the Pier Avenue crew were now there. Folks who lived on the Strand headed down, young and old. Even some of the Valley posers came. They were freaks as far as Logan was concerned, but it was a funeral so he let it go.

"Where's Emmie?" Logan asked.

"Don't know," shrugged Z-boy. "But she'll show up. You did."

Logan heard a roar coming from behind them. He turned and

saw three lifeguard boats coming toward them, their lights and sirens blazing. "What the—"

They were either in big trouble or—

"Isn't that Buddy on that boat?" Z-boy asked.

Logan squinted against the sun. Buddy stood on the bow of the leading boat, his gray blond hair blowing in the wind. Lined up behind him were maybe two dozen of Hermosa Beach's old-school legends, all with their boards.

"Damn, he brought The Hall . . . ," Logan said, impressed.

The Hall were the original South Bay surf legends immortalized by plaques in the Surfers Hall of Fame on the pier. These old-school pros had opened up surfing as a way of life in the late '50s and '60s. They preceded the hippies and the Beatniks, made the Beach Boys possible, gave meaning to words like *gnarly*, *bodacious*, and of course, the eternal *dude*. Back in the day, surfers were real mavericks—tough, wild, lawless. But they were also the first to discover the spiritual side of surfing. Surfing brought them closer to God than any church could.

"Kinda makes you proud to own a board," Z-boy said in awe.

All the surfers parted ways to let the boats through. All at once, Buddy and the members of The Hall jumped off the sides of the lead boat with their longboards. Then Buddy reached up to one of the lifeguards, who handed him an urn.

"Whoa . . . ," Logan said. "Is that . . . ?"

Z-boy squinted. "Yup . . . that's Fin, in a jar. That's messed up, man."

The locals moved to either side of the boat, forming an aisle for Buddy and The Hall. But all Logan could do was stare at Fin's urn balanced on the front of Buddy's board as they paddled slowly past him. All he could think was, What if the urn fell over?

Buddy stopped about twenty yards away from the boat. Logan and the others followed. They were out past the break point where the water was deep, turning black about two feet down. "Let's do it here," Buddy grunted.

Logan drifted in behind him. Buddy looked like he'd aged ten years overnight. His gray hair, weather-beaten skin and Hawaiian tattoos no longer had that look of eternal youth that Buddy had always carried with him. Instead, he just looked old.

Buddy held up the urn of his son's ashes.

Everyone sat up on their boards, waiting for Buddy to speak. His eyes were wet with tears. "*If you find the perfect wave, you can ride it forever.* That's what I used to tell Fin all the time." He wiped his eyes. "I've been riding that wave for a good long while, but now, it feels like I just went over the falls and ate it, big time."

He gazed into the water. "Life is that wave," he said matter-of-factly. "You paddle into it, thinking it's going to be the ride of your life. And it could be. Or it could kill you. You never know. That's why I respect anyone who heads into the ocean every day searching for that perfect wave. You're all riding into the great unknown, and that's what makes surfing . . . the next best thing to God."

Logan watched Buddy unscrew the lid of the urn. Dust from the ashes swirled into the air around him as he poured the remains of his son into the ocean.

Logan watched the ashes drift along the surface of the water, floating amongst him and the other surfers. It seemed weird that a person could turn into dust. But there it was. The remains slowly dissolved into the water, and just like that, Fin was gone. "Bye, Fin," he whispered.

When Logan glanced up, he noticed Buddy nod in appreciation. Buddy then turned his attention back to the urn, placing it gently in the Pacific till it filled to the brim with water. "Aloha, son. See you on the other side," he said quietly. He let the urn go, watching it disappear into the darkness below.

Buddy cleared his throat and spoke loudly. "Now every time you surf this beach, Fin will surf it too."

Buddy shook his head, as if to get any bad thoughts out. He raised his meaty fist, then struck it hard against his board. Raising his other fist, he brought it down with a thud and started beating his board to some mysteriously dark rhythm known only to him.

Ignoring the pain in his cold hands, Logan started pounding his board like a drum too, letting all his anger and frustrations come pouring out. Soon everyone was pounding away, an ancient drum circle in the sea. The lifeguard boats pointed their water cannons into the air and let it rain down on the procession. Buddy howled, and they all howled with him, like dogs lost in the wilderness, shouting at the moon. The sound rose all around them. They pounded faster and faster until the cacophony climaxed and came to a booming halt.

Suddenly, a wave appeared, forming slowly and rising before them. It wasn't a big wave like the ones Fin used to ride, but it was wide and smooth.

Buddy looked up to the clouds above. "Thanks, son." He started paddling to catch the wave.

All the surfers did the same. No one cut each other off or hotdogged. Logan, Z-boy and the crew spread out, rising in unison, as they rode the wave all the way in to shore.

5

WHEN LOGAN AND Z-boy arrived
that night, Buddy's party was already raging. Packed wall to wall
with four generations of surfers, it boasted everyone from The
Hall to Logan's crew to the latest newbies to take up the board.
The music was loud (Zeppelin) and everyone who had known Fin
was there. It was like a who's who from Logan's past.

They walked through the sea of red-eyed but grinning faces as
they were greeted with hugs, backslaps, beers and shouts of
"Logan! Z-boy! Whassup!" Logan moved in a daze, the faces beginning to blur from one to the next. He was looking for someone, then realized it was Emmie. *Why isn't she here?*

When he turned around, Z-boy was already deeply inhaling
from a homemade bong from one of Buddy's board shapers, an
older Hawaiian guy name Flea. Z-boy gave the thumbs-up.
"Smooth. A fine device from a master shaper."

"It's made of fiberglass, so the flavor sails right through, just like a board on water," explained Flea. "I made it myself."

"You should sell these at Buddy's shop," Z-boy said excitedly. "Can you imagine? An original Flea bong. *For you Valley boys who can't surf, now you can experience the true ride of a surfing legend.* Tasty, huh?"

Flea smiled his approval. "Brah, I see a future for you in marketing."

Z-boy held up the bong for Logan. "Dude, you should try this."

Logan shook his head. "Naw, not now," he said, dismissing him.

Z-boy's eyes grew wide. "Now I know you're depressed, refusing the herb from a local legend's bong!"

Flea put his hand on Logan's arm, surfer to surfer. "It's cool, brah. Flea is sad about Fin too. But Buddy, he'll be right happy to see ya."

Logan smiled uncomfortably. "Where is he?" he asked as he surveyed the scene. Buddy's place was a classic surfer's bachelor pad—surf memorabilia, beer posters, calendars with surfer chicks on them. Even at sixty, Buddy acted like he was seventeen. He always said that surfing was too good, too much fun and gave you a high like no other. Why would you want to grow up?

"So what're you gonna do with the shoe box, dude?" Z-boy said, nodding at the blue box Logan held in his hand.

"It's for Buddy. Something me and Fin made together in sixth grade," Logan said as he scanned the room.

"Buddy over der." Flea pointed to the balcony. "He's brooding. Be gentle, brah. His heart be broken."

Logan made his way to the balcony. He passed a makeshift

shrine for Fin in front of the fireplace. It included pictures, a few of Fin's things like his wet suit and his famous orange trunks, some articles that had appeared in surfing magazines, and a small prototype surfboard Buddy was working on for him: the Fin Hamilton Strato 3 Giant Rider. *Damn, Fin was only seventeen and already had his own board.*

Logan stepped out onto the balcony, his eyes adjusting to the darkness. He didn't see anyone. He slid the door closed behind him, leaving the party inside. It was quieter out here, and he could think. Logan looked down at the darkened beach below. The ocean had a faint glow to it; he couldn't tell if his eyes were playing tricks or not.

"Over here, Logan."

Logan could see Buddy's eyes peering at him from the darkness. He was hunched over in a corner all by himself.

"Long time, little brother," Buddy said. "I was glad to see you out there this afternoon."

Logan looked at his feet. "Sure thing, Buddy. Anything for Fin."

Buddy sat silent for a few moments before talking again. "Fin was always pissed at me for not teaching him to surf, but I didn't want him to get a free ride on my name, ya know? I wanted him to discover the wave on his own. You helped him do that, dude. He never forgot that."

Well, he had a funny way of showing his gratitude . . . As soon as Fin had started making a name for himself, he stopped hanging with the crew. He started treating Logan like he wasn't in the same league anymore . . . which was true, but—

"Fin was stubborn, though, that's for sure. But he always said you was the smartest kid he knew." Buddy grew silent again. "You going to college?"

"Supposed to . . ." was all he could muster. It all seemed so far away now, he thought. Looking through the glass door, he realized none of those guys had left Hermosa or gone away for school. What made him any different? "I don't know if I'm ready . . ."

Buddy shook his head. "Don't give up on that idea, Logan. You're a smart boy, be a smart boy. Leave surfing to the lunkheads like me and Z-boy."

"I'm a lunkhead too," he said in his defense.

Buddy laughed, nodding. "Yeah, I remember some of the things you three used to pull off. Like the time you guys broke into my shop and stuck all my boards out in the street with a FREE BOARDS sign in front of them. Remember that?"

Logan couldn't really make out his expression, so he didn't know if Buddy was pissed or not. But that had been Fin's idea, his revenge for being grounded and missing the Huntington Beach surf classic.

Logan noticed a board leaning against the wall behind Buddy. "Is that—?"

"Yeah, Fin's board. The one he was using when he . . ." Buddy looked off into the night sky.

Logan felt he had to touch it. He moved over and ran his hand along the board's edge. There was a flaw in the side of the board—a chunk that seemed newer than the rest. Buddy saw him staring at it.

"The guys tried to patch it up as good as before . . . It's not pretty, but it's sound."

Logan ran his hand along the fix. Logan had barely escaped getting smashed by his own board in several wipeouts over the years. To knock out a chunk of board that size with your head would take an incredible blow powered by a monster wave. A blow that could kill you.

Buddy's eyes got moist. "Coroner said he'd probably been knocked out and drowned." He wiped his face. "Crazy, huh? He was the best swimmer in Junior Lifeguards, and he's the one that . . ."

Logan didn't know what to say. Finally, he just held up the small box he had brought with him. "I brought this for you."

Buddy sat up. His big hands accepted the delicate box. "What is it?" He held it up and examined it closely.

"It's just an old school project I found last night. Me and Fin made it when we were kids." Logan pointed to the back of the box. "Go on, hold it up to the light and peek into the hole. Turn the knob."

Buddy held it in one hand and peered inside the box. "Fin . . . ," he whispered. He turned the knob, his mouth slowly opening.

Inside was a little plastic army soldier, painted to look like a surfer on his board and held in midair by a string. The back of the box was cut out and taped over with a blue translucent scroll, which made an endless wave for the surfing figure when turned. The surfer had on orange trunks, Fin's trademark.

"The wave never crashes. It just keeps going, forever," Logan explained, suddenly realizing that it might bring Buddy bad memories.

"It's . . . beautiful, Logan. I remember you and Fin making stuff like this." Logan could see Buddy's cheek glistening by the light. Buddy sat there like a little kid, transfixed by the magic box.

Logan wanted to say something, but didn't want to spoil the moment. So he quietly backed away, leaving Buddy in peace.

6

LOGAN SLID OPEN the door, stepping back into the roar of the party and straight into Billy "The King" Broza's beaming white teeth.

"LoganTomDudeWhatup!" Broza yelled, mashing his greeting into one word as usual.

Logan mocked him. "YoYoBrozaWhatup!"

Broza's way of greeting annoyed everyone, but he didn't care. He had the attitude and the cash to back up his strut. Although he was only a few years older than Logan, his status as the dealer with the biggest and best supply of pot made him a fixture at every party. It was his special connections to the best of Mexico's marijuana that made him the king of South Bay, and because of that, he made his minions call him "The King." Logan called him Broza just to spite him.

"What's your beef?" Broza spat back at Logan. "Still bummed that you drive a scooter?" Broza slicked his black hair out of his eyes. He was a tiny guy, maybe five foot four, but he made up for it with big ideas and a big mouth. "You know, people like to move up in the world. I mean, even Z-boy drives a car now."

Logan glared at him. Broza ignored his look. "Sad about Fin. Guy was a real pirate. Totally gonzo. And what a way to go. I miss him already."

Logan eyed him suspiciously. "Funny, I didn't see you earlier when we spread his ashes . . ."

Broza acted like he didn't hear him. "I got some business to discuss with you and Z-boy. Possible summer job for you guys."

A drunken partygoer bumped into Logan, gave him a hug and moved on. "Job? What makes you think I want a job?" Logan said.

"Oh, yeah, I forgot. You're Mr. Moneybags. You know, Cap'n Crunch doesn't grow on trees."

"I know. My mom buys it."

Broza smiled. "Thing is, I know your boy over there needs work." Logan looked over at Z-boy, who was commiserating with Flea. "Things haven't quite gone his way lately."

"So . . . what's that got to do with you?"

Broza leaned in close. "I like Z-boy. He's a good kid and his heart's in the right place. More important, he's a pirate with the right attitude. Willing to do anything. But he's a fuckup. You know that, so do I."

Logan glared back at Broza. "Why are you saying this to me?"

Broza looked around. Logan followed his gaze around the room. Nobody was paying attention to them.

"I have an opening," Broza said. "But I won't take Z-boy alone. Too risky. But if you two were a team . . . *that* could be of interest."

"A team?" Logan was lost. "What're you talking about?"

Broza smiled. "Opportunity."

Logan got it. "Are you—Jesus, are you asking me to work for you at Fin's wake?"

"I know. On the surface, it seems crass. But it's all connected. Fin. Z-boy. You. Maybe this is all happening for a reason."

Logan got up in Broza's face. "What possible frickin' reason would that be?!"

Broza held up his hands. A few members of The Hall were staring at them now. "Relax, man. Didn't mean anything disrespectful. I'm just saying, sometimes things happen for a reason. Our job is to figure out why, then act on it."

"Listen, man, I'm not interested. Show some class." He started to walk away.

Broza stepped in front of Logan, his smile disappearing. "I'm doing you and your pal a favor. At least try to act thankful."

"Thanks. But no thanks."

Broza stood his ground. "Fin liked you, despite whatever shit happened between you two. He said you had a good head on your shoulders, said he owed you for something. I think as the man is dead, the least you could do is hear me out."

Logan didn't have a response.

Broza eased up. "I know what's going on with your family. See, you're surrounded by people who could really use your help. Z-boy is lost without you. I know your mom is going through tough times financially—"

Logan gritted his teeth. "Leave her out of this."

Broza stepped back, nodding respectfully. "That's what I like about you, Logan. You're a no-bullshit kinda dude. You got loyalty, determination. That's the kind of guy I could use right now.

Just give me five minutes." He put his hand gently on Logan's shoulder. "Z-boy could really use a friend now. Just five minutes, if not for you, then for his sake. That's all I'm asking. If you're not interested after that, fine. What's five minutes for a friend?"

The light to Buddy's garage flickered on. There, in all its glory, sat a brand new yellow Hummer.

Z-boy was in awe. "No way!!"

Broza showed it off proudly. "Nice, huh. The H2 SUT. Eighty-six hundred pounds of power. You like?"

"What happened to your beat-up Ford Taurus?" Logan asked.

"That old thing? That's my cover. Can't be seen driving around in a Hummer without attracting attention, now, can I?"

Z-boy looked at his new hero. "Can't we just go for a little ride?"

"Sorry, Z, no can do. I'm just storing it here for now, but in a few years, when I'm retired, I'll give you a call and we'll go for a spin."

"So why buy it now?" Logan asked. "Especially with the price of gas."

"It's a hybrid, boy. Gotta launder the cash into real merchandise, which I can either use or sell at a later time. Can't stick it in a bank, ya know?"

Logan laughed. "How old are you, Broza?"

"Twenty-one and change. And I almost got my first million. Why?"

"Bitch."

Broza grinned. "Step inside." He clicked his remote and the car came to life, lights flashing and bass pounding. He held open the door, revealing the slick, black leather interior.

Z-boy nodded in appreciation. "Power."

Once they were all in the backseat, Logan cut to the chase. "So what is this great and glorious opportunity you are bestowing upon us?"

Broza shut the door.

"I have an opening. Now that Fin's left the company, I need someone."

Logan's jaw dropped. "*Fin* worked for you?"

"What, you didn't know? How do you think he supported his surfing habit? Being part of Shredder's surf team?" he scoffed. "You don't get paid when your dad's the sponsor. *I* gave him the opportunity to pursue his dream. He was smart enough to take it."

Now that Logan thought about it, Fin always seemed to disappear for four or five days at a time, especially last summer. Logan thought he was doing the surf tours. Fin always seemed to have enough cash on him.

"Bullshit. Fin won tournaments. That's how he got the cash," Logan said.

"How many tournaments do you think he won? After travel expenses, hotels, flights, parties . . . how much do you think was left? Buddy did okay, but he had to pay for marketing Fin, so earnings went back into the pot. Truth is, only a handful of surfers ever make any real money. Most are journeymen, just barely scraping by. Maybe he was top dog here, but around the world, he was just a good surfer, at best."

"But he was Buddy's top dog—"

"He's Buddy's son."

Logan shook his head, like it all made sense now. "So what'd he do for you?"

"He was a mule."

Logan gave him a odd look.

Broza elaborated. "You know, a driver."

"He drove you around?" Z-boy asked.

"No, dickweed. Deliveries. To the East Coast. Pennsylvania. Florida. Carolinas. Product is dry there, so they need to import."

Logan tilted his head. "Product? You mean—"

"Pot?" Z-boy said hungrily.

Broza smiled. "Only the best. Grade-A buds from Mexico. We have the contacts, the means to get it across the border, delivery routes to our clients on the East Coast, who give us clean cash. Easy for us, no hassle to them."

Logan let in all sink in. "Fin was dealing . . ."

Broza bristled at the suggestion. "Please. Pfizer, Merck, Johnson and Johnson—pharmaceutical companies are the pushers. Pot was put here on Earth by God and nature. Fin was just a driver, hauling our product across the country, just like any other trucker moving corn or soybeans. Only he muled pot."

"How much stuff?" Z-boy asked.

"Usually shipments of a hundred."

"A hundred what?"

"Pounds. A hundred pounds."

"Of weed?" Z-boy's eyes grew big. "Holy shit, brah, I had no idea you were so hooked up. I think I'm in love."

Logan hit Z-boy in the arm. "Shut up, man. That's your woody talking." He looked at Broza. "So this is a legal operation? I mean, is it tied into with the whole medical marijuana movement? Because I might be okay with that if it was, you know, not *illegal.*"

"You mean, do I run one of those new medical marijuana stores that take prescriptions and health plans? Are you kidding me? And pay taxes?" Broza shook his head. "I don't think so.

We're old-school distribution. First of all, medical marijuana is legal in only eleven states. Secondly, you have to have a prescription, which they don't give to kids under twenty-one, who are, by the way, about eighty-five percent of my clientele, people just like you two. Thirdly, that leaves thirty-nine states starving for product. And any Joe who thinks he can get enough legal weed to sell across state lines not only is stupid, but will get an even longer jail sentence if caught selling it." Broza spoke like a true salesman. "I can get pot in Mexico right now and sell it in places like Florida, Pennsylvania, the Carolinas, all the way up the coast. It's a total win-win for guys like me. That's called supply-side economics. They teach you that at Hermosa High?"

Z nodded in awe of Broza's economic theories. "The man's right. I never learned anything like that there, only bullshit I can't use in real life, like math and chemistry. Well, chemistry I suppose could come in handy for making hybrid plants and such—"

"Shut up, Z-boy." Logan turned his focus back to Broza. "So you want us to be drug runners?" he asked.

"Don't knock it, Logan Tom. Fin made three thousand dollars for five days' work. Ten to fifteen trips a year. That's a pretty hefty allowance for a seventeen-year-old. And tax free too."

Z-boy's eyes grew big. "Whoa. That's insane, man. I wish I had that kinda bling."

Broza stared at them. "You can. Interested?"

Z-boy looked at Logan and back at Broza. "In becoming mules?"

"Seriously. I got a run coming up to Orlando." Broza hit a button and a minibar appeared out of the floor. "I do very well for myself. We do two runs a month. You can use your imagination from there. But only if it's both of you."

Logan sat there silently. Broza continued. "You can take shifts on the road and make it across in two and a half days, three days tops. Fifteen hundred dollars each."

"Fifteen hundred dollars? What happened to three thousand dollars?" Logan asked.

"Now there are two of you. And it's only three days of work."

"But the risk is the same," Logan interjected.

Broza considered Logan, then nodded. "Okay. Two grand each. No more."

"Deal," Z-boy interrupted.

Broza looked at Logan. "Deal?"

Logan blinked. He thought of his dad and all the mysterious dealings he'd had trying to provide for his family. He could imagine his dad's downhill slide starting like this . . .

Logan stalled. "You really need two of us?"

"Two can keep an eye on the situation better than one. That way, if one is fucking up, the other can keep things on course. And taking shifts makes it quicker with less risk of falling asleep at the wheel. But mostly, it's because I had this vision that Republicans, like Jehovah's Witnesses, travel in pairs."

"Republicans?"

Broza smiled and winked. "Republicans."

7

LOGAN KNEW TROUBLE

when he smelled it, and it smelled like a hundred pounds of pot. He left the party without committing either way. Z-boy couldn't believe that he'd walk away from an opportunity like this. But things were coming out of left field, and Logan needed time to think. Something about Broza reminded him of his dad. Maybe it was his way of thinking he could skirt the rules forever and never pay for it.

Broza said he could sleep on it, then gave them his address and told them to come by around noon tomorrow. The address was somewhere in Compton. Not exactly surfer's paradise.

Logan wandered along the shore, chewing on his hair and leaving a line of glowing footprints in the wet sand. That was the red tide at work. When he, Z-boy and Fin were kids, they used to pick up handfuls of red tide mud and throw it at the ground, sending sparks flying in all directions. In those days, he had magic powers.

The foam from the waves glowed fluorescent green in the dark. There was some wave action, small but nice. Logan suddenly felt like bodysurfing because it always made him feel whole again. He stripped down and ran into the water. Even though the air was chilly, the water felt warm, like a bath, something you rarely felt in the cool Pacific. It was weird seeing the whitewash from a crashing wave at night but not the wave itself. He had to listen for the wave forming and feel for the current flowing away from him to know when the swell was coming. Then he dug his feet into the ocean floor to steady himself, launching his body in front of the invisible face of the wave. As he sailed downward on his belly, the wave broke, sending him to shore surrounded by glowing white water. It was like bodysurfing in lava, only without flesh-eating pain.

As soon as the wave petered out, he turned around and ran back through the water toward the break. Sparks went flying as he dove into the incoming waves. He felt free and happy.

The waves calmed for a minute and he floated by himself in the darkness. Suddenly, the water lit up about ten feet to his right.

A fin broke the surface.

For a second, Logan freaked. Thoughts of a shark attack at night sent a chill up his spine. Then the fin disappeared, and another popped up to his left. Then he knew.

Dolphins.

He'd seen plenty of them in his life. They always swam along the coast in the late afternoon. But he'd never seen them this close before. Plus with the eerie lighting from the phosphorescence . . . they looked like water angels as they circled him.

Logan laughed out loud as they kept glancing at him, their

eyes glowing. When the next wave came, he almost hated for the moment to end. But he was never one to pass up a good wave.

"See ya, Flippers," he saluted as he swam into the next break. He bodysurfed down the face of the wave. It was like flying. Then, one of the dolphins suddenly reappeared right alongside him, surfing the wave until it flipped and finally turned back.

Logan skimmed ashore and caught himself on the mud. He turned over onto his back and let the water recede around his body. The sudden chill from the night air gave him goose bumps. He scooped a handful of mud, stood up, and spun around, throwing the mud in a circle. The ground lit up like the Milky Way, then disappeared into darkness.

"That is so cool."

Logan turned and saw Emmie sitting on the shore watching. He hit the deck.

"I'm naked, Emmie," he said, embarrassed. "How long you been there?"

"Just a couple minutes. I saw you come down." She was dressed in her usual surfer-girl gear of Bermuda board shorts, slaps and a Billabong tank top. Her bleached-out hair blew freely in the breeze.

Logan didn't know what to say.

"You want your clothes?" she offered.

"Uh, yeah, if you don't mind."

"No, I don't mind." She smiled and held them up for him, but made no effort to get them into his hands.

Logan shook his head. "Funny. How 'bout tossing 'em over my way?"

Logan watched her mull it over. He laughed when she threw his clothes halfway between them. Then she sat back and waited.

Logan snaked his way over the cold sand like a soldier scrambling for cover. He snatched his boxers, then swung around to get them over his muddy feet, jumping up quickly to pull them to his waist.

"Nice butt." Emmie giggled.

Logan tried to shake the sand out of his shorts that now coated his nice butt. It was no use. He'd have to grin and bear it.

"Uh, thanks." If Emmie could see his face in the dark, she'd know it was redder than the tide that rose up around his ankles. Logan dressed quickly, getting more sand jammed in every nook and cranny of his body. He stood up and shook his wet hair like a dog, making sure Emmie got wet too.

"Hey!" she screamed.

"Oh, you don't like the water? Maybe I'll just throw you in then."

He made a fake lunge for her and she fell over backward. She scrambled to her feet, grabbed a handful of sand and threw it lamely at him. Sparks lit up the sand around his feet. Logan grabbed some mud and gave chase, their glowing footsteps lighting up the ground like fireflies in the night.

Emmie headed for the deep sand and, being lighter on her feet, managed to ditch Logan's every attempt to grab her. Finally, he fell to his knees, out of breath. She stood over him.

"Come on, old man. I thought you were an athlete."

Logan coughed for a few hacking moments. "Too much weed."

They both laughed, shivering in the breeze. Suddenly, he lunged for her, grabbing her waist and tackling her to the sand. He pinned her against the ground, laughing. "But I'm still pretty crafty."

He could feel her heart beating fast against his chest. He suddenly thought about kissing her. But she gave him a look, like she knew what he was thinking, and he let go. They lay there facing each other, smiling awkwardly. He could feel her breath on his face. It smelled of sweet fruit, like a peach or something.

"You seemed like a little kid out there in the water," she said, reaching over and moving his long hair out of his eyes. "You looked happy."

"I like the ocean," he said. He wanted to say that he loved shooting off the top of a wave or sailing down the face at incredible speeds, barely feeling the water below. Nothing made him happier or more at peace with himself than the ocean. But he thought that sounded stupid, so he changed the subject.

"So where were you?" he asked. "I didn't see you at Fin's ceremony. Or at the party."

Emmie stared at the sand. "No, it's just too weird. They all think I'm the girlfriend who got dumped or something . . . Now they'll feel even sorrier for me . . ."

"That's not true . . . I always felt sorry for you."

Emmie didn't laugh.

"Bad joke . . ."

He could see her lips trembling even in the dark. She rubbed her shoulder as an onshore breeze kicked up. She glanced around nervously.

"What?" Logan asked.

"It's just . . . weird, isn't it?" She sniffled. "Knowing someone who died? I never knew anyone . . . 'cept my piano teacher. But I hated piano, so that doesn't count."

"Tell me about it. I thought you had to be forty or something to kick the bucket. We shouldn't have to be thinking about this shit."

"Then let's not." She rolled onto her back, looking up at the night sky. "Can I ask you something else instead?"

Logan nodded.

"How come you never asked me to the prom?"

Logan blinked. Did she know that he'd almost called her, but chickened out at the last minute? "I . . . I just thought . . . you'd think it was weird 'cause we've known each other so long . . . and that maybe the last thing you'd want was to go out with another Pier Avenue surfer."

"So you asked a girl you barely knew? Was she worth fighting over?"

"No," Logan said matter-of-factly.

She nodded, surprised. "But I only . . ." She didn't say anything else.

"What?"

She shook her head. "Nothing. It's stupid."

Logan reached out and brought her close. She didn't resist. And even though they had never really touched in all the years they'd known each other, he felt comfortable being close to her.

"Nothing's stupid . . . ," he said.

He gazed at her slightly parted lips, feeling her breath on his chest. Logan brushed back her hair. He wanted to kiss her, to feel her warmth.

"I only went out with Fin because you never asked me," she whispered.

His lips gently touched hers. He could taste her breath now. It wasn't peach, but something like cinnamon. It was sweet either way.

They kissed. It was like everything he loved about the ocean—endless and exhilarating all at the same time. But something felt off. He opened his eyes and realized they were near the spot where Fin had lay dead. He jumped up.

"What is it?"

He looked at the lifeguard station and could see it all in his mind. "This is where Fin . . ."

She got it. "Where he . . . died?"

"I think so . . . He was lying right there, staring at me . . ." Logan felt woozy again—it was all too much. Fin, Emmie, Z-boy, the offer . . .

Emmie took his hand and pulled him away from the spot. They started moving back toward Buddy's house in silence. When he looked up, he saw Broza watching them from the balcony.

Logan panicked.

"I have to go, Em." He started walking away. "I'm sorry . . ."

"Hey, Logan—" she called out.

Logan broke into a run. When he glanced up at the house again, Broza was gone. Was his mind playing tricks?

"Logan!"

He was finished talking for today. It was too much to deal with right now. He had to get away before his head imploded.

Logan ran home and didn't look back.

8

LOGAN PUSHED OPEN the sliding glass door to his house, then quickly locked it behind him. He was out of breath, dizzy. He leaned over with his hands on his knees and tried to breathe deeply.

He heard some noises coming from upstairs. His mom should have been doing the night shift at work. He moved toward the stairs. "Mom?"

No answer. Then he saw the front door.

It had been jimmied open. Next to it was a pile of stuff. *His stuff.* A DVD player, the stereo, *his Xbox and PS2!*

He smelled pot.

Logan silently freaked. He thought about leaving, but that was his stuff, damn it! Logan grabbed the aluminum bat that stood by the front door and looked up the stairs. Nobody was going to steal his shit and get away with it.

When he got to the second floor, he heard sounds coming from his mom's bedroom. Logan tightened his grip on the bat, counting down quietly from *five* as he inched forward. When he hit *one*, he leaped in, bat raised for attack. "FREEZE, MUTHERFU—!"

Logan stopped in mid-motion when he saw a middle-aged man going through his mom's dresser drawers. The man wore only trunks and slaps, showing off his flabby belly and dirty feet. He had a joint dangling from his lips and a headset covering his thinning blond hair, plugged into an old Sony Walkman radio. When the man glanced over his shoulder and saw Logan, he froze—a kid caught with his hand in the cookie jar. He sighed, removed his headset and meekly held up his hand to ward off the questions that were about to come his way.

"Dad?" asked Logan in disbelief.

His dad slowly turned around, smiling meekly. "Is that how you greet your old man?" His face was puffy and red from the sun. He eyed the bat cautiously. "You gonna beat the crap outta me now, Logan?"

Logan didn't release his attack mode grip on the bat. It took him a few seconds to gather his thoughts enough to come out with a coherent sentence.

"What the fuck are you doing here?"

His dad stared at him for a beat. "Just reliving old times."

"What are you doing here?" Logan asked again.

"Toke?" He held out his joint for Logan.

Logan used to like his dad: a lifelong surfer, laid-back, always quick to laugh, chug a brew, go surfing. Problem was, he was a compulsive gambler and a lousy father who owed them money.

Logan furrowed his brow. "Does Mom know you're here?"

He shrugged, avoiding Logan's eyes, before stubbing out the joint on the bottom of his slaps and pocketing it. "Not exactly. I'm just collecting some things."

"You mean *my* things."

He paused. "I don't think you paid for them, Logan."

"Well, you sure as hell didn't, not since you maxed all our credit cards and forced Mom to work extra shifts! Were you just going to take everything?"

"Things aren't always black and white—" He smiled, but his eyes just seemed sad.

Logan saw red and raised his bat.

His dad flinched. "All right, man. I know I'm a bastard. I deserve your hatred. But it's not like I'm a junkie or fooled around on your mom. Things just got outta hand, you know?"

"Do you even *know* what we're going through? Do you even care that I'm *graduating*?"

"I heard you got accepted to Sacramento State. Hey man, good for you. But um . . ." He looked away.

Logan's instinct told him he was about to be screwed again.

"The money situation . . . you know, that we saved for you to go to school and all . . . That might be a bit of a problem . . ."

Logan could feel his blood boiling. "You spent that too, didn't you?" he hissed.

His dad slowly moved toward Logan and the door. "No, not exactly. I might be a bastard but I'm not a . . ." He searched for the right word.

"A bloodsucking, deadbeat dickweed?" Logan wasn't joking.

He inched closer to the doorway, nodding. Logan could smell alcohol.

"Well, maybe. It's just that the bank has . . ."

Logan raised his bat a few inches. "What?"

"Frozen those assets, you know, until all the debt has been cleared and we settle this thing about the bad checks—"

"Jesus Christ! Who *are* you?" Logan's eyes welled up. "Don't you even *think* about what you're doing to us?"

His dad squeezed past him into the hall and headed toward the stairs. Logan had images of pushing his father down the staircase, seeing him airborne until his head came smashing down on the tiles below.

Logan jabbed the bat in his dad's direction. "You know, I almost forgot about you. But now, I just hate you."

"Don't say that. You grew up all right. I treated you like a man. Like a real person. Like a friend. That's gotta be worth something."

"I'm not your friend. I'm not even your son anymore. There's nothing here for you. No money, nothing."

"So, you the man of the house now? You gonna run things?" He puffed up his chest even as he backed down to the first floor.

"Better than you."

"You have a job? Gonna take care of your mom? Doing what? What are you qualified for? Working at your uncle's restaurant?"

Logan watched his dad reach for the front doorknob.

"Well, I *was* going to go to college to *learn* something," Logan hissed.

"Hey man, I raised you, for better or worse. I could've left you a long time ago. But I didn't. I tried to show you a good time. I showed you the beauty of the ocean, the awesomeness of the wave. I wasn't one of those idiots who lectures their son about the evils of partying and having a good time. Those are things that make life worth living. Everything else . . . I kept from you. I kept you from seeing the dark side—"

He looked down at the pile of loot by the door.

They stood there silently.

His dad never finished the sentence. Instead, he just softly opened the door, giving one last glance around the house, and disappeared quietly and empty-handed into the night.

Logan stood there for five minutes. The whole day had been one long mind-fuck. His brain swirled about in his head—he needed to focus and set his mind straight. He had to get out, hit the open road and feel the wind on his face.

9

LOGAN DROVE HIS scooter along the coast toward Marina del Rey. This time of night, he was the only one on this dark, lonely stretch of road. A lot was happening . . . Fin, Emmie and now his dad. Everything was getting just a little too weird.

He wanted to feel free, like he did when he was in the ocean or like now, just him and the road, the wind sailing through his hair. He didn't want to think about what his dad had said about the family money. College seemed even further away now. So that left him with the Broza option. If he only had a sign—

BAM!

There was a loud smack—all Logan saw was a flash of white and a pair of red eyes frozen in the headlight. His rear wheel skidded out of control, and the scooter flung itself into the oncoming lane, barreling straight into the curb—

BAM!

Logan sailed over his handlebars, like a stuntman being shot out of a cannon. For a brief moment, Logan thought he was floating. One eye focused on the moon watching silently above, the other saw his bike flip up and over him in slow motion. There was only the sound of the ground rushing up to meet him—

THUD!!

Logan hit the dune on the side of the road at full force, sliding and skidding out of control until he came to a sudden stop when he slammed violently into a chain-link fence.

He couldn't breathe. Flailing around like a fish out of water, he gasped for air and tried to roll over on his side. Deep inside, he knew not to panic. He'd just gotten the wind knocked out of him and needed to relax. But it took a whole minute before he could say his first word: "FFUUUUUCCCKKKKK!"

Logan flopped onto his back and took short, deep breaths. His heart felt like it was going to explode, and his ankle shot a piercing pain up his leg.

"Goddamn it, goddamn it!" he kept saying over and over. When he finally got his breath back and calmed down, he lay there, trying to get his thoughts straight. He felt like he had been tossed off a train. When he tried to move his left ankle, a searing pain shot through his whole body.

Damn! It's busted!

Logan reached in his pocket for his cell phone, but it was gone. Strike three, he thought. He looked up at the light that he thought was the moon, but was really a light from the power plant that shined ominously across the road. Steam pumped out of the chimneys in huge billowing clouds that filled the night sky.

Logan had three options: cry like a wuss, scream for help or crawl back to the road and flag down a car. He decided on all three.

"HHHEEEELLLLLPPPPPPP!!!!!" he yelled till his voice gave out.

It was no use. The power plant drowned him out. So he just lay there. *What a wuss. Get up, get up off your ass and stop feeling sorry for yourself!*

Logan wiped his eyes, but only got sand in them. He stared up at the small hill he had slid down and saw the trail his body had left. *OK, I can do this. Fin's dead and you're not, so you got no right to complain! Now get up to that road, even if you have to crawl on your elbows!*

Logan started crawling. It took him an hour and his ankle hurt like hell, but he made it. When he got to the curb, he saw what he had hit: a big possum, spread out over twenty feet of skid marks. At the curb where his tire had hit, he saw a tiny claw clutching the edge. His eyes drifted over to his scooter, or what was left of it. The front wheel was bent in half, and the exhaust system and the seat were completely missing. And there was his phone, smashed to pieces. Great.

A light burned in his eyes. He looked up to see the headlights of a pickup approaching slowly. The truck stopped, and a pudgy power plant worker stepped out to survey the damage. He trained his flashlight on the skid mark and possum parts and followed them until it reached Logan.

"Roadkill" was all the guy said.

"D-do you think you could give me a ride home? My scooter's totaled," Logan asked.

The worker seemed tired and spent, like he'd just gotten off a twelve-hour shift. "Can you walk?"

"I don't think so." Logan tried to get up, but the pain forced him back onto his butt.

The guy stared into Logan's eyes like he was examining some machine. "Who's the president?" he asked.

"Of what?" Logan answered.

"Do you know what day it is?"

"Um . . ." He had never been good with dates. He took a guess. "Friday?"

The worker checked his watch. "Close enough."

10

LOGAN'S MOM WORKED the
night shift at the ER, and she wasn't happy to see Logan showing
up at 2:30 in the morning. She looked way too beat—tired eyes,
tired mouth, even her hair looked tired and strung out. Nurse
Wendy Tom had spent a good part of Logan's teenage years
patching up his wounds, or bringing him into work because he
had busted a wrist skateboarding in an empty pool or gotten
beaned by a surfboard. So she wasn't surprised when she found
him getting fitted for a cast around his broken ankle.

"Hairline fracture," he said.

She crossed her arms and sighed. This, Logan knew, was the
sign that she was waiting for The Explanation.

"Possum ran into me."

Wendy lowered her glasses and cross-examined. "Have you
been drinking?"

"No." He knew it was best to stick to the facts and not offer any justifications.

"Pot?"

"No, ma'am."

She wasn't buying the choirboy act. "Girl?"

He hesitated. He thought of Emmie and blushed.

She let him squirm and studied him closely. "Why were you headed up the coast at this hour? Where were you going?"

"I don't know . . . ," he whispered, trying to remember how it started. "Dad . . ." He looked up at her for the first time. "And Fin. And . . ."

He could see the concern in her eyes. He suddenly felt eight years old, scraped up and beaten. A little boy waiting for his mom to pick him up from the nurse's office.

She dropped her arms and took his hand in hers. He stared into her eyes for a long moment, and then she put her arm around him to help him to his feet.

She nodded. "Let's go home, Logan."

His mom tucked Logan into bed for the first time in ten years. Logan thought about how she used to read stories to him and talk about what was going to happen in the coming day. Back then, tomorrow was always full of hope.

His mom brushed the hair out of his eyes. She acted like she was going to say something, but stopped herself.

She pulled the sheets up to his shoulders. "I know your dad was here tonight. He left an IOU for all the stuff he was stealing from us."

Logan sighed. "Yeah, I kicked him out."

"I'm sorry you had to do that. But thanks for defending the house. I'll be applying for a restraining order on him."

Logan shook his head, defeated. *Has it really come to this?* "I don't understand what's going on. He said things—"

"I know. About the money. About your schooling. You're going. I talked to your uncle Keith about it."

Uncle Keith, the Seafood King. Logan and Z-boy had both worked in his restaurant in Fisherman's Wharf over the summers, sporting that ridiculous fish-head hat that caused no end of embarrassment. Luckily, the Pier Avenue crew never went in there. Keith always had it in for Logan's dad, even though they were brothers. He took every opportunity to show Logan how much better he was, even saying things like "If your ma hadn't married the wrong guy, you coulda inherited all this." Then he'd wave his hand, showing off his greasy restaurant like it was a kingdom or something.

Logan made a face, but his mom ignored it.

"Keith wants you to work at the restaurant this summer," she said. "Zane can work too. He said you boys need a man in your life."

"What does *that* mean?"

"You know what it means." She glanced around at all his surf posters. "I told him I don't want you hanging out with that surf crowd anymore. You're going to college to use your brain to become someone. If you need any incentive, just look what happened to your dad."

"Mom, I'm not Dad."

"I just don't want you falling back to bad habits. You're smart, Logan. Smarter than Fin, definitely smarter than that Z-boy. Just use your head, kid." She kissed him on the cheek. "I think the restaurant would be good for you this summer."

"I'm tired of busing tables every summer." He pulled the sheet up over his shoulder. "Besides, I can't do anything with this busted ankle."

He imagined telling her about the job offer he'd had tonight. *I got a job as a pot smuggler though. The pay is excellent and I get to see the country. Pretty bitchin', huh?*

He could feel her staring at the back of his head. He knew she was trying to think of something supportive and loving to say, with maybe just the right amount of parental advice to keep him on the straight and narrow.

"Your uncle said you should be driving a car now. I'm sure when he hears about tonight, he'll come down here and kick your butt."

Logan shook his head. "Yeah, the Seafood King is gonna kick my butt."

His mom rose and headed for the door. "I told him if he wanted you to have a car so bad, he should buy one for you."

"What'd he say?"

"He laughed."

She turned off the lights. Logan looked at her shadow standing over him. The door closed. He thought he heard her whisper, "Please don't let him end up like his father." He lay there in the darkness, his ankle throbbing.

11

LOGAN OPENED HIS eyes. He winced from the sun and the pain shooting through his ankle. He reached down, feeling his cast, and it all came back to him.

Something hit his head. He sat up in bed and saw a few acorns lying in his lap. Confused, he looked up at the ceiling. Just then, an acorn flew through an open window across from him, smacking him on the nose.

Goddamn—

Logan awkwardly stumbled over to the window and saw Z-boy standing down below with a handful of acorns.

"Dude!" he shouted in a whisper. "Where were you last night? I had to crash at Buddy's."

"It's a long story . . ." He yawned, rubbing the sleep from his eyes.

"Come on, man. Get your ass in gear. We're supposed to be at Broza's at noon. It's already ten."

"Hold on," Logan bitched back. He chugged down a couple of painkillers. They had worked wonders last night. Then he grabbed the crutches that the nurse had given him and steadied himself. He snagged some smokes off the dresser and slowly managed his way downstairs.

When he opened the kitchen door, Z-boy was looking down at a freshly done tattoo on his shoulder.

"Check it out, dude! Me and Flea got branded last night!"

Logan stared at the tattoo, a cross stuck in the sands of a beach. The cross said F.H.—R.I.P. and underneath said SURF OR DIE.

Logan couldn't believe it. "You're kidding, right?"

"What're you talking about? Fin was like a brother—" Z-boy glanced up for the first time, saw Logan's cast and gasped.

"No . . . *way*" was all he said. He moved in closer for a better look. Z-boy shook his head as if someone had just killed his cat. "Muther . . . goddamn . . . bitch! What is *this*?!" he hissed.

"Shut up! My mom's still asleep." Logan hobbled through the yard into the back alley. Z-boy watched in shock, then dashed after him.

"What the—I just saw you last night!" He noticed the scrapes on Logan's face. "What happened?"

Logan leaned against the garage door, took a cigarette out of his pocket and lit up. "I hit a possum."

Z-boy looked at him in disbelief. "You hit . . . a possum? Why? What'd it do to *you*?"

Logan took a drag. "On my scooter, idiot. I wiped out. Busted my ankle."

Z-boy stared at his cast. "You hit a possum . . ."

"Yeah . . . after the party. I flipped, man. You shoulda seen it . . ."

"What about our job offer? We're still going to see Broza,

right? But he can't see you like this." Z-boy kept staring at the cast. "Does it hurt?"

"Yeah, it hurts. And to hell with Broza. I'm not going now."

Z-boy panicked. "What?! *What?* Don't say that! Of course you're going. You're just in shock is all—"

"I'm not in shock." Logan thought about it. "Well, maybe I am. But I'm still not going. What would I say to my mom? 'I'll just be gone for a few days while I smuggle a hundred pounds of marijuana across state lines. Oh, and if I get caught, I guess I'll see you when I get out of prison.'"

Z-boy took a deep breath and analyzed the situation. Logan could see his thinking process as he kept coming up with arguments and shooting them down before he could finish the thought. It was a war zone in Z-boy's head, and intelligence was losing.

"You can't work at the restaurant where you have to stand all the time or carry trays of fish." Z-boy rubbed his chin, thinking. "On this job, you can sit. And since you broke your left ankle, you can still drive."

Logan took another drag. "I'm not supposed to drive. Doctor's orders."

Z-boy was not deterred. "You and I both know that a broken ankle is death to a surfer. You'll sit around and watch guys like me hit the waves every day, and you'll go psycho. You'll get depressed like you did before."

Logan remembered the summer he'd busted his wrist skating an empty pool. He'd sat around in a cast, staring at the wall, getting angry every time a surfer walked past his house.

Z-boy looked him in the eye. "Dude, I just want to surf. I know I'm not good enough to tour or compete. But surfing's all I got. I can't do a nine-to-five job or wear a suit. And if I worked at

7-Eleven, I'd never hear the end of it. I got nothing going for me. I'm not like you. You got talent. You're smart—"

"Okay, I get it."

"No, you don't, brah." Z-boy looked him straight in the eyes. "I need a way to live. This is my only chance. Dude, I could make some real money here and only have to work a few months a year and still surf most of the time. After a few years, I'll have enough money set up to retire—"

"Whoa, Z. You haven't even done this yet and you're already signing up for the retirement plan?"

"I've been thinking. I'm a perfect match for this. I could move up the ranks and when Broza retires, take over and run my own business. With you, of course."

Logan put his hand on Z-boy's shoulder. "Z, I am not a drug dealer."

Z-boy frowned. "Dude, pot isn't a drug, it's a plant, as in God's nature. You should know that, man. It's not dealing, it's distribution."

"Whatever. Police might have a different take on it."

"Hey, it's a well-known fact that George Washington grew hemp as a cash crop. Did you know the Constitution was written on hemp?"

Logan was dubious. "What are you, a historian now?"

"Hey, it's a fact. Well, at least on the Internet. But what's even more bogus is the fact that the ciggie you're smoking is okay, but pot isn't. How many people kick the bucket each year from smoking and boozing?" Z-boy paced back and forth. "A lot. Hundreds of thousands. Dead, every year. And how many die from pot? Zero. Nada. But pot is illegal, and alcohol and cigarettes are sponsoring NASCAR. Go figure that shit out."

Logan slowly exhaled, wondering what to say to that.

"Forget that, forget that. I got off track." Z-boy collected his thoughts and stopped pacing. "Logan. This'll fund our dream. Isn't that what we always wanted? Enough money so we can surf the rest of our lives without wearing a monkey suit and working for some corporation? Get a little beach hut in Mexico with some *bonita* chickitas, drinking mai tais, smoking weed, and surfing those long Baja waves . . ." Z-boy was transfixed by the thought. "Man, that would be awesome."

Logan took a deep breath. He liked that vision too. They had talked about somehow getting a million dollars and retiring before they hit twenty-five. That's all they'd spoken about last summer when they were down in Baja—how to win the Lotto, play the stock market or maybe even rob a bank.

Logan considered the dream while Z-boy took the opening and launched a new attack. "Look at Broza, man. Twenty-one and he's almost got a million. What's not to like?"

"Broza. Broza's not to like. You wanna end up like him?"

"What, rich? Uh, yeah."

"Don't be a smart-ass, Z-boy. He's just . . . so full of himself. I mean, calling himself The King? Who is he, Elvis?"

Z-boy rubbed his chin. "Maybe you just don't like successful people . . ."

Logan let that one pass.

Z-boy sighed. "The thing is"—he paused dramatically—"he really wants *you*. Not me. I'm just the bait. I can see that, I'm not stupid. Without you, it's a no go."

Logan took a few deep drags on his cigarette. Z-boy was right. "I don't think the university's gonna take kindly to me being a felon."

Z-boy put his hand on Logan's shoulder. "Look. Do it once. Just help me get in. Do it just this once, then quit, and I'll have proven myself and that'll be it. I'll be in. You can still go to school, whatever." He stood up, ready for action. "Besides, you need a new scooter. That costs big money."

"My mom says Uncle Keith is gonna take care of me. Maybe even buy me a car."

"Oh, so you want your mom to be in debt to your dad *and* uncle Keith? How selfish is that?"

Logan stewed, sucking on his cigarette, the ash growing long and red.

Z-boy nudged him. "Maybe I'm wrong. But I don't think you're ready to move away. Maybe this could be good for you, give you perspective, ya know? You need to do something to shake whatever's sticking up your ass, 'cause you're starting to stress *me* out, and I got nothing going for me!"

Logan ran his hands through his hair. "I wish I had a time machine, you know? Go back maybe two years and freeze it. Remember then? You, me and Fin, the Three Musketeers. Plus, my parents were still together."

"Those were killer days, brah," Z-boy said, smiling. "And they could be again. Come on . . ."

Logan felt stressed-out big-time about his future and knew deep down that he needed a break. He flicked his cigarette across the alley. "Maybe I could take a little time . . ."

Z-boy nodded. "That's right, dude. Just chill out a bit, take it easy, help your mom out . . ." He held his hands out, weighing the options. "What's better, wearing a fish hat and coming home stinking of red snapper or . . . working a few days here and there and making some real cash? Enough to take a few trips to Baja and start scoping out the terrain for Z-boy and Logan's Surf Shack!"

Z-boy was right. Logan knew he was never gonna wear his

uncle's fish hat again. "You mean, Logan and Z-boy's Surf Shack . . ."

Z-boy smiled. "Uh, that could work too."

Logan closed his eyes. He thought about his mom, about everything she'd sacrificed for him. He'd once asked her why she put up with his dad for all those years. She simply said, "Sometimes you just do what you have to in order to get by."

He took a deep breath, let everything out. "Okay."

"Okay?" Z-boy raised his eyebrows. "Okay what?" he said eagerly.

Logan opened his eyes. "Okay . . . let's go."

"Thank you, Jesus!" Z-boy hugged him. "Damn, boy! You won't regret this!"

Logan looked at Z-boy's hopeful face and prayed he wouldn't.

12

"*TOTO, 1 DON'T* think we're in Kansas any-more," Z-boy said.

Clearly lost, Z-boy's white-boy Geo Metro chugged slowly through the gray streets of Compton.

"Ya think?" Logan said sarcastically. "What the hell does Broza live out here for?" Logan slouched down, trying not to be too conspicuous. He recognized a burnt-out street corner from the news. "Isn't this where the riots started?" he asked nervously.

"Almost. A few blocks south, I think. But I saw this street in *Boyz N the Hood.*"

"That makes me feel better. Maybe you should ask for directions," Logan said.

"Are you crazy? I'm not gonna stop here. They'll kill us."

"What're you, afraid? I thought you were a tough guy," Logan said.

"Tough guy? I'm not tough. I just like living is all." Z-boy's eyes darted left and right to make sure no one was sneaking up on him.

"You're exaggerating."

"Exaggerating? Okay, *you* ask directions. Look, there's a little girl." Z-boy slowed the car close to the curb.

A black girl dressed in pink overalls stood alone on a street corner. She eyed the approaching car suspiciously.

Logan hesitated. "What's a little girl doing out by herself in this neighborhood?"

"What, are you afraid of a little girl too?" Z-boy snorted.

"Shut up. I'm not afraid." Logan rolled down his window.

"Excuse me. Little girl. Hey, could you tell us where Chester Avenue is?" Logan used his choirboy looks to make himself seem as innocent as possible.

The girl examined Logan closely. She leaned forward and peered into the car at Z-boy.

Z-boy gave a little wave. "Hello, little gi—"

"WHITEY'S HERE!" She screamed at the top of her lungs. "WHITEY'S HERE!!"

Logan froze. "No, no, we're just lost—"

Her eyes went wide as she waved her arms about. "WHITIES!!"

Z-boy held his hands up. "Listen! We're not gonna hurt you! We just need directions!"

"WHITIES!!"

"*Please!*" Logan begged. "We don't want trouble."

The girl looked him straight in the eye. "You in the wrong place, mister. The only white peoples that come here is looking for trouble, believe me."

"But—"

"WHITIES! WHITEY'S HERE!"

Logan saw trouble coming fast. Three hard-core gangbangers were strutting up from the rear and they were not happy.

"Go. Z-boy. *Now.*"

"What?" Z-boy muttered, frozen in fear.

Logan rolled up his window and yelled in Z-boy's face. *"GO!!"*

Z-boy saw four other homies running across the street toward them. He hit the gas without putting the clutch in gear. The car seized and died.

"No! No, no, no!" Z-boy tried to restart the car, grinding the clutch.

"Start the goddamn car!" Logan shouted in full panic mode.

"I'm trying!"

Gangbangers surrounded the car, guns in hand.

Z-boy tried desperately to coordinate the clutch and the ignition, but the car failed him every time.

A meaty-looking gangbanger tapped on the window with the tip of his gat.

"Dang!" Z-boy threw up his hands. He then put on his most friendly face, grinning in a mixture of fear and desperation as he turned to face his end.

"We're dead," Logan muttered. He started chewing on his hair.

"Shut up! I can do this," Z-boy said through his teeth.

The gangbanger, wearing a tight tank top that showed off all his tattoos and muscles, indicated that Z should roll down his window.

Z-boy opened his window a crack and began his pitch. "Hello, friend. We were just asking the young lady for directions and I think she thought—"

"Shut up, wigger. What'ya say to her?" the gangbanger demanded.

Z-boy began to sweat. "Well, sir, we merely asked if she knew where Chester Avenue was—"

"Chester Avenue? Now, what would two white boys want on Chester Avenue?" he asked as he lowered his shades.

Z-boy took a deep breath. "Well, we're friends with Mr. Broza—"

The gangbanger laughed. "King Broza? You in with him?" The others laughed too. "I guess the surfer hair shoulda tipped us off!"

Z-boy looked at Logan, shrugged slightly, then turned back to his tormentor. "Uh, yeah. Is that a good thing?"

"Hell, you right there. That's his house over there. The ugly one."

Z-boy and Logan turned their attention to the street corner fifteen feet in front of them. The street sign said Chester Avenue. Three houses in, an ugly, unpainted shack stood behind a rusty chain-link fence. Broza's boring white Ford Taurus sat in the driveway. A pit bull lay asleep on the porch.

Logan shook his head. "You're such an idiot."

"Look, don't be hard on yourself," Z-boy said out of the side of his mouth.

Logan stared at Z-boy without expression.

"Let me just finish with my man here . . ." Z-boy turned back to the gangbanger and smiled. "Well, I guess we're not lost anymore."

The gangbangers glared at them through the windows. "Bit far from the beach, ain't ya?"

Z-boy nodded. "That's us, just a couple of surfer boys lost in Compton."

The gangbanger put his gun back in his pants. "Yeah, well, you do your business with The King and you surf the hell outta here. Understand?"

"Oh, yes, sir. Absolutely."

"All right then. The name's Goldie. I guess we'll be seeing ya." He smiled, showing off a mouthful of gold-plated front teeth.

"Nice grill, man," Z-boy said.

Goldie stopped smiling. "Try your car now," he said as he signaled his guys to return to their posts.

Z-boy turned the ignition. The car started up.

"Thanks." He waved meekly to their backs.

"Just go, will ya? Jeez." Logan shook his head.

"Okay, okay. It's right there." He put the car in gear and chugged around the corner.

Z-boy stopped in front of Broza's house and killed the engine. "Well, we're here!"

Logan looked around. It was not the kind of neighborhood they had grown up in. No beach houses, quaint streets with sidewalk cafés or white people for that matter. Only run-down bungalows with barred-up windows and graffitied walls.

Logan reached in his pocket and pulled out his painkillers. "I have a feeling I'm gonna need these." He popped one into his mouth. "Let's do this before I wake up and change my mind."

13

LOGAN AND Z-BOY stood in front of the chain-link gate, staring at an overweight pit bull who bared its teeth every time it snored. The yard stank of warmed-over crap.

"Think he'll bite?" Z-boy whispered.

Logan looked at Z-boy. "Only one way to find out."

"Me? Why me?"

"Your idea. Your connection. *You're* going." Logan smiled sadistically.

"Okay, okay. I can handle a little doggie."

"Just like you handled that little girl, huh?" Logan unlatched the gate for Z-boy.

"Hey, I'm the one who got us outta there after you totally choked." Z-boy slowly opened the rusty gate, which squealed like a pig. Wincing, he cracked it open just wide enough to squeeze through. The dog stirred, glancing at them through half-closed eyes. He didn't bother getting up.

"See? He's just a friendly pooch," Z-boy said. "Aren't you, little fella?"

The dog didn't react.

"Just move slowly," Logan warned. "Don't get him excited."

Z-boy padded quietly toward the porch, glancing back at Logan. "Thanks, brah. If he attacks, I'm gonna take you down with me."

Logan's face went gray. "Uh-oh."

When Z-boy turned around, the pit bull was standing on all fours, eyes blazing and teeth snarling. Z-boy froze. "Oh, crap. I think I pissed myself," he said through his teeth.

The pit bull jumped off the porch and landed in front of Z-boy. He took a step and sniffed at Z-boy's crotch. The dog started growling the kind of growl you hear only before a vicious attack.

Z-boy let out a high-pitched squeal. "Heeerrrre, pooochie . . ."

Logan panicked. He hopped through the gate, screaming, "HEY, UGLY!"

The pit bull seemed confused. Logan hopped a few feet to the left of Z-boy, waving his crutches at the dog's face. "HEY! HEY! OVER HERE!"

"What are you doing?" Z-boy hissed.

"Diversion!" Logan started hopping around the yard. The pit bull leaped at him, snapping and yapping. Logan stumbled out of the way, quickly trying to master the art of Crutch Fu. He waved his crutch in front of him while balancing on one foot. "Go get Broza! Quick!" he yelled.

"I'm already here."

Logan looked up to see Broza standing on the porch in a robe and boxer shorts. Broza yelled out, "General! GetYourBigBlack AssOverHereRightNow!"

The dog stumbled to a stop and ambled up to his master. When Logan realized the dog wasn't going to kill him, he collapsed, out of breath.

Z-boy smiled dumbly, as if nothing had happened. "Hey, King. We're here!"

Broza grinned as he slapped his pooch affectionately on the back. "I see you passed the first test."

"Test?" Logan said angrily. "We coulda been killed!"

"A mule has to be able to think quickly in the face of disaster," Broza explained like a field commander. "Only in crisis can you find the true character of a man."

"Who said that?" Logan asked.

"My screenwriting teacher. I'm thinking of making a movie about my life." Broza glanced down at Logan's cast. "What the hell happened to your leg?"

Logan used his crutches to slowly get up. "I hit a possum on my scooter."

Broza sighed. "Can you drive?"

"Yeah."

"You sure?"

"Yeah, man. Didn't you just see me almost take out your dog?"

Broza shook his head. "A possum! For real?" He chuckled. "Maybe we can use it."

As Logan moved past Z-boy, he whispered, "I shoulda let the dog have you for dinner."

Z-boy shrugged. "Hey, it was a test. That means we acted like partners. It was all part of the plan."

"Well, you're here, that's what counts." Broza held out his hand for a high-five with Logan. "LoganTomWhatupBro!"

Logan frowned, but slapped his hand anyway.

"Hey, can I be in your movie?" Z-boy asked as he entered.

"You already are." Broza closed the door behind them and locked all six dead bolts.

Logan looked around. To say the place was a dump was being kind. The floor showed the remains of a green shag carpet that had probably been white at some point. The walls were a mixture of water-stained plywood and old newspaper. The kitchen had a week's worth of dirty dishes and smelly, overflowing trash.

"So, uh, this is your kingdom, Mr. King?" Logan said. His gut wrenched. This guy was a millionaire?

Z-boy stared at a black velvet painting of Denzel Washington on the wall. "Cool painting . . ." was all he could muster.

Broza looked pissed. "You . . . don't like my crib?"

Logan and Z-boy glanced at each other. "No, I like what you did with the place. Very . . . urban." Logan tried to hint to Z-boy that they should get the hell out.

"Yeah . . . urban," Z-boy agreed, trying to decipher Logan's facial tics. "What?"

Broza burst out laughing. "You idiots. It's a front."

"I knew it," Z-boy said.

"So living out here is like a disguise?" Logan asked, doubtful.

Broza smiled deviously. "Well, if you're dealing in illegal substances, you need a safe house to do business in. This is one neighborhood even the cops are afraid to go into. I pay off Goldie and the boys for protection, keep a low profile and nobody knows I'm here. If the cops ever check it out, all they'll see is poor white trash."

"But you're the only whitey around."

Broza laughed. "So you met Tanisha? She's my level-one alarm system."

Z-boy jumped in. "I knew it! She acted too innocent to be real."

"Locals know I'm in with the gang. They don't bother me, I don't bother them. It's a perfect setup."

"I guess . . . ," Logan reasoned, "if you want to live a lie."

"Careful there, boy. I'm just a small-business man doing what he has to in order to compete. We are providing a valuable service."

"I told him that too. Great minds think alike," said Z-boy.

Logan nodded. "And I'm guessing maybe the laws are different for minors if they get caught?"

Broza smiled. "I knew you were smart, Logan Tom. You're putting that education to good use. That's why I want you!"

"Employing underage mules to do your shipping . . . Too bad there're no pot unions . . ." Logan laughed cynically.

"Hey, if they have their heads on straight, clean records and can pass for adults to avoid suspicion, why not? Beats working at 7-Eleven."

Logan was about to say something, but couldn't come up with a counterargument to that. So he just shut his mouth.

"Exactly," said Broza. "Now come with me." He turned and headed down a dark hallway.

Logan didn't like it. The peeling wallpaper and dim lighting reminded him of some horror movie—the ones where the victims never return.

He looked at Z-boy. "What do you think?" he whispered.

Z-boy could barely contain his awe. "It's like *Mission Impossible*, man. I bet we get disguises."

Logan shook his head. "I don't know about this . . ."

"Come on, man. Don't be such a girl. We're having a little adventure." Z-boy slapped his buddy on the back. "Hey, you came this far. Let's just try it."

Logan took a deep breath and followed Broza.

Broza stopped suddenly in the middle of the darkened hallway and showed them a ratty old rug. "Most houses in So-Cal don't have basements. This one does. That's why I bought it."

He lifted the rug and Logan saw the trapdoor. It was hard to notice except for the small keyhole in the floor. Broza pulled out a key that hung on a chain around his neck.

"I am assuming now that you've come all this way, you're in. I can't show you this if you still got doubts." Broza held up the key. "This is my business and I need to protect it."

Logan looked at the key. It was a plain old key, nothing special. He had always heard expressions like "the key to happiness is . . ." or "the key to success . . ." Now he stared at a key that could change everything.

And then something in his mind suddenly clicked. It was like that little key had opened a door in his head and the fear drained right out. Maybe he was a character in Broza's movie. And just like in a movie, everything would be okay in the end and he'd go on his way, all the wiser for his adventures.

"Let's do it."

"Good," Broza said.

"I'm in too," Z-boy said.

"I know it, brah. But there's just one thing." He glared hard at them. "If you ever rat me out, Goldie will hunt you down like dogs and get medieval on your ass, got it?"

Logan and Z-boy nodded dumbly. "Got it," they muttered.

"Damn straight." Broza opened a laundry closet to his left. "Here, you'll need these." He pulled out a brown paper bag and held it open for them. Inside were plastic sunglasses, the kind used for watching 3-D movies.

"We gonna watch movies?" Z-boy asked.

"Oh, this is better than a movie," Broza said. "You better put them on."

Broza unlocked the door and lifted it open. An intense light flooded the hallway from below.

"Damn, that's bright!" Z-boy said, shielding his eyes. Logan and Z-boy quickly put on their glasses.

"These glasses really help. I bought them in Amsterdam. They were designed to look at eclipses."

When Logan's eyes adjusted, he saw a stairway leading down into the light. He could smell the pungent scent of pot. Lots and lots of pot.

14

"**SO THIS IS** what heaven is like," Z-boy said.

"Welcome to the home office," Broza said proudly.

What Logan saw took his breath away.

They were standing in a large room, the size of the entire house. The room was covered in what looked like aluminum foil. On one side of the room was a forest—a forest of marijuana plants, all about four to six feet tall, maybe five hundred plants in all. A special irrigation system connected their base, and above that was an elaborate system of brilliant fluorescent lamps that flooded the room with light.

"Jesus, Broz," Logan said.

"They're nice, aren't they?" Broza said, admiring his own handiwork.

Z-boy wandered among the plants like a blind man who had just regained his sight. He softly caressed the leaves as if they were too sacred to hold. "You are now officially my role model, Broza. I've never seen anything more beautiful in all my life."

"That's my personal stock you're stroking. Premium high-blend Kush from Afghanistan. Actually, it's a special hybrid strain, genetically altered for a twelve-hour buzz. Only for my *very* special clients," said Broza. "Five thousand dollars a pound."

Broza lowered the light level and took off his glasses. "We just blast it when we're not down here. Check this out."

Broza opened up a long black case that was sitting on the floor. Inside were maybe a hundred different vials containing seeds. Each was labeled with a funky name: Stella Blue, Sticky Fingers, El Magico Haze, L.A. Confidential, Skunk Kush and Swiss Miss.

"My babies. I try to keep up and experiment with different varieties. Every year we go to the Cannabis Cup in Amsterdam. That's like the Olympics for guys like me. Over two thousand varieties, farmers from all over the world, and best of all, free samples."

Z-boy hyperventilated. "Dude, I read about that shit in *High Times*. When I get some *dinero,* I'm booking my next vacation there."

"Hey, man, Amsterdam is serious business," Broza said.

"I'm totally serious. I gotta do research, don't I?"

"What's with the shiny walls?" Logan asked.

Broza slapped the fortification. "It's moon nylon, what they use at NASA. Keeps the heat in. See, the DEA likes to patrol by helicopters. They use these infrared heat scanners to see if any house is giving off unusual amounts of heat. It's a good sign there might be a greenhouse or meth lab," Broza explained. "But get this—I tied this room's power into the city's grid, so this house has a really low electrical bill, thanks to the city of Compton. I'm not even on their radar."

Broza pointed to a machine in the corner. "We got CO_2 tanks, with carbon filters that rotate the oxygen three times every minute. That keeps the plants super healthy. Then we suck up all the heat from this room into a duct and put it to work!" He opened a curtained-off area, revealing a hot tub. "That's called recycling energy!"

Z-boy slapped hands with Broza. "Dude, you gotta show this place off in *MTV Cribs*. Put the others to shame!"

Broza grinned. "Damn straight. Now let's go over here and talk business."

Logan and Z-boy walked over to the largest part of the room. It really did look like an MTV crib: a huge wraparound white leather couch, a plasma-screen TV with PlayStation and Xbox, a killer surround sound system, laptops, foosball, a wet bar and a huge white bearskin rug to rest their feet on.

"*Niiice!*" Z-boy said, nodding. "Now we *talkin'*!"

Z-boy and Logan planted themselves on the couch.

"What happened to deception?" Logan asked.

Broza headed over to the bar. "If the cops ever get this far, it'll be too late anyways. Might as well live a little where it's safe."

"Thought of everything, huh?" Logan asked.

Broza pulled out a large box and dragged it over to the table. "If you don't think of everything, you get in trouble. It's that simple, dude."

Broza looked at his watch. "Production team will be here tomorrow. I'll be getting a fresh load from Mexico then. I've made arrangements for a drive-away. That gives you twenty-four hours to get ready."

"Whoa. What about my graduation?" Logan asked. "It's tomorrow morning."

"Graduation? What's that good for?" shot back Broza.

"Hey, just 'cause you guys didn't—"

"Hear that, Z-boy, he's gonna insult us." Broza laughed. "But then again, I got almost a million dollars and no degree. Them college kids? All they get is a hundred thousand dollars in debt and a job waiting tables."

"Amen," Z-boy said.

Logan brooded. "Look, I can't miss the ceremony. It's important to my mom."

"Your mom? That's sweet," Broza said. "Okay. Just because it's your first time, I'll help you out. You can go to your little ceremony. Just get your butts over here afterward. Did you tell your moms what kind of summer job you're getting into?"

"No," Logan said.

Broza chuckled. "I'm just giving you a hard time. She'll be fine once you got some of this in your pocket." He whipped out a wad of cash from his pocket about two inches thick and waved it in front of them. "Gree-e-en."

"That's beautiful, dude," Z-boy said.

"You guys play your cards right, you could have the same thing too. Hell, I might even pass the business on to you if you do well by me."

"Oh yeah, baby . . ." Z-boy said, grinning.

"Don't wave that in front of him," Logan said. "Let's just talk about the job we have to do right now."

Broza smiled. "Fine. Here's the deal. Like I said: four thousand dollars a trip. Three days to complete the deal. Here's how it works. We arrange to get a drive-away car for you—"

"The drive-away car, what's that?" Logan asked.

"It's like a delivery service," explained Broza. "Someone has a car they need transported from one coast to the other and they go through a service to find drivers at a very low cost, to drive their car across country. And we get a way to distribute our goods across state lines."

Logan was surprised. "So you just borrow someone's car and drive across the country with a hundred pounds of pot in the backseat?"

Z-boy shook his head. "Such an amateur. It's in the trunk, dork."

Broza shook his head in amazement. "Actually, it's all packed away in the panels of the car. Cop stops you, he won't find anything."

"What about drug-sniffing dogs?"

Broza nodded. "You'll find out tomorrow."

Logan was dubious. "And when we get there?"

"Our East Coast guys take apart the car, get the goods, reassemble it and you deliver the car in perfect shape. Everyone's happy."

"And then we get the money?"

"Our clients will give you approximately a hundred and forty thousand dollars in exchange."

"Holy mother! A hundred and forty grand for pot?" Z-boy exclaimed.

"We do pretty well for ourselves. I only grow here for my special clients. But for the bigger market, I can buy a hundred pounds from the Mexicans for under a hundred thousand dollars and turn it around for a hundred and forty thousand. Minus operational costs, salaries, like I said, we're doing pretty good for a few days' work."

"But how do we get back?" asked Logan.

"You fly."

"What about security? I mean we can't just walk onto a plane with a hundred and forty thousand dollar. Especially after 9/11."

"Relax. They're looking for nail clippers and liquid Nyquil—*making the world safe from the terrorists.*" He chuckled. "No, you're right. Fact is, it's not illegal to carry that much cash, but if they find you with that, it'll raise suspicions and they will confiscate the money. They won't arrest you, but if you want it back, you have to appear in court to prove it's yours."

"Okay, Boss. So how do we carry a hundred and forty thousand dollars past security? Baggage?" asked Z-boy.

"Hell, no." Broza said. "Never, *ever* let the money leave your side. No, you'll be wearing these."

Broza peered into the large box he'd dragged over and pulled out a pair of long underwear.

"Long johns? In the summer?" Logan was confused.

"Ah, these are special. There are pockets sewn in along the legs, stomach and back. Each pocket holds three to five grand in cash. Each of you will carry seventy thousand dollars on your body and you'll just walk through security."

"Uh, just like that? Isn't that a little, you know, risky?" asked Z-boy.

"That's how we've been doing it. Sometimes the simple ways work best." He looked at Z-boy and Logan. "'Course, you don't want to do anything stupid that would cause them to search you. Then it'll really be suspicious."

"So, we just act normal," Logan said.

"No, not normal for you, you potheads . . . normal like this." Broza reached in his pocket and produced a small plastic pin of an American flag.

Z-boy pointed to the flag pin. "And the flag is . . . what?"

"This, my friend, is the membership pin worn by all Young Republicans."

"Young Republicans? You gotta be shitting me. I'm not wearing that," Logan protested.

"*Exactly.*" Broza nodded, as if it were so obvious. "Pothead surf mules do *not* belong to the Young Republicans. That's why it's fucking genius. Cops, security . . . they won't hassle a Young Republican because he *must* be conservative, religious and righteous, dig? Besides, those born-again neocons are desperate these days to get young people into their ranks, so it makes sense that you'd be traveling around recruiting."

Logan laughed. "So not only do I have to risk my neck, but I gotta sell out too."

Broza held the flag pin up to the light, where it gleamed like gold. "It's not selling out if you're beating the system . . ."

15

"I'M GONNA ENJOY this," snickered Broza.

He clicked on the electric razor and then held it in front of Z-boy, who was sitting on a stool with a sheet covering his body.

"Dude, this hair took me years to perfect," Z-boy pleaded.

"Yeah, I can see that," Broza said as he examined Z-boy's dried-out dreads. "Anyways, it's all part of going undercover, my friend. Dreads might be a tipoff to the DEA that you're a pot-smoking surfer dude, don'tcha think?"

"Oh, man. It's my whole look."

"You want in, you gotta pay your dues. Why do you think Fin had short hair? Or me?" Broza said.

"I just thought you were from O.C. . . . ," Z-boy said.

"You know, the shaved noggin *is* in style," Logan piped in.

"Hey, you're next, funny man." Z-boy shut his eyes tight. "Oh, hell. Get on with it. I can't bear to watch."

Broza grabbed his remote and cranked up the tunes. Some badass gangsta rap that Logan didn't know pounded on the speakers.

While Broza attended to Z-boy's mane, Logan picked through the box that Broza had provided for them. He pulled a suit out of the box. Dark blue Sears special with a red-and-blue striped tie. The short-sleeve white button-down shirt was a nice touch. He held the suit in front of him and glanced in a mirror.

"Damn, that's scary," he said to himself. The only time he had ever worn a regular suit in his life (excluding his prom tux) was at his Catholic confirmation. Would he really end up wearing one of these later in life, like all those sellouts he saw taking their breaks every day at the downtown Starbucks? He shook the thought from his head and dropped the suit like it was made of Kryptonite.

Z-boy was making noise again. "Hey, asshole! That's too short, man!"

But Broza ignored him and danced around, waving his shears like they were a sword doing battle with Medusa's snakes.

Logan dug deeper in the box and tossed out a few other items: A Young Republicans handbook, magazines like *The Republic*, *Guns & Ammo*, and *Soldiers of Truth*, a Bible, pins from the last Republican National Convention, a map of Orlando, insect repellent, a baseball cap that said *God Bless America*, a framed picture of Ronald Reagan and Billy Graham, and some nonprescription glasses.

Logan put on the glasses for Broza to see. "How do I look?"

Broza shrugged. "You could pass for twenty-one. Those glasses will only help you feel older and more conservative."

"I feel ridiculous," Logan said.

"Beats jail," Broza added.

"True that," nodded Z-boy.

"All done! What d'ya think?" Broza shouted.

Logan turned around and laughed out loud. "Holy crap! It's that little choirboy, Zaney Adams! Nice ears, dude!" Logan had forgotten why Z-boy had worn his hair long for so many years: he had ears that stuck out like a mouse.

Z-boy looked in the mirror and screamed at the crew cut Broza had given him. "Goddamn it, Broza! I said not too short!!"

Broza chuckled. "Just tell your pals you got a job at Sears."

Z-boy tried pressing his ears flat against his head, but they sprang back out as soon as he let go. "I hate you."

"Okay, Logan. You're up." Broza fired up the clippers.

Z-boy leapt to his feet and threw the sheet at Logan. "Oh, let's see who's gonna cry now, pinhead."

Logan felt the top of his head. "I don't have a pinhead. And I sure don't have elephant ears, freak."

Logan sat down and tucked the sheet up around his neck. "Do your worst, King."

Broza did his best gay hairstylist impression. "I think we should go for a feathered, eighties look. Short and sassy and verrry chic!"

Logan stared at his long dark hair and took a deep breath. It had taken him a while to get it that long. On the bright side, maybe his mom would think he was turning over a new leaf, getting ready for college.

"How many mules have you employed?" Logan asked.

Broza thought about it as he clipped away. "Maybe six over the last four years. But I had Fin the longest. He was the best mule ever."

"What happened to the others?"

"You can't keep a mule too long. They get lazy and start to

think they're immune to danger. Got to keep 'em fresh and afraid. Fear will save your butt more times than not."

Logan wondered how long they would last.

Broza stopped cutting. "'Course, Milo got snagged a couple of years ago. Decided he wanted to sample some of the merchandise as he passed through the Grand Canyon. Doofus actually unpacked part of his car in the parking lot of the national park and sparked up on the hood as he looked out over the canyon. Dumbshit. That's a federal bust 'cause it's on federal land. Mandatory sentencing."

Z-boy piped in. "What happened to him?"

"I sicced our lawyer Donny on his ass. Persuaded him not to talk. He'll have a nice 401(k) set up for him when he gets out."

Logan's mouth went dry. "He got sent up?"

"Yeah, but he only got fifteen years."

Logan jumped up. "Fifteen years?!"

"Well, that was the minimum. He was over twenty-one. He'll be out in five with good behavior."

Logan took a deep breath.

"Relax, Logan," Broza purred in his ear. "You're a smart cat. That's why I picked you. You play by the rules and you won't get caught."

Logan tried to swallow, but his throat was dry. "And what exactly are the rules?"

Broza gave his best evil laugh. "All in good time, all in good time . . ."

16

LOGAN AND Z-BOY sat uncomfortably in their Sears slacks and jackets. Their hair, short and conservative, plus the glasses, gave them a look of young men in their first lower-management jobs.

Broza paced back and forth, studying the results of his masterful work. "Not bad. Not bad at all."

Broza aimed a digital camera at them one at a time and snapped away.

"What's that for?" Logan asked.

"Your fake driver's license and company I.D. cards. You'll be working for Goldie's Transport Service. We'll also have Young Republican cards made up for you."

"Come on, Broza. I feel like an idiot," Z-boy said as he tore off his clip-on tie.

"Hey, man. It's the Bible Belt look we're after here. Get used to it, Z."

Logan took his glasses off and rubbed his eyes. "Okay, so tell us these rules that'll keep us out of jail."

Broza put the camera down. "The Rules. Check it out . . ." He walked over to a whiteboard in the corner.

"I like to call them DISSD," Broza said as he wrote the letters out on the board. "As in 'You be *dissed* if I get pissed at you.'"

"Dissed, yeah . . ." said Z-boy. "Should we take notes?"

"No. But burn them into your brains, because ignoring any one of these rules puts you in danger and me at risk. And I don't take risks."

Z-boy sat up and focused. "Okay. Shoot."

"*D* is for *Driving*. This is the main part of your job. The rule here is simple: Never, *ever* break any traffic laws. Period. Don't speed, don't drive too slow. Don't swerve when you drive. Check to make sure your brake lights and turn signals are working. Obey all traffic signs. Pay attention and don't *ever* give a cop a reason to pull you over."

"We can do that," Logan said, looking to Z-boy for confirmation.

Broza leaned into their faces. "DO NOT PICK UP HITCHHIKERS." He eyed Z-boy. "What did I just say?"

"No hitchhikers. Right." Z-boy tapped his finger against his own forehead.

"Right," said Broza as stood up straight. "Now *IF* you are ever stopped by a police officer, pull over in the first and safest place available. Remain calm. Have easy-listening music playing on the radio. Casually have some of these fine publications I have provided for you lying on the backseat. But be *subtle* about it. You don't want to overplay it. Just think boring. Take a ticket, pay a fine if need be. But never give them a reason to search the car."

Logan imagined a cop grilling them for information. "What if they ask us where we're going?" he asked.

"Well, that leads me to our next letter: *I. Invest* in your character. The plates of the car will say California on them. That's normally a tip-off for interstate patrol. So you must invest in your purpose: you two are canvassing different states on behalf of the Republican Party. Read the handbook. Know the jargon. Practice talking in the car."

"Do Republicans really recruit like that?" Z-boy asked.

"You ever meet a Republican who didn't like to push his views on you? It's in their blood."

Z-boy nodded. "That's like my cousin Pete in Anaheim," he said as he tried to comb back his phantom dreadlocks with his hand. "He's a born-again. Talks about God and how abortion is evil and how welfare keeps poor people on crack. Shit like that."

"Well, pretend you're him. Remember, you're on legit business. You're doing a drive-away. You'll have proper papers. Just try not to talk unless you have to."

"Okay. What're the two *S*'s?" Logan asked, ready for more.

Broza circled the two *S*'s on the board. "*SS. Stopping* and *sleeping.* Never stop to sleep. You have a backseat. You will take turns and keep driving. I once made it across country in two and a half days driving tandem."

"That's harsh. Can we stop to eat at least?" Z-boy asked.

"Yeah, sure. But stick to drive-thrus. Try to stay away from places that attract cops: 7-Eleven. Denny's, Dunkin' Donuts. Stay away from crowds. If you're around people and trouble breaks out, leave. Rest stops are good. But don't hang there too long. They have security. And above all, no sightseeing. This is a job, not vacation."

"Got it. No fun," Z-boy said. "Not even the Grand Canyon?"

Broza stared at Z-boy. "Was that a joke? I hope so."

"Relax, man," Z-boy said. "I've already been to the Grand Canyon."

Logan hit Z-boy in the arm. "And the final *D*?"

Broza pointed to the *D* on the board. "The final *D* stands for *Delivery*. Now don't mess this up."

He sat down facing Logan and Z-boy. "I will give you the number for the guy you are delivering to in Orlando."

"Orlando, as in Disney World, as in Florida?" Z-boy asked.

Broza smiled. "Boy knows his geography. Yes, Orlando, Florida, as in, the drop-off point. Now if you don't mind?"

Z-boy bowed. "Please continue, professor."

"Your contact is Randy. He's a cool dude. But you need to call first to make sure the coast is clear. The phone may be tapped, so you're gonna use code."

"Cool," Z-boy said, rubbing his hands together. "Just like spies."

"You call when you are thirty minutes away. You'll say this is Rick's Furniture and you are calling to confirm delivery of a La-Z-Boy chair. Will anyone be home tomorrow? If he says yes, you go. If he says no, Friday will be better, the deal's off."

"The deal's off? But we got a car full of pot!" Logan said excitedly.

Broza held up his hands. "Call me from any pay phone, no cells. I'll give you further instructions. Just tell me the customer isn't home."

Logan and Z-boy looked at each other.

"If you get an okay, you go to Randy's house. Pull into their garage, they'll be waiting. One of you goes inside, one of you stays with the car. Randy will hand you a bag of money. Probably in a shopping bag. There will be a hundred and forty thousand dollars inside it."

"In small unmarked bills?" Z-boy joked.

"You watch a lot of movies, don't ya? Hold on, I'll show you." Broza went to a cupboard over the bar. When he opened it, Logan saw a shelf full of boxes of cereal and other items. He grabbed a box of Lucky Charms.

"You got any Cap'n Crunch back there?" Z-boy asked.

"Shut up and listen." Broza opened the box. Inside was a normal bag of cereal, but when he pulled it out, the cereal covered only the top half of the box. He dumped the rest of its contents onto the coffee table.

Twenty small bricks of cash wrapped in rubber bands fell out in front of their eyes. "This is what twenty grand looks like. Count it."

"Damn. I like Lucky Charms now," Z-boy said, gazing with his mouth open.

Logan stared at the cash spread out on the table. It was more money than he had seen in his entire life. He slowly reached down and picked up a stack of twenties. He fanned them quickly. He could buy a nice car with all this . . .

"No, organize the piles. Stack them here," Broza said, laying them out. "Now take the first pile and peel back the corner of each bill one at a time. How much is there?"

Logan counted the bills. "A thousand."

"Right. Now mark it on the paper band and count the next stack."

Logan carefully counted each stack. Z-boy watched closely. He glanced up at the cupboard full of cereal boxes. "Are all those filled . . . ?"

"No. I just really like Lucky Charms. My cash, I disperse in different places. Unlikely places."

"You don't put it in the bank?" Z-boy asked.

Broza frowned. "People get curious when you start depositing large sums of cash on a regular basis. I prefer burying it."

Logan couldn't believe it. "Burying it?"

"I'm not talking the front yard, nimrod," Broza said. "These are remote locations where people aren't building or repairing pipes or anything."

Z-boy nodded in approval. "Like treasure, huh? How much you got underground?"

Broza smiled, enjoying the attention. "Maybe eight hundred."

"Eight hundred what?" Z-boy asked.

"Thousand."

Logan lost count. "You put eight hundred thousand dollars in the ground?"

"Yeah. All over the state. And in Mexico. I have a property down there under a friend's name. You never know where you're gonna need some cash."

Logan and Z-boy looked at each other.

"It pays to play, boys. Keep your eyes on the prize and do well, you could be like me."

Logan glanced at the money on the table. *Maybe this was better than college.*

17

BROZA BEAMED. "NOW go home, get some rest. Pretend you have a job because starting now, you do. Goldie will bring you back here tomorrow. We'll have the crew here to get the car ready, and we'll go through your travel route and discuss any last details. We cool?"

Inside his head, Logan felt anything but cool. His ankle ached and so did his brain. But he nodded and got up with Z-boy's help, maneuvering his way awkwardly up the stairs. *What had he just committed himself to?*

Logan stepped outside onto the front porch. General panted heavily from the corner of the yard, watching him warily.

Broza patted Logan on the back. "Don't sweat it too much, man. It's all right, you'll see."

Famous last words. Logan waved good-bye to Broza and made his way to the car. He noticed the gangbangers across the street.

Goldie, the one who'd accosted them earlier, walked toward them.

"Damn, that Broza sho' do clean up you white boys. What're you selling, Bibles now?" He laughed, his gold teeth sparkling.

"Almost. We're Republicans," Z-boy said, blushing from embarrassment.

Goldie laughed even louder. "Republicans! HA! Last one was a Mormon. Before that, Jehovah's Witnesses. That Broza sure has a wicked mind. Say, what happened to that last mule, anyways? The surfer guy who thought he was hot shit? Ain't seen him around for a few weeks."

"He died," said Logan.

Goldie shook his head slowly. "Too bad . . . That boy was all right."

Logan lowered himself into the front seat. "Let's go, Z."

Goldie closed the door after Logan and leaned in through the window. "Seems like if we gonna be in business together, we should understand each other. We got financial relations with The King. If you're in good wit' him, you're good wit' me. You get on his bad side, I'm the one comin' for ya. And I won't be all smiles neither. Dig?"

Z-boy nodded. "We dig, we dig."

Goldie smiled. "Okay then. Have a nice day." He headed back across the street.

Logan watched him closely. "Well, I guess we'll stay on Mr. Broza's good side then," he muttered sarcastically.

Z-boy started the car and took a deep breath, pulling out slowly. "So, what'd you think?"

Logan slumped down in his seat. "Aside from hanging out with dealers and gangbangers, and getting ready to commit a felony, things are going nicely."

Z-boy gritted his teeth. "I'm gonna make this thing work, Logan. You'll see. I'll make enough money so I don't have to get a real job. Then one day, I'll show up at a high school reunion in a Hummer, just like Broza's. And my old teachers will be standing there, shittin' in their pants when I step out. I'll walk up to them and say, 'Dudes, I guess that diploma wasn't worth squat after all.'"

Logan thought that if he made that much money, all he'd want to do is see his mom happy again.

"In three months, you'll see," Z-boy continued. "We'll have plenty of dough, you'll have a new car, and we'll be taking trips down to Baja, just you and me, the waves, and our bonita chickitas."

Z-boy drove in silence, letting the dream hover before them. As they wound through the streets of South Central, Logan had a thought.

"There's only one problem," Logan said. "What do I tell my mom?"

"That we signed up to be camp counselors?"

"Camp counselors?" Logan laughed.

"Has a nice ring, don't it?" Z-boy asked. "Actually, it's kinda perfect in a way. They think we're away for a few weeks, earning cash and doing some good. And we are. Only we'll be down in Baja surfing after we make our delivery."

"My mom might think that's a bit of a stretch."

"We can make up a letter with a camp logo on it with all the details. Grab some nice mountain shots off the Web with some happy kids. The camp won't take calls, of course, but we'll check in every once in a while."

Logan shook his head. He could feel the last traces of morality slipping out the window. "You're the devil, aren't you?"

Z-boy gave his best devilish laugh. "I will corrupt you yet, Logan Tom!"

18

LOGAN WAS IN no hurry to get back to Hermosa. He didn't feel like explaining things to his mom. So they took surface streets, stopping at In-N-Out Burger, the Mall and the arcade along the way. He and Z-boy didn't talk much. They ended up watching the sunset from the Hermosa Pier. When Logan tried to get him to come to his house, Z-boy declined. "It's a full moon and it's pretty warm out. Besides, I don't wanna be a leech . . ."

Maybe Z-boy just wanted to be alone. They were going to be spending an awful lot of time together in the next few days, Logan thought.

Logan's mom was already asleep by the time he got inside. Her shifts at the hospital kept bouncing back and forth between night and morning. He never knew anymore when she was going to be home. He thought about waking her to explain his whole scheme while she wasn't fully alert. That might help. Let's see: *I look like a clean-cut doofus because I got a job as a camp counselor and I leave tomorrow* . . . Maybe he could drug her coffee in the morning.

Logan sat alone in the living room. He had his work cut out for him. As long as there were no more distractions—

When he glanced up, he saw Emmie's face hovering in the window. He nearly fell over. He stared for a moment to make sure she wasn't a ghost. Emmie motioned toward the front door.

Logan hobbled over to meet her. He pressed his ear to the door and listened. There was a faint tap on the other side.

Logan opened the door a crack. Emmie stood there in the darkness, her scrunched-up face peering in. Even though it was dark out, he could still see her jaw drop.

"Oh my God! What *happened* to you?" she whispered.

Logan stepped back, puzzled. Then he ran his hand through his hair and realized he didn't have any. He saw he was still dressed in that god-awful suit. *And* he was wearing a cast. He laughed.

"Well, since you last saw me, I busted my ankle when my scooter turned a possum into roadkill. Then I decided to become a Republican. What's up with you?"

"Your beautiful hair . . ." was all she could say. "What happened?" She reached up and felt his short cropped mane. He let her.

"It's a long story . . . It's just, there's a lot going on right now."

Emmie shook her head. "Listen, Logan, I don't know what happened the other night. I'm sorry if I did something to upset you . . ."

Logan remembered running off and leaving her alone on the beach. That look on her face said she felt it was all her fault somehow. She stepped into the light of the doorway. Logan could see how totally fine she was—the perfect surfer chick: bleached-out hair, freckles and big blue eyes, which were in shock at the moment.

She gazed sadly down at his cast. "Your poor foot . . . Are you okay?"

Logan sighed. "I don't know. If I can just survive the summer . . . The last few days have been . . ." He couldn't even begin to describe them. "Rough."

He looked at her for a moment, trying to decide whether he should tell her everything that had happened and everything that was going to happen. "It seems like the summer . . . is going to be a little different than I thought."

Suddenly, he found his own eyes getting moist. *Oh, no you don't!* He shut his eyes. *Don't you dare wuss out in front of a chick!* He lowered his head and tried to back off, but Emmie reeled him in, slowly, softly, and he let go.

He fell into her shoulder and let her arms engulf him. He didn't know what anything meant anymore; he had given up trying to figure it all out. She held him close, her lips finding his. She smelled of the sea, of everything that made him happy. Logan gave in. He was heading into the ride of his life and suddenly felt she was the only thing keeping him afloat as he plummeted into the darkness of the waves below.

19

WHEN HE AWOKE, Logan heard his mother shuffling around in the kitchen below. It was still dark outside. He remembered that he had to tell her something important, some story about summer camp. Did kids even go to summer camp anymore? He sat up on his elbows, rubbing the sleep out of his eyes.

Logan smelled the ocean. When he glanced over next to him, there she was, his mermaid. Emmie had a slight smile on her sleeping face. He softly brushed back her hair, watching her breathe.

Logan gazed at her slightly parted lips. He'd kissed those lips on the beach and run. Now he couldn't believe he was lying with her in his bed. He wanted to stay with her forever. But he kept hearing the sounds of his mother below and knew that moment was gone. He'd have to deal with his life.

Logan gave Emmie a quiet kiss on the nose, then sat up on the bed to collect his thoughts. What would his mom say about this? He was sure she had heard them during the night. What had he been thinking? It was like Emmie had made him drunk with giddiness.

Throwing on his trunks, he grabbed his crutches and hobbled downstairs. His mom sat at the kitchen table, drinking—whiskey, he thought by the smell of it. She didn't even notice him until he stood right next to her. When she glanced up, she seemed ten years older. He hadn't seen her like this since Dad left.

"Where's your hair?" she asked as if in a dream.

"It's gone" was all he said. Suddenly, all his explanations seemed lame. "What's wrong?"

She laughed. Actually, it was kind of a snort, the kind that said *What isn't?* She analyzed his new look. "You look like you did when you were eight."

"Mom, what's wrong?"

"Everything."

Logan waited.

She took a drink and let it settle in her gut. "I don't think your uncle is going to help us right now. Seems you can't trust your dad's side of the family, period."

"Why?"

A dark shadow passed over her eyes. "All men are bastards."

Logan didn't want to argue that point. Here he was, about to lie to her. "What'd he do?"

"Seems he was interested in more than us helping him out at the restaurant. I guess he figured since his brother was done with me—"

Logan scrunched his face up in disbelief. "Did he make a pass at you?"

She took another drink and didn't say anything.

"You didn't sleep with him, did you?"

She shot him a red-hot look that told him to back off.

"Well, what then?"

She winced. "I told him to go to hell. I-I kicked him . . . hard . . . where it counts." She snorted again.

Logan couldn't believe what he was hearing. "You kicked Uncle Keith in the nuts?"

Mom snickered like a little girl, but it quickly passed. "It was satisfying . . ."

Logan shook his head. "I knew you were a ballbuster, but . . ."

She wiped away a tear. "Hey, kid. Maybe college can wait a year, huh? I know you were on the fence about going to Sacramento . . ." She held his hand. "Just till all this gets settled, then next year, you'll see . . ."

Logan sat there. He didn't know whether to feel pissed off or elated. No college fund, no college. Now he was in Z-boy's shoes too.

He looked at his mom's drink. "What's that?"

"Johnnie Walker."

He grabbed the glass and gulped it down. It felt like someone shoved a hot poker down his throat. It burned, sinking deep into his belly, where it ate away at the bad feelings in the pit of his stomach.

"Easy there, cowboy," she said, looking a bit surprised. "Feeling grown up, are we?"

He breathed hard. "Just old." He sat down next to her.

"You have no idea what's in store for you . . ." She nodded quietly to herself. "So who's the girl?"

Logan had planned to lie about everything else, but he didn't have a cover for Emmie.

"Don't be embarrassed. I could hear you." She poured herself another drink. "At least someone should be having sex in this house."

Logan had never talked about sex with his parents. The closest he'd ever come to it was when his dad gave him his old porn magazines.

"You don't have to think so hard about it, kid. You're an adult now, right?"

"It's Emmie."

His mom raised her eyebrows, impressed. "Well, she always seemed like she could hold her own with you boys. Has this been going on long?"

"No. It's the first time."

His mom poured herself another drink. "It must be nice to be young and in love." A tear rolled down her cheek. "I always liked Emmie."

"We're not in love. We're just . . . friends." Logan felt embarrassed saying these things.

"Spoken like a true man. Only seventeen and already talking like your dad."

He didn't like being compared to his dad. Truth was, he didn't know exactly how he felt about Emmie. Even if he did, he wasn't about to tell his mom about it. "You're mad at him, not me."

She sat back and looked at her drink. "I guess it's none of my business anyways."

He tried to steer the conversation away from Emmie. "What happens now?"

"A date has been set in court for arbitration. But I've been told that trying to cut a deal may not change anything in the end. We might lose all the savings anyways to pay your dad's debts. And since the house is still in both of our names . . ."

"What . . . they want the house too?"

"We may have to sell." She glanced around the room, clenching her jaw. "Right now, I'm not sure how we're even going to pay for this month's mortgage with all the damn legal costs . . ."

Logan felt hollow. "It's not fair."

His mom raised her glass for a toast. "Welcome to the real world."

Watching her drink at the kitchen table, Logan suddenly realized that she wasn't just his mother anymore. She was a person struggling to make things work. The sooner he stopped being an expense to her, the better.

"If I'm not going to college right now"—Logan put his hand on hers—"at least I can help."

His mother looked up into his eyes, waiting. "Yeah, how's that?"

"I got a job."

20

LOGAN DID HIS best to calm his mom's fears without giving too much away. He used a line about his being an adult now and that she'd have to trust him . . . if only this once. She hated mysteries, but he said that he loved her and that he needed to do this. She let him go with a tight hug that seemed to last forever.

When he finally made it to the top of the stairs, he found Emmie peeking out of his bedroom. He quickly ducked inside and shut the door behind them.

"What was that about?" she whispered.

"You heard *that*?" he asked.

"Well, just a little. You're going away?"

He shook his head. "No. Florida. Just for a few days."

"Can I come?"

"No! It's . . . business."

"Business? Excuse me, Mr. Executive. I didn't know you was sucha playa! Come on, spill the beans."

"It's just a thing I gotta do with Z-boy is all . . ."

Emmie wrinkled her brow. "A 'thing'? We haven't been going out long enough to have secrets."

He dumped his crutches and fell onto the bed. She joined him and pulled the covers over them.

"Well, I did tell my mom about us—"

"You told her!?" she whispered in his ear.

"Well, I think she heard you screaming—"

"I did not scream!"

"Shh! She'll hear you screaming again."

She hit him in the arm. "Dick."

"Wannabe."

Emmie smiled, then launched an all-out tickle assault.

Logan squirmed. "Stop!"

"Who's a wannabe?"

Logan grabbed her and planted a big kiss on her lips. She stopped tickling.

"Give?" she asked.

"Give," he replied with more kisses.

She lay on top of him, staring into his eyes. "What did you tell her?"

"She asked who I was with, and I said you."

Her eyes opened wide. "You said *me?*"

"She seemed surprised . . . but impressed. She likes you."

Emmie covered her eyes. "I can't believe you told your mom that we just had sex in her house. God, I'll never be able to look at her again."

Logan covered his face with his pillow. "Well, it was definitely not a normal conversation."

"My mom thinks I'm a virgin."

Logan acted shocked. "You mean, you're *not*?"

Emmie returned his scandalous look. "Oh, and I suppose you are?"

"I swear, I've never been with another girl. Now another *man* . . ."

He kissed her. They both cracked up.

Emmie smelled his breath. "Were you drinking?"

Logan grew serious. "She's under a lot of pressure. Things are . . . weird right now."

"No kidding . . ." Emmie laid her head on Logan's chest. "Look, you do your thing with Z-boy . . . Get it out of your system. Probably involves some strip clubs and stuff I don't wanna know about anyways. But after that, you're mine."

Logan felt his heartbeat flutter and didn't know if it was because of her, his mom or the alcohol. "Thanks. But don't worry. There're no girls on this trip."

"Hmm," she mused. "Maybe I should be more worried then."

"Don't. I only like women." He leaned in and kissed her.

Logan had never felt so much pain, pleasure and confusion all at once.

21

LOGAN WORE ONLY trunks and his beach slaps under his graduation gown. His little form of rebellion. Besides, it was hotter than hell out on the football field. What idiot thought it would be a good idea to dress everyone in black and sit them under the hot baking sun at noon for a graduation ceremony? Maybe it was the administration's last form of torture.

Logan's mom sat in the bleachers, smiling for the first time in a year. That was the only reason Logan had come, really, was to see her smile, maybe tear up in a good way, not like she did every other night. He thought maybe for just a day, she could enjoy life again.

Logan sat in the sixth row between two people he'd never met before. He scanned the crowd until he spotted the back of Emmie's head three rows up. He wanted to go up and grab her from behind, maybe take her under the bleachers to make out—

The music fanfare kicked in as the line of faculty marched onto the stage. First was an address from Principal Watson, also known as Bill, depending on how much time you spent in his office.

Logan's thoughts drifted during Watson's "inspirational" speech, which was filled with lots of talk about how they were at the crossroads of their lives, how life was full of choices, and how these choices determined everyone's future. Logan thought about how much had changed in the last few months and what choices he'd had to make. Never in a million years could he have imagined what he was about to do in a few hours. He glanced at everyone around him and wondered what choices they'd made. Did anyone else have a big secret like he did?

He zoned out on all the other speeches, unable to focus. But when a black woman with graying dreadlocks stepped on stage, he sat up. The final talk by Fatima Oliver Hamweed, the poet, actually made Logan think. She had been the first black graduate back in '67, the first to organize the minority students and demand they be heard. Because of that experience, she had no room for the BS institutional garbage they fed the students. Said she couldn't remember a damn thing about high school. Her life began after that, after she lived awhile as a true person on the Earth, open to life's adventures, tragedies and miracles. She spoke about making mistakes, many of them, and of all the disappointments she'd had. But she embraced those moments and made them her own. When she said that, Logan felt she was looking straight into his soul.

The speeches ended. It was time to cross the stage and receive the diplomas. The parents and the families in the audience rose, proudly clapping when the student body was announced.

Logan searched for his mom in the audience. After a minute,

he saw her, beaming. What surprised him was who sat next to her: Z-boy.

Damn, Z. You didn't have to come. If Logan had been the one to flunk out, he would've been too embarrassed to show his face. But not good ol' Z-boy.

After fifteen minutes of calling out names, Principal Watson finally said, "Logan Tom."

Logan straightened his cap and strode across the stage, raising his arms to the cheering section of his mom and Z-boy, who both jumped up on the bench and made fools of themselves. Logan was touched.

Logan accepted his diploma and shook Watson's hand, grinning.

"Good luck," Watson said, smiling through his teeth. Logan detected a bit of sarcasm in the comment. *Did he know?* He let it go and walked off stage to Z-boy's chants of *Lo-gan, Lo-gan* that continued for ten seconds.

"God, who's that idiot?" someone said behind him.

Logan didn't even look back. "That idiot," he said proudly, "is my best friend." And for the first time, he knew he'd made the right choice.

22

THREE HOURS AFTER graduation, instead of partying with the rest of the seniors, Logan and Z-boy found themselves dressed in their Republican suits, waiting for their ride from Logan's house. Luckily, his mom had to go to work right after the ceremony. She understood he wouldn't be there when he got home.

They each had a small suitcase for three days of travel. Logan had spent the last hour reviewing his Republican handbook and smoking one of Z-boy's joints to calm his nerves.

"So how's your Party agenda coming?" Logan asked in a Republican sort of way.

"Excellent. I'm throwing an NRA fund-raiser next week. How's your portfolio these days?" Z-boy asked.

"Corn is up, oil is up, technology, up."

"And your dick?"

"Down," said Logan, very businesslike. "But it's likely to rise again in the near future."

They sat in his living room, practicing their conservative-speak, when they felt the walls start to shake.

"What's that?" Logan asked.

The rumbling grew louder. *Doesn't seem like an earthquake,* he thought. Logan and Z-boy gazed out the window to the street.

A pimped-out, black Cadillac Escalade slowly pulled up to the curb in front of the house. The bass from its massive sound system made Logan's fillings ache.

"I think it's our ride . . . ," Z-boy said, unsure.

The driver door opened. Out popped Goldie. He lowered his shades and scoped out the neighborhood.

"Yep. Looks like our ride." Logan turned to Z-boy. "You understand once we step out this door, there's no turning back? We're on our way."

Z-boy nodded. He held out his hand. Logan took it. "It's the beginning of our big adventure."

"Z-boy and Logan's Big Adventure," Logan said, laughing. "Isn't that the movie where we end up on some exotic beach with a couple of girls and all the loot?"

"You know it, dude."

Goldie smiled when he saw them. "Still can't get over the new look. This your crib?"

Logan suddenly regretted having told him where he lived. He locked the front door. "My family's."

"That's nice. Living with your mama."

Logan thought about giving Goldie some lip for talking about his mama, but Goldie's bulging biceps convinced him otherwise.

Z-boy eyed Goldie's wheels. "Nice SUV, man. What happened to keeping a low profile?" he shouted.

"That's Broza's thing. Cops know I got the bling. Who's gonna stop me?"

Logan opened the back door and was blasted by the wall of sound. "Not me! Say, can we lower the music a little?!" he yelled.

Goldie shook his head. "I forget, you white boys can't handle the gansta shit." Ignoring Logan's request, Goldie started the engine. Logan shrugged and got in.

A half hour later, Goldie finally turned off the music and pulled into the Long Beach home of Art Bandini, a real estate broker who was moving to Orlando. He needed his car transported across country.

Goldie stopped in front of the driveway. He reached into the glove compartment and pulled out some papers, handing them to Z-boy. "These are the transportation orders for the car. Just take it up to him, have him sign page two and he'll give you the keys. Be sure to give him the receipt. If he asks if you've done this before, you say, 'Many times.' Tell him the car will be there in three days."

Z-boy looked at the papers. It said Goldie's Transport Services on top. "Is this for real?" he asked.

"'Course it is. Man's got to have a front, don't he? Besides, it brings in the cash, and I can't argue with that."

Z-boy read on. "Who's Lance McDaniels?"

"Almost forgot." Goldie took an envelope out of his jacket pocket. He held up two sets of I.D. cards—driver's license, Young Republican membership and company I.D. One set had a picture of Z-boy on them and said Lance McDaniels.

"Lance? Do I gotta be Lance? Why not . . . Keir or . . . Laird . . . something."

Logan checked out his I.D. *"Dick Johnson?* Who picked these friggin' names?"

"I did," Goldie said proudly. "Got a problem with that? At least you don't got two first names now, Logan Tom." Goldie laughed.

"Fine. Dick Johnson, whatever." Logan started to get out of the car.

"Where you going?" Goldie asked. "You stay here. Don't want to worry the owner about your broken foot an' all."

Logan turned to Z-boy, who was straightening his tie. "It's okay, brah. I got it. Watch and learn from the master, Lance McDaniels." He put on his glasses, checked his hair and walked cockily to the front door.

Z-boy knocked, looked back at the boys and waved. The door opened. He was face to face with a squat brick of a man with oily hair and a pencil-thin mustache.

Logan watched Z-boy explain that he was here for the car. Bandini closed the door in his face. Z-boy stood there staring at the knocker. When he heard the garage door opening, he smiled and jogged over.

Inside the garage was a gleaming white sedan. Logan had seen that kind of car before, but wasn't sure where.

"The Crown Victoria. Police car of choice," Goldie said. "Good pickup, fast as a muther." He smirked. "That bitch acts like Five-0 too."

Logan studied Bandini. "A cop? You think so?"

"Who knows?" Goldie said. "The real estate thing could be a cover. Could be an undercover agent working a sting operation against Broza." He winked. "Wouldn't it feel good to stick it to The Man for once? Use his car to mule." Goldie dreamed. "You could always claim he was crooked, if ya got caught."

Logan couldn't tell if Goldie was serious or just yanking his chain. But he didn't like it either way. *Great*, he thought. *Just one more thing to add to the fire . . .*

23

BROZA WAS STANDING in his robe in front of his garage, drinking a Corona Light, when Z-boy drove the Crown Vic into his driveway. Broza hauled up the squealing old garage door and waved them in.

The garage door closed quickly behind the car. Logan hobbled into the house, following Z-boy and Broza as they disappeared down into the basement.

When Logan peered down the stairs, he saw lots of activity. A big Samoan dude clomped up the stairs toward him, lugging a tool kit. He sweated profusely and smelled of taco sauce.

"'Sup?" he said as he passed Logan. "You here to wrap or strike?"

"Uh, not sure. I'm a mule," Logan asked.

The Samoan stopped and gave Logan the once-over. "You must be new. Go down and wrap." The Samoan turned and headed into the garage.

"Sure." Logan managed his way downstairs. Then he got it. Laid out on the floor was a whole lot of weed, all packed down into one-kilo bricks. Two surfer chicks were wrapping the bricks in cellophane. Another Samoan smothered the bricks with motor oil. These were wrapped again. Another surfer dude was spraying those bricks with perfume. Those were wrapped one last time. Broza paced back and forth, inspecting the packages, then writing a number on each brick with a big red pen. He logged each one in a small black book.

Logan spotted Z-boy in the corner and made his way over.

"Look at all that. That's like six years' worth of highs, dude," said Z-boy. "Broza says it's from Oaxaca. The valley there is supposed to be the most fertile in Mexico. He says the soil makes it spicy, like a mole sauce or something."

Logan smiled. "Sounds tasty . . ."

When all the bricks were finished and logged, Broza snapped at Z-boy. "YoZaneAdams,GoGetTheDog."

"You mean the dog that almost killed us?" Z-boy asked.

Broza smiled. "Yeah, the General, the drug-sniffing dog. He's our final test."

"I ain't getting near that thing," Z-boy said as he covered his nuts. "I might wanna have kids one day."

Broza shook his head. "I gotta do everything." He moved past Z-boy to the base of the stairs. Then he gave an ear-piercing whistle, right next to Z-boy's ear.

"Goddamn, you trying to make me go deaf!?" Z-boy yelled.

General came rampaging down the stairs, sending Z-boy and Logan flying up against the wall. Everyone cleared the way.

"General! Drugs!" Broza pointed toward the wrapped bricks.

General's ear perked up and he scanned the room. Logan noticed that all the plants that were there before were now gone. "What happened to the forest?" he whispered to Z-boy.

Z-boy shrugged. "I guess he harvested for his well-to-do clientele . . ."

The place was spotless. "I guess he cleaned too."

General sniffed eagerly around each brick, meticulously working his way across the room. Finally, he returned to Broza with a puzzled look on his face. Broza gave him a treat. "Good boy. No drugs here, right General?" Broza clapped his hands. "Let's rock and roll, boys and girls."

They started an assembly line as the bricks were hauled up the stairs and into the garage. When Logan entered the garage, he saw the Samoan had taken apart the entire inside of the car: seats, side paneling, carpets. "Jeez, don't you think Bandini will notice?"

Broza supervised the scene. "Hell, no. Anything that is put together can be taken apart and put together again. We've done more than thirty runs and the owners have never batted an eye. In fact, I think we even managed to deliver them in better shape than when we picked them up."

Logan watched the bricks being packed into the side and floor paneling of the car. The Samoan then reattached all the paneling until it was as good as new.

"You'd never guess there was a hundred pounds of pot in here," Logan said, peering into the car.

"That's the idea." Broza took out a roll of twenties and counted out a small stack. "Here's a hundred and twenty dollars for your per diems. That's forty dollars a day for food, tolls, whatever. Don't go over or you'll starve. This"—he pulled out an envelope with more cash—"is for gas only. *Never* use it for any other purpose, *comprende*? And I want receipts."

Logan took the cash. "Receipts, huh? What happened to keeping secrets?"

"I don't want you to keep secrets from me; that's how it works!" Broza winked and slapped him on the shoulder. "Don't worry, brah, it's good to go. Now go earn your pay!"

24

LOGAN HAD TAKEN only two road trips in his life. Once, when he was nine, the whole family had driven an RV through the Southwest—Las Vegas, the Grand Canyon, Four Corners, Zion, Arches, Santa Fe, the Giant Crater, Route 66, the whole bit. That was before his dad and mom started fighting, back when they were actually a family. Seemed like a million years ago to Logan.

Then, there was the trip to Baja last summer. That was Logan's reward trip for having made honor roll during his junior year. His mom let him drive, but went along to make sure he and Z-boy behaved. Even worse, they had to camp on a surfers' beach with his mom. Once, he had to turn down a joint from another surfer because she was watching him. Still, the waves were tasty and the days were long. His mom sat on the beach reading trashy romance novels, and by the end of the trip, she started loosening up a bit. She even let Logan drink a brewski in front of the locals to prove his worth.

Aside from that, Z-boy had driven every day since he got his license and Logan made sure to never get a ticket or in an accident, in hopes of inheriting the Volvo someday soon.

"You ready?" Z-boy said.

Logan had printed out online maps from Broza's computer. He laid the hard copies out on the hood of the car, tracing the route with his finger. It seemed simple enough: a straight shot on Interstate 10 from L.A. to Orlando. Twenty-five hundred and twelve miles, according to Mapquest, a thirty-nine-hour and thirteen-minute drive. Logan wondered if that included piss breaks and breakfast, lunch and dinner at Taco Bell.

"Check this out." Logan pointed to the main section of the journey. "Ever see *Deliverance*?"

Interstate 10 drove straight through fourteen hundred miles of hillbilly territory: Texas, Louisiana, Mississippi and Alabama.

"Maybe with our short hair, our necks'll get red enough," Z-boy said.

Logan had never been to the Deep South. He'd only seen in the movies that they didn't take kindly to hippie types. They'd probably beat him up if he went there looking like a surfer. But as a Republican? Maybe they'd welcome him as a brother-in-arms.

After all the waiting and preparation and mental psych-up to do this trip, Logan and Z-boy were finally ready to go. Z-boy volunteered to start in the driver's spot.

As Logan hobbled toward the passenger seat, Broza came up behind him.

"Hold up. Take this."

He handed Logan a small device that looked like a pager with a little speaker on it.

"What's this for?" Logan asked.

"Emergencies. Call me on a pay phone, hold it up to the phone and push the button. It'll make a free call and you won't be traced. Those bastards are listening everywhere."

Logan studied it more closely. He had never seen this at Radio Shack. "Does the phone company know about this?"

"Shut up, bitch." Broza leaned in close. "And uh, don't give it to Z-boy. He might get carried away with it."

Logan nodded. "Got it, chief. Should we use some sort of code language?"

"Just don't be a dumbass. Don't say *pot* or *drop-off point* or *I'm driving a white Crown Victoria filled with a hundred pounds of marijuana.* Okay?"

Logan pocketed the device. "I'll see you when I see you, then."

"Not if I see you first." Broza held open the door for Logan, then retreated to the porch.

"What was that about?" Z-boy asked.

"Nothing. Just a little pep talk," Logan said. "Ready?"

"Let's rock and roll!" Z-boy wailed.

They pulled out slowly from Broza's driveway, even turning on the right-hand blinker to make a legal turn onto the street.

"That'll impress him," Z-boy said.

Logan turned and waved good-bye to Broza, who stood there shaking his head.

"Well, we're off," said Logan with a sense of finality. They had a hundred pounds of pot on them, some questionable disguises and a lame excuse. They could get caught here or in Florida, it didn't matter now.

"Nervous?" Z-boy asked.

Logan studied himself in the mirror and saw how stupid he looked. "Who're we kidding? I feel like an idiot." He studied his face. "Do you really think I look older like this?"

"You could pass for twenty, anyways," Z-boy said. "Hell, in that suit, you might as well be fifty." He laughed nervously. "Hey, let's hope none of our buds see us on the way out of town."

Z-boy turned the corner and passed Goldie and his boys polishing his SUV. Goldie watched them go, his eyes hidden behind his shades. Logan gave a little wave, but Goldie didn't budge.

"You don't think I offended him with what I said about his music, do ya?"

Z-boy glanced at Goldie through his rearview. "Him? Nah. He's just playing it cool. He can't pretend to know two Republicans now, can he?" Z-boy laughed and flipped Goldie off, making sure they were far enough away so that he'd never see the gesture. "You'll be my bitch soon, my man."

Z-boy turned back onto Crenshaw Boulevard and headed toward the freeway. Logan looked over at a bus stop on the side of the road and saw the little black girl who'd yelled at them the day before. The girl's eyes followed Logan as she waved slowly and said something he couldn't quite make out.

Logan thought she said, "See ya, whitey."

They made their way to Interstate 10, leaving the ghetto behind and heading out onto the open road.

25

THE OPEN ROAD didn't last long. As soon as they hit Interstate 10, they met with a mess of traffic that would surround them for the next four hours.

"This sucks," Z-boy said. "How can there be traffic at this time of the day?"

"Welcome to L.A. You should've checked the traffic report," Logan said matter-of-factly.

"No, *you* should have checked the traffic reports. I'm the driver. You're the navigator. The navigator navigates, the driver drives."

Stuck in a standstill, Logan glanced over at a Lexus waiting next to them. A pasty-white manager-type nodded at him. Logan realized he was one of them now. He nodded back.

"How 'bout some tunes at least?" Z-boy asked. "Goldie said Bandini left us quite a collection."

Logan popped the glove compartment, where he found a CD case. When he opened it, he laughed. "Hope you like the classics.

Kenny Rogers . . . Hall and Oates . . . Christopher Cross . . . Oh, man. John Tesh!"

"Jesus, this drive is torture enough, now we have to listen to this music too?"

"All to keep us in character, I guess."

By the time they made it past Riverside, they were on track 22 of *Chicago's Greatest Hits* and making good time. Z-boy started singing the high notes from *If You Leave Me Now*, forcing Logan to switch to the radio.

"Hey, I like that song!" Z-boy complained.

Logan stared at him. "What are you, a clone? What do you mean, you *like* that song?"

"It's kind of catchy . . . ," Z-boy said.

"Catchy? Z, don't get too carried away with this Lance McDaniel character thing."

Z-boy straightened his tie. "I happen to know for a fact that Dick Johnson likes Chicago."

"That's close to blasphemy. What happened to the dude who requested *Stairway to Heaven* as his confirmation song?"

Z-boy laughed at the memory. "*That* was funny."

Logan cracked up. "The monsignor thought it was a Christian song—"

"Man, when those drums kicked in—!"

Logan and Z-boy flashed back to the moment. Z-boy started to rock out. "*And as we wind on down the ro-ou-oad . . .*" He smiled at Logan, who took the bait.

"Now that's more like it . . . *Shadows taller than our sou-ouls . . .*"

They were about to launch into the next line when they both saw a highway patrolman pull up alongside them. They immediately disposed of their air guitars and tried to act normal.

"How fast are you going?" Logan asked nervously, trying not to look at the cop.

"Seventy," Z-boy answered quietly.

"What's the speed limit?"

"I don't know, isn't it seventy out here?"

Just then, they passed a speed sign that said 65.

Logan gulped. "Slow down, man . . . but don't use the brakes."

Z-boy eased off the gas until the speedometer dipped below sixty-five. The cop waved, then continued past them.

Logan watched until the patrol car pulled ahead by a few lengths. "Get over into the slow lane. Use your blinkers!"

Z-boy pulled over and maintained his speed. "Maybe I should use the cruise control?"

"I thought that was the plan, Z-boy. Why didn't you use it before?"

"I guess Zeppelin gets me going . . . but don't sweat it, brah. Cruise control . . . on!" Z-boy set the control at sixty-five and let his foot off the gas. "Steady as she goes, captain."

Logan breathed again. "Okay from now on, we are sticking to the plan, right? Lay low, don't attract attention."

"But now you see that I'm good luck, don'tcha?" Z-boy smiled.

"Good luck? You're always messing up. How's that good luck?" Logan asked.

"Yeah but, I never get caught. It always turns out good in the end. I mean, look: I flunk out of school, I get a job. I can't get the job unless I get you to come along, you come! You break your ankle . . . you still come! We almost get killed by gun-totin' gang-stas and they become our pals."

Logan tried not to bust his bubble. "Whatever, Z."

"You'll see. I'm like the village idiot in ancient times. Good luck for the entire village."

"Now you're reaching, but hey, who am I to argue with the village idiot?"

Z-boy nodded. After a few moments, he added: "You don't really think I'm an idiot, do you?"

"Z, that was your word, not mine—"

"Yeah, but really . . ."

Logan thought about it. "If you really were an idiot, do you think I'd risk my neck by going on this trip with you?"

Z-boy smiled. "Thanks, brah. That means a lot to me."

Logan gazed into the endless void of the interstate, wondering what waited for them down the road.

26

"**WINDMILLS!**" **Z-BOY** shouted.

Logan's eyes popped open. He had drifted off somewhere near the beginning of the desert. His eyes scanned the landscape where he saw thousands of giant windmills, their whiteness gleaming in the clear desert sun, whirling at top speed as the wind came barreling down through the valley.

"Pretty cool, huh?" Z-boy asked. "Hey, we must be close to Palm Springs. Maybe we should stop there," he suggested, rubbing his eyes.

Logan felt the wind pushing the car all over the lane. "I thought we weren't supposed to stop."

"Well, we gotta stretch, don't we?" asked Z-boy. "I think Broza meant for us to take short breaks and not go sightseeing or nuthin'. Let's stop and refresh our Big Gulps."

For the next ten miles, Logan saw nothing but billboards for golf and leisure. He had never been to Palm Springs. All he knew was that it was nothing but old people driving their little golf carts around. No temptations there. As long as Interstate 10 delivered boring scenery, they'd get through this trip intact.

When they reached the city limit, the first thing Logan noticed were all the young chickitas driving around in convertibles.

Z-boy noticed too. "There're sure a lot of fine babes here for a city full of old geezers."

Logan waved at a VW Beetle filled with five coeds. "Maybe they're visiting their grandparents or something."

When they hit the main street, Logan thought he was dreaming. He rolled down his window—the dry heat surprised him. The main strip, packed with women, smelled of Coppertone and sage. The sidewalks bustled with females. Every car on the street oozed femininity.

"I think we hit the mother lode," Z-boy said in amazement.

"Easy, cowboy. Remember, we're working," Logan said, distracted by the sea of women before him.

"Yeah, but we gotta take a break. We've already been on the road five hours."

"And we're already four hours behind schedule because of that friggin' traffic."

Z-boy shook his head. "Don't act like such an old man. We'll make it up."

Logan eyed some of the women passing by. "Okay, okay. But let's just be aware of the time."

They slowly passed under a banner proclaiming THE HOT DESERT NIGHTS WOMEN'S WEEKEND AND GOLF TOURNAMENT. Logan noticed a lot of the girls wearing golf clothes. "Wow, these girls must really like golf."

Z-boy winked at a few women passing by. "Yeah, I think I'm

starting to like golf too." He spotted an open parking spot and pulled in. "We'll just stop for ten minutes, right?"

"Sure. But only ten minutes." Logan's eyes swept the field. There were a lot of women, but now he saw that they weren't all young hotties. He noticed a lot of older women too.

"They're staring at us," Logan said.

"Sure. This is Republican country. All these fine conservative chickitas are zooming in on the real deal." Z-boy ran his hand through his hair. "Let's go stretch our legs."

Logan felt uneasy. "Did you notice there aren't very many men around?"

Z-boy shrugged. "So what? Maybe all the men are old farts who don't move around in the day. That leaves more for us."

Logan felt something gnawing at his gut. "Maybe we should just stick to the plan."

Z-boy pointed out two women in their early twenties staring at them. "Yeah, we will. But I think somebody wants to play," Z-boy said, already on the move.

Logan checked his breath. It smelled like the In-N-Out Burger he had devoured a couple hours ago. He took the last swig of a warm Mountain Dew, swishing it around in his mouth. He swallowed, then hobbled out of the car.

"Hey there," the girls said in unison. Both were dark skinned with short black hair, nose rings and boots.

"Howz it going, ladies?" said Z-boy all suavelike.

"Hi," Logan said, unable to come up with anything else.

"My friend has a question for you," the one on the left said, giggling. The other one looked at Logan curiously.

"We like questions," Z-boy injected.

"Are you guys . . . cops?" she asked.

Z-boy broke up laughing. "Cops? Are you kidding? Do we look like cops?"

Logan remembered they did.

"Uh, yeah. You do kinda." She scoped out their suits.

Logan frowned. "We're not cops, we're . . . just passing through."

Z-boy tried to play it cool. "I heard there was great golf here."

The women glanced at each other. "We hate golf. We're here for the action." They winked playfully, then giggled.

Z-boy grinned. "Action. I like that. We're active guys . . . and we don't really like golf either. Too much . . . grass."

Logan couldn't help it. "Never thought I'd hear you say *that* . . . ," he whispered.

The women laughed. "You guys are funny," said the tall one.

The other one looked at Logan's cast. "What happened to your leg?"

"Motorcycle accident," Logan answered. "You shoulda seen the other guy. Roadkill."

The tall girl checked out their car. She nudged the other one and they whispered back and forth. Finally, the tall girl spoke up. "Say, you think you guys could give us a lift to our guesthouse? We've been shopping all day and it's just a little farther than we want to walk right now."

Z-boy smiled. "We'll make up the time later, brah, *and* have a story to tell," he said out of the side of his mouth.

Alarms rang in Logan's head and one of the DISSD rules flashed through his thoughts: no hitchhikers.

"Sure," he found himself saying. He thought of Emmie and wanted to take it back, but it was too late. He vowed to himself not to do anything stupid.

"Maybe we could have a drink first," offered Z-boy. "That desert sure makes a man awful thirsty."

Logan wanted to strangle him.

The women looked at each other doubtfully. "Hmm . . . Maybe we'll just walk. Thanks anyways." They started to gather their things to leave.

Z-boy turned on the charm. "Come on . . . one drink. You must be parched too, all this . . . hot . . . weather . . . all that walking." He couldn't help letting his eyes wander to the wide variety of booty at hand.

The tall girl shrugged. "I *am* thirsty," Logan heard her whisper to the other one.

She rolled her eyes. "Fine. One drink, your treat. Then the ride, yeah?"

"Sure thing. It's on me. What's your names?"

The taller one said, "My name's Camilia. This is Marjane."

Z-boy extended his hand. "Hey there, girls. I'm uh . . . Lance, and this is my partner in crime, um . . ."

"Richard," nodded Logan, holding on to his crutches.

Z-boy nodded. "Oh, right. I usually call him Dick."

The girls snickered. "Dick? That's kind of an old man's name," said Marjane.

"Yeah, well, my dad was kind of a dick. I think he thought he could just pass on his misery," Logan said.

"And I was named after Lance Armstrong," Z-boy interjected.

Camilia made a funny face. "Aren't you a little old to be named after him?"

"Oh, you mean the bike racer dude. I'm talking about the astronaut, you know, first man on the moon an' all."

The girls gave each other a look. "Whatever."

They wandered into a cantina across the street. Except for Logan, who hobbled, trying to keep up.

Logan went through the motions, even though he felt like a cheap bastard for even thinking about cheating on Emmie. He scanned the cantina for a table. They needed to sit where they could see the car.

Z-boy offered to get the drinks. Logan grabbed Z-boy by the arm and whispered into his ear. "Twenty minutes, okay? Then we hit the road again."

Z-boy frowned. "Man, I'm sure we could score with these babes in a couple of hours. Don't be an old man."

"You're gonna be an old man in jail." Logan stared daggers. "Z, are we on a mission or what?" he hissed.

"You agreed to stop!" he growled.

"Yeah, that was before I knew you were seriously thinking of going hunting," Logan muttered back.

"All right, *Dick*. We'll have a drink and go. But if there's any touching within the next twenty minutes, we renegotiate. How old do you think they are? My guess is they're only six or seven years older than us."

Logan looked at the girls, who were whispering to each other. He checked his watch. "Twenty minutes. Go."

Z-boy rushed to the bar and ordered drinks, even though his driver's license said he was under twenty-one. He returned only with a round of Cokes. "God, that guy was weird. I asked for rum and Cokes, but he forgot the rum. I think he was trying to hit on me or something." He winked at Logan.

"That's okay. Coke is fine." They giggled to each other again.

"So, what are you guys doing here?" asked Marjane.

"Um, we're passing through town on our way to Florida," Logan said.

"What's in Florida?" asked Camilia.

"Business. We have business in Florida," added Z-boy.

Marjane and Camilia seemed confused. "How old are you guys anyways?"

"Twenty . . . one," Logan answered.

Z-boy interjected, "Twenty-two, actually. We just had birthdays this week."

"Both of you?" asked Camilia.

Z-boy breezed by the question. "Say, why *are* all these girls in town anyways? I thought this place was for old fogies."

"You mean you don't know?" Camilia asked.

Logan and Z-boy shrugged.

"Um . . . the golf?" Logan asked.

When Marjane and Camilia laughed, Logan knew something was wrong. He was a handsome guy and a surfer to boot. He wasn't used to girls laughing at him.

"Oh, I'm sorry," said Marjane. "You thought you were gonna get laid tonight."

Z-boy looked at them for a long beat as it sank in. "It could happen."

"Not with this crowd. Not unless you're a lesbian."

Logan and Z-boy slowly gazed around at all the women in the bar. "You mean . . . they're *all* lesbians?" Logan asked.

"You too?" Z-boy added.

"Don't be so shocked. It's no big thing." Marjane nodded. "The Hot Desert Nights Weekend is kind of like spring break for us."

"Wow, that's . . . I didn't know . . . ," Logan said. "That's a lot of lesbos . . . I mean . . . lesbian-Americans."

"Lesbians," Z-boy added, as he processed the information. "Who woulda thunk?"

"Yeah, maybe we should be going . . . ," Logan said.

Z-boy held up his hand. "Well, now Richard, how many chances do we have to hang out with a bunch of lesbians?" He turned and looked at the girls slyly. "Maybe we could watch instead."

"Uh, did you guys park in a loading zone or something?"

Z-boy was too busy calculating the possibilities in his head, but Logan followed the girls' gaze until it came upon a tow truck. A tow truck that happened to be towing their car.

"Oh shit."

"I think that's your car," Marjane said.

Logan took off in a sprint. Or as much of a sprint as he could with two crutches and a cast. By the time he hit the sidewalk, the truck was just pulling out.

"Hey!" Logan screamed. "Hey, stop!!"

He tried forcing his way through the crowds, but it was too late. When he reached the street, he could only barely make out the tow truck's company name before it disappeared around the corner:

Speed of Light Towing, Inc.

27

A CAR HORN blasted in his ear. Logan turned around and realized he was standing in the middle of the street, a line of cars waiting to get by.

"What?! You late for something?" He snapped at the elderly woman behind the wheel of her Lexus. He thought about taking her car right there and running down that truck. He could do it. Just whack her with his crutch. Because if he didn't—

"What happened?" Z-boy asked.

Logan turned his wrath toward his buddy. "What happened? We just lost a car full of marijuana, that's what happened. Because of you—"

"Hey, Logan, hold up. No one made you—"

"You made me. You made us deviate from the plan. You." Logan marched straight over to Z-boy, letting the cars free again. The old lady flipped Logan off.

"Dude. It's just a minor setback is all. We'll get it back."

"Get it back? Remember when my mom's car got towed?"

"You mean when you parked in the red—"

Logan held up his hand. "When we picked it up two hours later, my CDs and my phone were gone, remember? Those mofos will strip that car to the ground!"

Z-boy stood there staring at the spot where the car used to be. "We're fucked."

"Thank you. Thanks for that opinion," Logan said, pacing back and forth.

"Should we call Broza?" Z-boy asked sheepishly.

"No. He's gonna kill us if we say anything. Goldie will hunt us down like dogs." His mind raced. "We gotta solve this ourselves. How much cash we got?"

"Well, our per diem is forty dollars a day, minus twenty dollars for the drinks—"

"You paid twenty dollars for four Cokes?"

"I had to tip the guy. I say we got a hundred and change."

Logan sighed. "We're fucked. Last time it cost me a hundred and seventy-five dollars to get the car out."

He thought about using the gas money Broza had given him. But if he got the car and ran out of gas, they'd be fucked anyways.

"Maybe we could ask the girls for a little loan?" asked Z-boy.

They both turned back to the cantina and noticed their table was empty.

The cab set them back another fifteen dollars. Even another pain-killer didn't make Logan feel better. When they were dropped down the street from Speed of Light Towing, their car was sitting in the parking lot, unhooked behind the tow truck and waiting to be processed. The tow driver, a burly dude with long greasy hair, was clearly going through the glove box.

Logan stared. "Bastard! Look at him, in broad daylight!"

The driver tossed aside the CDs, then turned his attention toward their bags in the backseat.

"He's going for the bags," moaned Z-boy. "What're we gonna do?"

"You got the keys?" Logan asked.

"Yep. You gotta plan?" Z-boy asked.

Logan took the keys. "You distract the greaser, I steal the car back."

"What? Why do I gotta take on the greaser?" Z-boy asked.

"'Cause you can run."

"Fine," Z-boy said. "We're fucked anyways, so we might as well go for it. What's my angle?"

"Just start arguing with the guy, accuse him of stealing and say that you're gonna talk to the manager."

"And should I? I mean, talk to the manager, 'cause maybe—"

"Improvise," Logan said.

Z-boy shook his head. "Man, we could've had those girls."

"Z, even if you were gay, you couldn't have had those girls."

Z-boy tried to do that equation in his head.

"Just go," Logan said.

Z-boy took a step and stopped. "You really think this'll work, dude? This ain't a movie."

"Hey, you gotta better idea, go for it. But we don't have the cash or the time for anything else, Z."

"But what if we get caught?"

Logan thought hard. "Well, at least we're stealing our own car. I don't know," he said, frustrated. "Who're we kidding? We weren't cut out for this shit. It's the first day, and we've already fucked it all up."

Z-boy stopped Logan. "So, maybe we got nowhere to go then . . . but up?"

Logan sighed. "Unless we go to jail."

While Z-boy sneaked up on the driver and surprised him, Logan hung back and waited. Z-boy argued and ranted, pointing at the bags that had been rifled through. He pointed back to the ticket office and finally stomped off toward it. The grease monkey looked around, then followed Z-boy, leaving the car alone in the parking lot.

Logan moved into action, hopping and trying not to drag his crutches. He kept his eye on Z-boy, who was doing his best WrestleMania bit of overacting. Logan opened the driver side door as quietly as he could, slipping his crutches behind the seat.

As he was fishing for the keys from his pocket, Logan glanced up and saw the grease monkey running at the car full speed.

"Oh, shit . . . ," Logan whispered.

Logan fumbled for the keys, dropping them on the floor.

"Logan!" Z-boy yelled from behind the grease monkey.

The greaser reached for the passenger door, pulling it open before Logan lunged and pulled it back shut. With his left hand he reached for the auto lock, hitting it with his fist.

Z-boy was running around the car in circles. "Start the frigging car!"

When Logan dived back down to find the keys, his head hit the steering wheel, setting off the horn.

The grease monkey started banging on the window.

"Start the car!" Z-boy squealed.

Key. In the ignition. Logan grabbed the key off the floor, shoved it in the ignition, turned it on. The engine roared to life. The greaser was getting ready to put his fist through the window when Logan put the pedal to the metal. The car took off like a rocket.

"Damn, these cop cars can fly!" Logan shouted.

In the rearview mirror, Logan saw Z-boy chasing him, leaving the fat, out-of-shape greaser behind in the distance. Logan slowed up a little, popping open the door with his right hand.

Z-boy lunged for the door, crashing into Logan on the way into the car. Logan swerved, the door slamming shut and pushing Z-boy back in his seat.

"Goddamn! Did you see that?! He was ready to kill you!" Z-boy howled. "That was fucking rad, man!"

Logan sped up. "We are so fucked."

"He's not chasing us," Z-boy said, glancing back. "I don't think he'll call the cops."

"Yeah? Why not?"

Z-boy watched the grease monkey flip them off. "He won't call. I mean, we got him too, right? We saw him going through our shit. There's two of us."

Logan kept shifting his focus to the rearview mirror, looking for signs of trouble. "I don't know. Maybe the manager will call."

"Dude, they hadn't even logged the car in yet, so they got no records, no registration, nothing. The lady at the ticket office, she could give a shit. I think we're home free."

Logan turned the corner, following a sign back to the interstate. He gave Z-boy a sideways glance, then whip-snapped him in the gut with the back of his hand.

"Ow! What was that for?" Z-boy asked. "That hurt."

"Good," Logan said. "Remember that the next time you want to break the rules. Ass."

Z-boy frowned. "I'm still good luck," he mumbled. "Without me, you wouldn't've been able to get the car back."

"What kind of logic is *that*?" Logan said. "If we're gonna be professional about this, we gotta behave like pros."

"I know, I know." Z-boy nodded. "How's that foot of yours? You ran outta that cantina pretty fast."

"Don't worry about me. Just worry about us not getting caught, okay?"

His ankle throbbed. He couldn't find a comfortable position for it. Lucky for him, the painkiller was starting to set in.

Logan got back on the interstate, staring ahead to the open highway. It looked like the ocean with that never-ending horizon and big sky. Only it was the opposite of L.A.—the sky was blue, the ground brown.

Logan checked his rearview mirror. Only a lone car trailed behind them.

28

LOGAN'S KNUCKLES were white from squeezing the steering wheel too tightly. He expected any minute to see a cop pull up behind him, lights flashing. At that point, he could either try to outgun him (after all, he was in a cop car) or give up and hope to share a cell with Z-boy and not someone like Goldie.

"It's kind of hot in here, isn't it?" he asked.

"It's the desert, dude. Gets hot." Z-boy looked at Logan's forehead. "Damn, you're really sweating this, aren't you?"

"Aren't *you*?" Logan said.

"Yeah, I guess. But I just feel like, okay, we messed up a little back there. It was a wake-up call. Now we're straight arrows headed for Orlando. No more messing around. So, why worry now?"

"Uh, jail?" Logan adjusted the mirror.

"Stop looking back, Lo. Forward. That's where we're headed." Z-boy cranked up the A/C a notch. "Chill, dude . . ."

They rode quietly for two hours, focused and determined to act like pros.

Then they got bored. Z-boy started making rap noises with his mouth. Logan started laughing when Z-boy added some drums and scratches to his beat.

He winked at Logan. "You know where I'm going with this, brah."

"That's what I'm afraid of."

Z-boy started singing. "And we went through the desert in a car full o' *weed* . . ."

Logan raised his eyebrows.

"With *Mary Jane* by my side and a bag full o' *seed*..." Z-boy egged Logan on.

Sometimes when they were bored, Logan and Z-boy made up free-verse raps to pass the time. Coming up with names for marijuana and dropping them into choice sentences was a specialty.

"Okay, okay . . ." Logan shrugged. He listened to Z's thumping beat. "Um . . . *Mary Jane* liked to nap on a hill full of *grass* . . ." He threw it back to Z-boy.

Z-boy struggled to suppress his smirk. "With *Bud* and *Herb*, who all sat on their ass . . ."

Logan snapped "We called him *Cripple* 'cause he had *chronic* back pain . . ."

Z-boy changed the beat. "'Cause he got *whacked* one day up in the state of Maine."

"With a *Buddha stick* owned by the groovy *Doobie* Brothers," thumped Logan.

"Who sang *Dank Dinkie dow* and danced like your mother."

Logan and Z-boy broke down in laughter. "Now that was some homegrown schwag right there," Z-boy said, impressed. "We should start our own rap label."

"Bong Records," Logan suggested. They cackled, like they were stoned. Logan's laugh petered out until he was left staring at the road.

Then he looked in the rearview mirror. There was the black Lincoln Town Car he thought he had seen before. "That car's been following us."

"Duh . . . there's only one road here," Z-boy said, still imagining being an executive at Bong Records.

"No, really. Everyone else is passing us, except that car."

Z-boy turned around and saw the car. "Seems okay to me. Probably some old lady."

"I think it's a cop," he said, adjusting the mirror.

Z-boy squinted. "You're crazy."

Logan panicked. "Don't look back. I think it's one of those unmarked cars."

Z-boy was skeptical. "Unmarked? In the middle of the desert? You're just paranoid, man."

"I think he's been behind us since Palm Springs."

"Hey, maybe it's a lesbian cop."

"Shut up. We have anything suspicious showing?"

"Check you out, man. All calm and collected one minute, now you're gettin' all freaky on me," Z-boy said.

"We just have to be on guard. I'm not gonna blow this again."

Z-boy squinted. "I don't think that's a cop . . ."

"Will you stop? Let's just get out of California, okay? You have your seat belt on?"

"Seat belt, roger that. Speed?"

Logan glanced at the speedometer. "Sixty-five. What's the first rule of muling?"

"Never break any traffic laws."

"And don't ever give a cop a reason to pull you over."

Logan stared into the rearview mirror at the Lincoln. "I'm a model driver. Never got a ticket. Never speed, always use my blinker. In fact, I'm so good—"

"Look out!" Z-boy yelled.

For a split second, all Logan saw was the IF YOU CAN READ THIS, YOU'RE TOO CLOSE! bumper sticker about to smash into their car.

Logan slammed the brakes. He swerved to the side of the interstate, struggling to keep the vehicle from going off the side of the road. They stopped inches from the guardrail, the smell of burnt rubber seeping into the car.

"Goddamn!" Logan yelled. "Frickin' old ladies!" He glared at the grandma driving the Chrysler K car ahead of them as it teetered on, unaware of the close call. "Isn't there a minimum speed of forty?"

"You okay?" Z-boy asked.

Logan took a deep breath. "Yeah, I'm fine." Then he saw Z-boy's white shirt covered with blood. "Z! You're bleeding!"

Z-boy dipped his finger into the red goo. "Cherry Slurpee," he said, pointing at the empty cup on the floor. "You made me spill."

Logan leaned back and breathed. They were safely on the side of the road. Cars passed by without a second look.

"We got company," Z-boy said, looking in the side-view mirror.

Logan turned around. The Lincoln was parked right behind them.

"Shit, let's—"

Someone rapped on the window to his left.

When Logan spun around, he saw an older guy with a crew cut and pale white skin staring at him through mirrored glasses. His black windbreaker fluttered in the breeze from the traffic. Logan didn't know what do to. The guy acted like The Man if ever there was one. He made a slow circular gesture with his finger.

"He wants you to roll down the window," Z-boy said.

Logan searched around for the window button and couldn't find it on the door. How could there be no button for the window?

The stranger pointed to the panel next to the automatic stick. The button was there. Logan lowered the window.

The man stared in, making a visual sweep of the situation. He looked at Z-boy's bloodred shirt.

"You boys okay?" He had a bland accent that betrayed no origin.

Logan saw his own reflection in the guy's shades. "Yeah, we're okay. Someone was driving pretty slow in front of us and it took me by surprise."

"I saw. What about him?" he said, glancing at Z-boy.

"Cherry Slurpee," Z-boy said, running his finger up the shirt and licking it for effect.

"Tastes better in a cup, I hear," he said. His gaze came to rest on a copy of the Republican handbook on the backseat. "You boys with the Party?"

Logan saw the book.

Z-boy scrambled for the right answer. "No, sir, we don't like to party. We do the Lord's work."

Logan shot Z-boy a look. "Actually, if you're referring to the *Republican Party*, the answer is yes. We're trying to sign up young people to vote come November."

Logan beamed his pearly white teeth for effect.

"Really? I didn't know the young people were so involved."

"Oh, yeah. Unfortunately, a lot of people our age have gone to the liberals. The GOP has asked for young volunteers from all over the country to help the cause. Mostly college kids like us. So instead of working at Quickee Freeze, we decided to work for our country."

Logan was a little disturbed at how easy it was for him to lie.

The guy smiled. "Republicans, huh?" He stood up and gave the car the once-over. "So how much are you packing?"

Logan's face went blank, like a deer lost in the headlights. "What?"

The stranger nodded like he was talking to a child. "It's okay, you can tell me."

Logan's brain rewound through his training session with Broza. All he could remember was *Stick to the story*.

"We have to go now. They're expecting us." Logan started the car. "Have a nice day."

He hit the gas, quickly swerving back onto the interstate. He could feel the sweat trickling down his neck. Logan watched the mystery man slowly disappear in his rearview mirror.

"Jesus, what was that all about?" Z-boy asked.

"Don't know. Don't wanna know. All I know is, if he's a cop, he can't follow us across the state line, right?"

Z-boy shrugged. "I guess. You really think he was a cop?"

"He coulda been. He coulda been a retired drug smuggler. We gotta take precautions is all I know." Logan checked the rearview mirror again.

"Maybe he'll call ahead to the border guards."

Logan's face went white. "Do they have guards on the California borders?"

"Shit. How should I know?" Z-boy looked down at the map. "We could take a little detour. Maybe they only have them on the interstate. There's a little road that runs north a few miles . . . crosses the Colorado River at Lake Havasu. Then we could cut back down and meet the 10 again in Arizona."

Logan was in no mood for taking chances. "Let's do it."

The sun was setting by the time they left the interstate behind. Logan was getting bleary-eyed from constantly checking his rear-view mirror for cops.

When they got to Lake Havasu, Logan thought he was hallucinating. He rubbed his eyes to make sure.

He saw the London Bridge in the middle of the desert.

29

"I KNOW WE'VE been driving for seven hours, but I'm starting to see things. Are we in England?" Logan asked, looking around a quaint English village.

Z-boy gazed at the bridge in admiration. "Hold on . . ."

He riffled through his backpack and pulled out a little travel guide. "I bought this book before we left. *Traveling Interstate 10: Highlights and Other Oddities.*"

"You . . . bought a book?" Logan asked in disbelief.

"Just a little something to help pass the time."

"Read away, senior navigator . . ."

Z-boy flipped through the tome. "Lake Havasu . . . Aha! The London Bridge." He perused the page, then announced: "When London Bridge was sinking into the River Thames in London, an Arizona businessman bought it, dismantled it and shipped it to America, where it was rebuilt brick by brick in the middle of the desert."

Logan glanced at Z-boy. "That's freakin' bizarre."

Z-boy smiled. "Reading is a powerful tool, dude."

Logan shook his head. "All right, genius, I guess if we cross the river here, we'll be safe in Arizona."

"Well . . ."

"Cough it up, Z."

"I also searched for the state drug laws online, 'cause Broza said some are worse than others. Arizona and Texas deal out the worst prison times for first-time offenders."

"Reading and researching. Huh," said Logan.

Z-boy shrugged. "Didn't want to spook you, brah. I know you were on the fence about this whole thing. Now we're in it together, for real." Z-boy waited for a reaction, but Logan gave him none. "But hey, now we can say we been to England. And look, they even have a 7-Eleven."

He pointed across the bridge to Arizona and the familiar green-and-red sign. "Can't be all bad then. Tell you what, brah. Next Big Gulp's on me."

"What else you keeping secret in that head of yours?" Logan asked, glancing sideways.

"Nothing. Ain't nothing in my head."

Logan grunted. "You said it . . ."

"Check it out, Lo. Stars," Z-boy said.

Logan looked up through the windshield. He noticed the stars for the first time.

"You don't see that in L.A. Hey, the Big Dipper!" yelled Z-boy.

Logan smiled as he watched his childhood pal sticking his head out the window like a dog, feeling the cool night air against his face. It reminded Logan of when they were kids on summer vacation. He, Z and Fin used to act like one another's dogs, since none of them had pets.

They stocked up on the essential supplies at 7-Eleven: cherry Slurpees, a two-liter bottle of Mountain Dew, four Big Bite jumbo dogs, spicy Doritos, miniature powdered doughnuts, some beef jerky and an assortment of candy ranging from peanut M&M's to grape-flavored Bubble Yum.

Of course, there were cops sitting in the parking lot, having a coffee. Logan kept an eye on them as he filled up the tank. From now on, no friendly banter with anyone, even the 7-Eleven attendants.

When they reconnected with the 10 in Arizona, Logan drove, keeping his eyes glued to the rearview mirror for that Lincoln Town Car. Since it was night, and all the cars looked alike, he thought every car coming up on them would be the cops or someone who knew their secret. His eyes soon grew tired with all the back-and-forth.

The next 170 miles took them through the warm desert night. Nothing but a lonely stretch of interstate and a caravan of long-distance truckers to keep them company. Phoenix was the next rest stop to break up the monotony.

"This is pretty crazy, us driving all this way by ourselves. What's the farthest you ever drove before?" Z-boy asked.

Logan was still tense but didn't want Z-boy to know it. "My mom doesn't want me to even drive east of Highway 1. But we did drive to Santa Barbara that one time, remember? For that party?"

"Yeah. I drove the Geo down to Oceanside once. That was like an hour and a half," Z-boy said.

"Well, I'm pretty sure I broke my record. And we're still in one piece."

Z-boy rubbed his eyes and took a swig of Dew. A mighty Mack

truck hauling oranges across the state kicked up a whirl of dust that sprayed the windshield.

"I don't know how those guys do it. Driving across America by themselves. And then back again? I'd go crazy."

Logan sat up. "And yet, that's exactly what we're doing."

Z-boy shrugged. "Well, I guess it's one-way travel for us. And there're two of us to share the duty and entertain each other. That's a big difference."

"Maybe. But mules haul stuff. So all these guys are mules too. Not much difference if you look at it that way."

Z-boy thought about it. "But the cargo sure is different. Can't get high on oranges."

"Can't get high on our stuff either," added Logan. "Right, Z-boy?"

Z-boy cracked a slight smile. "Not on what we're *delivering*, no."

Logan thought that was an odd answer. "What do you mean by that?"

Z-boy chose his words carefully. "We can't get high on Broza's stash."

"Good," Logan said.

Z-boy was silent for a long moment, staring out the side window.

"Still, it's a long drive . . .," Z-boy said.

"Don't get any ideas, Z."

"Dude, I'm not stupid," Z-boy said. "I'd never touch Broza's stash. I know he's got it weighed to the gram."

Logan sensed something else. "But?"

"But . . . if we had a separate stash, hypothetically, to help us relax while driving . . ."

Logan stared at Z-boy. "You didn't . . ."

Z-boy sniffed. Then hemmed. Then hawed . . . "Uhh . . . maybe . . . a little."

"You brought some weed?! What're you, crazy??" yelled Logan.

"Listen, technically, they're hash brownies—"

"You brought hash brownies?!"

"Dude, we're sittin' on a hundred pounds of pot. I don't think two or three brownies are gonna make a difference. You'll thank me later—"

Logan had heard enough. "I'm pulling over."

"Logan, you're overreacting."

"Overreacting? Try . . ." He couldn't think of the word.

"Paranoid? Crazy? You're juiced on caffeine and sugar, brah, which, by the way, is way worse than—"

"How about *smart?* Or *using my brain?* I'm stopping!" Logan yelled.

"Okay, okay. Don't have a shit fit, man."

Logan pulled the car over to the side of the interstate. Beyond their headlights, the edge of the road drifted off into total darkness.

"Where is it?" asked Logan.

"You're not my mother. I can take care of it."

"Where is it?" he asked again.

"Look, Broza said don't think about smoking any of *his* product," Z-boy said in his defense.

Logan was all business. "He also said, don't act stupid. Which means *don't get high.*"

"That's one man's interpretation."

"It's the *only* interpretation, Z. No wonder you flunked out." Logan regretted saying it the minute it popped out. "I didn't mean that."

Z-boy just stared at him. "So it's like that, huh? You're the brains of the outfit 'cause I flunked out?"

Logan gazed off into the darkness looking for an answer. "I just mean that we can't take chances. You know that. So why is this such a hard concept to get?"

"I dunno. Maybe I'm too stupid to get it."

Logan hated when Z-boy played the guilt card. "Hey, when we get back, I'll smoke a few J's with you. Hell, I'll buy you a brick and you can fry your brain. But not here. Not on this trip."

Z-boy seemed downcast. "You know I get nervous when things go wrong. It helps me relax."

"Things will go wrong when you're on that shit. Just tell me where it is, please?" Logan pleaded.

Z-boy thought about it. "It's inside my Bible."

Logan shook his head. "You have no limits, do you?"

"Hey, who's gonna search a Bible? It's sacred."

"Not anymore."

"Check it out." Z-boy reached into his backpack and pulled out a worn black Bible. When he opened the cover, Logan saw that he had hollowed out the insides. Z-boy pulled out a baggie with three small brownies in it.

"You can't even get arrested for this in California."

"How 'bout Arizona?"

Z-boy shrugged.

"Z, we can't take chances. Look, I swear, when we get back, chronic's on me. We'll get some loco weed and get wasted beyond repair. I swear."

"Just one bite?" Z-boy asked, hopeful.

Logan rolled down the window, grabbed the bag from him and tossed it into the darkness.

Z-boy was melancholy. "That's just sad, man. What a waste."

"You sure that's all?"

Z-boy thought about it. "Yep."

Logan had his doubts. "Good. I know that was hard. It takes a big man to own up. You're a big man."

Z-boy sat up straight. "You're just saying that 'cause you know it's true."

"Goddamn right. You wanna drive?"

Z-boy drove the rest of the way to Phoenix in silence.

Secretly, Logan wondered how much he would be able to rely on him. He wondered if Z-boy had a chip on his shoulder about the whole school thing and if, deep down, he had gotten Logan into all this just to prove something.

Phoenix itself was just another concoction of desert, tract houses and golf courses, with a few skyscrapers to boot.

"I hear Phoenix is one of the best places to live in the country. But why would you *want* to live out here?" Logan asked.

Z-boy read off a passing billboard. "The CrackerJax Family Fun and Sports Park?"

They drove through Phoenix and headed down to Tucson without incident. Z-boy stayed at the wheel. It was nothing but long, straight highway. Logan didn't ask to take over. It was almost midnight and he was drifting off.

"You tired?" Logan asked, yawning. He could see Z's eyes drooping.

Z-boy shook his head slowly. "Nah . . . I like driving."

"Should we stop or just plow through?"

Z-boy breathed slowly. "I say . . . let's keep going." He slurred his words. "Later on . . . maybe we'll stop . . . You catch a few zzz's . . ."

Z-boy gazed ahead into the darkness. Logan hesitated. "We

should be in New Mexico in a few hours. Wake me up, then we can switch."

Z-boy laughed strangely. "Just don't . . . wake the penguin . . . The penguin hates tequila."

Penguin? Logan studied Z-boy's vacant eyes. *Jesus!* "Zane!" he shouted, punching him in the shoulder.

"Ow!" Z-boy yelped. The car swerved into the next lane. Logan grabbed the steering wheel.

"You were sleeping!"

Z-boy looked around in a panic. "I was not! Are you crazy, hitting me while I'm driving?" He swatted Logan's hand away.

"What were we talking about then?" Logan glared.

"Fuck, man. I don't know. I was in the zone is all." He rubbed his eyes.

"I'll put you in the zone, if you fall asleep again."

Z-boy rolled down the window and let the wind blow in his face. "I wasn't asleep."

Logan rolled his eyes. But he was too tired to take over. He handed Z a Mountain Dew. "Drink this. And stay awake. If you can't, pull over at least. Jeez . . ."

Zane chugged the Dew. His eyes were wide open now. "You go to sleep, Logan. I got this."

Logan would have to sleep with one eye open. He fiddled with the radio until he found a Mexican station playing a Spanish pop ballad.

Despite the happiness in the music, Logan, with his Level Two Spanish, thought the song was about a drug dealer who dies in a hail of bullets from the *Federales*. He stayed awake as long as he could, until he slowly drifted off into an uneasy sleep, with visions of himself and Z-boy going down like Butch and Sundance, alone in a foreign land with no place to run.

30

LOGAN DREAMED HE was on his board fighting his way through a series of monster waves. The breakers were rough and vicious, slamming him repeatedly as he held on to his board for dear life. He saw Emmie watching helplessly from the shore. She waved and shouted at him, but he couldn't hear what she was saying.

Then he heard another voice. It came from beyond the waves, far off in the distance. Logan searched the horizon in vain, but the voice drifted farther and farther away, disappearing into the roar of the surf. He thought it might be Z-boy.

When Logan awoke from his dream, he felt the wind rocking the car in sudden bursts. What he thought was rain turned out to be sand blowing against the windshield.

He slowly realized they weren't moving.

Z-boy was nowhere to be seen. It was early, 4:30 A.M. by his watch. Faint echoes of morning light were starting to peek up behind some massive mountains. He quickly looked at his map of New Mexico and didn't see any mountains.

He pushed open the car door. He was in a parking lot. Far to the south, he could see the dim lights of a decent-sized city. He glanced up at the mountains, where he saw a figure. Logan stepped away from the car, shielding his eyes from the wind.

He watched the sand blowing across his feet. Those weren't mountains.

They were dunes.

"Z-boy?!" Logan shouted, but his voice was swallowed up by the gusts. He grabbed a crutch and started moving toward the dune. "Zane?"

The figure didn't move. Logan got to the base of the dune and thought he must be about thirty yards away. Even in the soft light, he could see the sand was incredibly white.

"Z?"

Still no answer.

Logan tried making his way up the side of the dune, but his crutch was useless. He ditched it and crawled up using his hands and one good leg. The sand was deep; it felt like for every step he took, he slid back two. His eyes adjusted to the darkness. The higher he got, the more dunes he could see.

After about five minutes of scrambling, he squinted into the wind and saw Z-boy's still body, highlighted by the coming dawn.

"Z, what are you doing?" he yelled. Z-boy didn't answer.

Logan sat down next to his friend. Z-boy had the thousand-yard stare. Logan followed Z-boy's gaze. It floated out over hundreds of dunes toward a sunrise that was about to creep up on them.

"Z, what's going on?"

"I was just driving through the desert . . . ."

"Where are we?" Logan asked.

"White Sands," Z-boy said. "Did you know . . . that right over there, they exploded the first A-bomb?"

"What's going on, Z-boy?"

"I don't know. I was driving and I thought, we're only in New Mexico for a hundred and fifty miles, then it's nothing but boring Texas. So when I saw a sign for White Sands, I turned and came here instead. I've always heard how great this place is . . ."

"How far are we from the highway?"

Z-boy thought. "Maybe an hour or two . . ."

"Goddamn it . . ." Logan sighed. He didn't want to probe too much, but they did have a schedule to keep. "Are you okay?"

"No."

The sun peeped up from under the horizon, lighting up the top of the dune in a brilliant orange light.

"What's wrong?"

"That sure is beautiful, isn't it?" Z-boy asked.

Logan looked at his friend in the light and noticed the dark rings around his eyes. He nodded. "It sure is."

Logan and Z-boy watched the sun rise until they could see empty desert around them for miles.

"Hey, you know what?" Logan asked softly.

"What?"

Logan smiled. "We survived our first day. That's something, huh?"

Z-boy smiled too. "We did, didn't we? We musta drove eight hundred miles or so . . ."

"That's a long way. I guess that makes us real mules then."

Z-boy laughed. "Ya think?"

They listened to the wind until they could feel the warmth of the sun on their faces. When the wind died down, it was suddenly quiet.

"I can drive now. You need some sleep," Logan said.

Z-boy kept staring at the sunrise. "Who am I kidding?"

"Nobody," Logan answered. "Come on, Z-boy. Let's get off of this dune and get going."

Logan stood up and offered his hand out. Z-boy looked at it.

"Sometimes I hate you," he said. "I don't know why I bothered trying to save your ass in the ocean."

Logan froze. He kept his hand out, but felt like slapping Z-boy.

"You tried to save my ass because I'm your best friend, dick."

"You're Dick, remember?" Z-boy smiled weakly. "You're my only friend. That's why I hate you."

Logan laughed. "You hate me 'cause of my good looks."

Z-boy shook his head. "When I saw you go under and not come up, I wasn't sure if I wanted to pull you out. But I didn't want to find you dead too . . ."

Logan grabbed Z-boy's arm and pulled him to his feet. "But you did pull me up . . ."

"But I failed at it like everything else. You ended up saving me."

"We saved each other," said Logan.

Z-Boy shrugged.

"Look: who's sitting here now, at five in the morning on some sand dune in the middle of New Mexico hauling pot across the country with you. Doesn't that tell you what you mean to me?"

Z-boy and Logan stood facing each other.

"It's funny that you survived and Fin didn't," Z-boy said. "What if it had been the other way around? Would I be here with Fin?"

"If it had happened the other way around, you'd be sitting by yourself on the beach, crying your eyes out about how you didn't save *me*!" Logan poked Z-boy in the shoulder. "Besides, if Fin had lived, Broza wouldn't have asked you."

Z-boy poked him back. "I guess."

Logan added, "As long as we're around to save each other, we'll be okay. You got my back, I got yours. Right?"

There was an awkward pause.

"I guess we should hug or something . . . ," Z-boy offered.

Logan grinned, shaking his head. "Maybe this once . . ."

Z-boy looked warmly at his longtime friend, then suddenly pushed Logan off the lip of the dune.

"Assho—" Logan laughed as he went tumbling, sliding almost all the way down. An avalanche of sand followed that threatened to swallow Logan. Z-boy and Logan ended up together in a heap at the bottom.

Z-boy jumped up. "Oh, sorry about your leg—"

Logan winced from the pain. "Thanks, partner. Now my cast is full of sand."

"Good."

Logan brushed the sand off his face. "How 'bout a hand?"

Z-boy started clapping.

"Funny." Logan stuck out his mitt. Z-boy took it and they stumbled back to the car together.

31

2-BOY FELL ASLEEP within minutes of getting back in the car. As Logan drove toward the dawn, he felt he needed to hear a voice of reason. Someone to tell him he hadn't made a huge mistake in taking this job. Someone to tell him he'd make it through in one piece. Confessing to Broza what had happened to them in the last twenty-four hours would not be a good thing. But he had someone else in mind as he pulled off at a lonely gas station to make a call.

He reached into his pocket and pulled out the secret device Broza had given him. Logan dialed the long-distance number, then when the automated voice asked for $2.75, he held the device up to the phone speaker. He pushed the speaker button as Broza instructed, and it made the beep sounds that happen when a bunch of change is dropped into the phone. A moment passed and the voice operator said, "Thank you."

Logan was impressed. "Damn thing works . . ."

The phone rang five times before someone picked up. "Yeah?"

"Buddy?"

There was a pause. "Who is this?"

"It's, um, Logan. Logan Tom?"

"Logan . . . ," he exhaled. "What's going on? You okay?"

Logan hesitated. "I just . . . I wanted to talk . . ."

"You on a pay phone?"

Logan looked around at the empty gas station. "Yeah."

"I heard you got in some sort of accident?" Buddy asked. The reception was weak, like he was walking on the Strand in front of his house.

"Scooter wiped out."

"That sucks. Should have stayed at the party. You disappeared on me."

"Yeah, I guess I was trippin' too much," Logan said.

Buddy sighed. "Yeah, I know . . . it wasn't quite the house party we intended to have around graduation . . ."

Logan felt like a schmuck. No matter how hard he had it, at least he hadn't lost his son.

"Logan, Z-boy told me about your mission . . ."

Now he really didn't know what to say to Buddy. "He wasn't supposed to . . ."

"It's cool, man," Buddy said. "I have no judgments to make. Z just needed to confide in someone, unload, ya know? We're all going through hard times, it seems . . ."

Logan bit his lower lip. "So . . . you think we're doing the right thing, with our mission?"

There was a long pause. Logan could hear the ocean in the background. "Thing is, Logan, I can never be you, so I can't tell you what's right for you or not. Ever hear that expression, life is like a river?"

"Not really . . ."

"It doesn't matter. I like water metaphors. The Indians say it, or maybe it was the Chinese . . . *Life is like a river*. And each of us is in our own little boat, going down a treacherous river, but you can't see what's around the bend."

Logan shrugged. "I've never been rafting."

Buddy laughed to himself. "It's the unknown that scares the shit out of people. Some people just can't put their trust in the river. They fight it. *What if there're rapids, or some killer waterfall that's gonna smash us to pieces?*"

Logan gazed down at his cast. "I think I already hit the rapids."

Buddy snorted. "I hit a few rocks in my time. A lot, actually. The point is, life hands you things and you can do them or not. But you'll never know unless you try."

"And what about Fin? He rode the river and look where it got him. I mean, what good is that?" Logan immediately regretted saying it.

Buddy was silent for a long moment. Logan imagined him all alone, surrounded by Fin's things. Finally, he said, "I got no answer for that. You have to take the good with the bad. Sometimes, you just end up on the rocks and that's it. No explanation."

Logan didn't like the sound of that.

Buddy continued. "You're a man now, Logan. You gotta make your own calls. I have no judgment either way."

"Really?"

"Hey, you know me. Pot is as natural as surfing. If it grows in the ground, it's probably okay, ya know? So you want to sell plants? There are worse ways of making a living."

"You make it sound harmless."

"It is. It's only the perceptions people put on it that make it harmful."

Logan nodded, then asked cautiously, "So what's your relationship with . . . The King?" The phone hissed and buzzed. Logan thought they'd lost contact. "Hello?"

"Let's just say, I'm an investor," Buddy said. "I mean, I could invest in some multinational corporation that's pillaging the earth and sending our country into the shitcan, or I could invest in local entrepreneurs and double my cash without Uncle Sam taking his share to fund some illegal war."

That seemed to make as much sense as anything. "And you trust him?"

"You've heard of organized crime, right? Well, this is disorganized crime. Broza puts up a good front, but he's just a kid, ya know? Thinks he's The King and shit. But he's smart, even if he's surrounded by stoners. He may not know everything, but he's gutsy. And he gets it done. It's a surfer's business. That's what I like about it." Buddy laughed. "Where else but in America could a twenty-one-year-old dropout become a millionaire?"

Logan didn't know if that was a good thing or not. "So you wouldn't say I was stupid to be doing what we're doing?" he asked.

"Crossing state lines with illegal narcotics, that's DEA territory, my friend," Buddy said. "But then again, you are a minor, I guess, old enough to be driving across country, seeing the lay of the land as a young man, doing the whole Kerouac thing." Logan could hear him scratching his grizzled chin. "The feds are too busy looking for terrorists these days to bother with a couple of white kids seeing America one state at a time."

Logan rested his head against the phone. Maybe Buddy was right.

"The real question you want to ask yourself, Logan, is this: Now that you're on the road, do you—" The phone suddenly went dead.

"Hello? Buddy?" There was white noise on the line. "The real question? What's the question?"

The phone started beeping loudly in his ear. He hung up.

He glanced over at Z-boy asleep in the car. The real question was, could he really trust Z-boy not to fuck up?

LOGAN DROVE slowly into Texas, a sense of dread shrouding the car. The ache in his ankle was dulled by another painkiller, but the sand in his cast itched like hell. The sun was only a quarter ways into the sky, and it was already 100 degrees.

Worse, Logan started getting that feeling they were being followed again.

Z-boy studied the map. "Man, for the next hour or so, we're gonna be driving only a mile away from Mexico. That means Border Patrol."

Logan's paranoia started to resurface. "I think I see that Lincoln behind us again."

Z-boy looked back, then shrugged. "I dunno. I think that's a different car. Why would he tail us all this way?"

"To rob us. How could he stay with us so long?"

Z-boy squinted. "Can't be the same guy."

Logan sped up a little. So did his pursuer. "See?"

He noticed a rest stop ahead. "I'm pulling over. See if he follows."

Logan pulled into the rest stop. The car followed. "Shit."

Instead of stopping, Logan just drove through and back out onto the interstate. The pursuer parked in the rest area.

"He stopped. I don't think it was him," Z-boy said nervously. "That was a good move though. I'll have to remember that."

"Yeah, but what if he had followed us?"

Z-boy paused for reflection. "Then we'd have to kill him. Dump the body somewhere in the desert."

"Funny. You're laughing now. Wait until they slit our throats and take everything. Then where will we be?"

"Hopefully dead. Otherwise, Broza will kill us."

Logan snorted. "Let's just keep moving for now. How long till we're outta Texas?"

"Eight hundred miles across," said Z-boy as he examined the map. "Broza said it's the one place we need to be extra careful. He said we shouldn't stop unless we absolutely have to. Texas has the harshest drug laws in the country."

"That's like eleven hours. Great, I hate it already."

They traveled past El Paso and continued through the burning desert. Logan concentrated hard on the interstate ahead. The heat waves coming off the highway caused the road to waver before his eyes. The horizon began to melt into a mirage, and for a moment, Logan thought he saw Fin surfing across the highway. He snapped out of it, rubbing his eyes.

"I don't know how Fin handled this by himself," he muttered. He stared hard at the horizon, waiting for the mirage to return.

Z-boy looked annoyed. "What's it matter to you?"

It took him a second to realize Z-boy was talking to him. "What?"

"You heard me . . ."

"Hey, I was just talking to myself," said Logan. "I thought of Fin is all. Chill."

Z-boy crossed his arms. "Fine. You go on thinking . . ."

Logan knew he had something on his mind. "What?"

"Nothing."

Now Logan wanted to know. "What?"

Z-boy exhaled slowly. "I just don't understand why you had to fight the dude."

Logan rolled his eyes. "Again? What do you want me to say? It was fucked up. I know that. How many times do I gotta say it?"

"Yeah, but . . . why fight, brah? I mean yeah, it was a shitty thing he did, stealing your date, but you were leading him on, calling him a sellout in front of everyone. We used to be the Three Musketeers, you, me and him. But you had to go ruin a good thing, ya know?"

Logan nodded. "I know you think I just couldn't handle all the attention he got. But he was also tuning us out. He stopped surfing with us way before the fight. And getting cocky and shit. Remember at the Open? He wouldn't even talk to us in front of the tournament people. It was like he was embarrassed."

Z-boy shrugged. "Maybe. But didn't we always say that's what we wanted? To be sponsored, hit the tour, get a name for ourselves? He just did what we always dreamed about. Maybe he just needed our support more—"

"He didn't need us anymore. That's fine. But he cut us off and that hurt. But I guess sometimes you just gotta let go, Z. Things change. I guess that's how it works . . ."

Z-boy gazed out the window. After about a minute, he said, "You're still *my* best friend, you know."

"Yeah, I know." Logan felt he needed to say something else. "Hey, wasn't there a movie about the Two Musketeers?" was all he could muster.

Z-boy didn't answer. Maybe he knew there was no such thing . . .

A half hour later, Logan felt like hearing Emmie's voice again. He needed her calmness.

"I need to make another call," Logan said.

"Another call?" Z looked at him funny.

"Just a call." He didn't feel like mentioning Buddy.

"To who? Broza?"

"No . . ." Logan blushed.

Z-boy eyed him. "Aahh, could only be a girl then. You been holding out on me, dude?"

Logan grinned shyly. "Maybe it's none of your goddamn business." He spotted a gas station ahead.

"So, why don't you use your cell?"

"Didn't bring it," Logan lied. "Besides . . ." He grinned.

"What, you dog? Give it up."

Logan couldn't resist. "I got something better."

Logan reached into his pocket and pulled out the secret calling device.

"What's that?"

"Broza gave it to me before we left. Free calls from anywhere in the U.S."

"He gave you a spy device and you didn't tell me about it?" Z-boy said, incredulous.

Logan pulled into the station and stopped. "Wait here."

"I get to make a call too."

"Who do you need to call?"

Z-boy couldn't think of anyone. Logan got out. "Why don't you fill it up?"

Logan heard Z-boy mutter "I'm not the one who's full of it" as he headed to the pump.

The phone rang four times before Emmie picked up.

"Hello?" she asked, her voice husky from sleep.

Logan breathed her in. "It's me."

"Logan?" she asked, unsure.

"Yeah," he said, imagining her in her underwear, stretched out on her bed. "I just wanted to . . ." He lost his train of thought, closed his eyes and pretended he was lying next to her.

"Hello? Logan, where are you?"

"Texas. I—"

"What are you doing in Texas? I thought you were going to Florida."

"I am. Texas is on the way."

"You're *driving* to Florida? I thought you were going to be back in a few days."

Logan wanted to explain but knew he couldn't. "I will be. We'll be in Florida in a day and a half. Then—"

"But how—"

"Emmie—"

"—how—"

"Emmie, I can't explain right now. I'll tell you all about it when we get back. I just . . . I just wanted to hear your voice."

There was a long pause on the other end.

"Hello?" Logan asked.

He heard her take a deep breath and relax. "I miss you," she whispered.

He missed her too. "Emmie . . . did you know about Fin?"

There was another long pause. "What about him?"

"About . . . what he was doing when he would disappear for a few days."

"Just what he told me. That he had business . . . I thought it was surfing tour stuff, but sometimes he was so secretive, it didn't make sense." Emmie sighed. "Are you—"

"Don't ask . . . please." Logan exhaled. "Just don't."

There was silence on the other end. Then she spoke very quietly. "Fin never let me in that close. But he seemed kind of lost before he died. Acting out in weird ways. The way he ended it with me just didn't make sense." She paused, like she was thinking of what to say next. "Are you okay, Logan?"

Logan rested his forehead against the phone. "Will you do me a favor?"

"What is it?"

"If I ever do anything really stupid, will you kick my ass for me?"

He could hear her breathing. "Sure. Will I need to?"

Logan couldn't think of a good reply. "I dunno . . . You will wait for me, won't you?"

"You're only going to be a few days, aren't you?" she asked, confused.

"I mean, if something happens . . ." He almost hung up. "Fuck, just ignore what I'm saying. I'm just tired is all."

"Logan . . ."

Logan saw Z-boy walking toward him. "Emmie, I gotta go. I'll call again."

"I'll be here. Don't do anything—"

"Lates." He hung up.

Z-boy stepped in front of him, squinting to assess the situation. "Have you been gettin' some on the side?"

"It's just a girl."

"I hope so. Otherwise, I'd leave you here. Who is it?" Z-boy leaned in. "You know I'll find out sooner or later. We got about two thousand miles to go—"

"It's Emmie."

Z-boy's jaw dropped. "Emmie? Emmie Slater?" Z-boy whistled. "Wow . . . I always wanted to bang her."

"Nice, Z-boy. Whatever happened to never sleep with one of your own?"

Z-boy laughed. "Where'd you hear that? It's the other way around, brah. *Only* sleep with your own kind!"

"Well, your people did come from the South . . ."

"Shit, Southern California, dude. But no worries, it's not like I ever did anything with her."

"No?"

Z-boy scratched his head. "Well, at that Fourth of July party at her parents' house three years ago, I did try to kiss her. But she threw up on me."

Logan shook his head. "Well, I hope it was because she was drunk and not 'cause you made her sick."

Z-boy didn't answer. "She's cool though. Got the moves. Hell, she can surf better than you!"

"Not quite. But . . ." He smiled softly. "She found me on the beach that night at Buddy's, and well, after that . . ."

Z-boy nodded in approval. "A surfer dude with a surfer chick. What could be better?" He had that devilish look in his eyes. "So . . . how 'bout it?"

"What?"

"Did you do it?"

"Dude, forget it, I ain't telling you." Logan pushed his way past Z-boy.

Z-boy followed. "Oh, you did. You dog! I want details!"

"I said I'm not talking."

"It's a looong way to Florida. You're gonna confess sooner or later . . . ," Z-boy said gleefully.

It was almost 600 miles from El Paso to San Antonio, by far the longest stretch of wasteland Logan had ever seen. And for 400 of those miles, Z-boy would not let up.

Finally, Logan spilled the details of his first and only night with Emmie.

Afterward, Z-boy sighed with a faraway look on his face. "That's just like I imagined it, dude."

Logan shook his head. "From now on, I don't need to hear about your fantasies."

"Come on, man. Don't be so tight. You need to share these treasures with your best friend." Z-boy closed his eyes and rubbed himself. "Oh, nice . . ."

"You're a sick bastard," Logan said, thinking of a way to get him back. "Still, when I did it with your mom . . ."

Z-boy stopped rubbing. "Man, you sure know how to ruin a boy's fantasy."

"Good. Keep that image in your head. Me and your mom gettin' it on . . ."

Z-boy covered his eyes. "Enough! I give!"

Logan's smile disappeared when he realized that he had to get that image out of his head too.

"DUDE, CHECK IT out. Surfers!" Z-boy pointed to a Jeep ahead of them. Strapped to the top of the truck were three surfboards.

"I wonder what they're doing out here," Logan said.

"Pull up alongside them."

Logan noticed the bumper sticker on the Jeep that said SURF NAZIS KICK ASS. "Let's keep going."

"Come on, man. When are we ever gonna get to talk to Texas surfers? That's kind of like . . . running into Bigfoot or something. Hey, they're even wearing cowboy hats!" Z-boy said. "Yeehaw!"

They were a motley crew of sunburnt cowboys—Ray-Bans and hillbilly tattoos. "They don't look like they want to play . . . ," said Logan.

"It's the brotherhood, dude," Z-boy said. "Maybe they know some sweet spot they can turn us on to."

Logan knew that unless you were trying to weasel in on a *locals only* surf spot, surfers were a truly friendly breed, always welcoming to another wave rider.

Z-boy rolled down the window. "Yo!" He flashed the back of his fist with his thumb and pinkie finger extended, proudly saluting the universal surfer hand gesture. "Shock 'em, brah!"

In the backseat of the Jeep, a big chiseled ape of a guy glanced over, baffled. He nudged his squirrelly tattooed friend next to him, who pointed at Z-boy and laughed.

Z-boy hung halfway out the window, pretending to surf, using his hands to sail through the wind.

"They're laughing at you, Z. What're you gonna do?" Logan asked.

He yelled, "We're surfers too. Hermosa Beach *rules*!"

All three looked over, talking amongst themselves. Then they all flipped the bird at Z-boy.

"What's up with that?" Z-boy asked Logan.

"I guess they figure you're moving in on their secret spot." Logan adjusted his sunglasses with his middle finger, sending a subtle message back their way.

The Surf Nazis laughed. The big guy rolled down his window. "Where you boys from?" he yelled.

"Cali, brah. South Bay. You know Shredder Hamilton?"

He checked out Z-boy's get-up. "What's with the monkey suit?"

Logan glanced at Z-boy's polyester suit and close-cropped hair. "Uh, you don't really look like a surfer anymore, Z."

Z-boy loosened his tie. "Oh, that! We're on business. Look!" He rolled up his sleeve to show them the SURF OR DIE tattoo on his arm. "Dude!"

The big guy blew Z-boy off. "Posers!" He rolled his window back up.

Logan snickered. "Oh, man! Dissed by a Texan!"

Z-boy ground his teeth. "No friggin' Texan is gonna tell *me* about surfing."

Logan saw the Jeep pulling off to a small exit ramp.

"Follow them."

"Come on, Z-boy. We both know you're the bigger surfer here."

"Logan, we gotta set the record straight. He dissed you too."

"Forget it."

Z-boy reached over and grabbed the steering wheel, swerving the car toward the off-ramp.

"Are you crazy!?" Logan yelled. "We're pros, remember!"

"We're not gonna be dissed by some Texas yahoos . . ."

Z-boy released the wheel. Logan had no recourse except to follow them.

The boys in the Jeep must have seen them coming, because their vehicle slowed down and stopped in the middle of the exit ramp, forcing Logan to stop too. "Great. Now we get to have our asses kicked by Texans too."

The exit ramp was quiet, since it dropped them off in the middle of nowhere. The big guy got out and threw off his hat, revealing a Mohawk. The squirrelly dude followed as they rushed the car. The third guy, who was shirtless and sporting a SURF NAZI tattoo on his chest, hung back in front of the car while the other two stood on each side.

Mohawk kicked the car. "What's your problem, man?"

Z-boy held up his hands in a sign of peace. "Bros. We just wanted to set the record straight."

The squirrelly dude did a double take when he saw Logan up

close. "Fuck, he's just a kid. Both of 'em. What're you, in high school?"

Logan noticed the dude was wearing an unbuttoned gas station attendant shirt two sizes too big, with a name tag that said BRAD. "Uh, Brad . . . my friend here just felt that you didn't think he was a surfer, that's all. And he is. Big time."

Z-boy continued. "We're in disguise—"

Logan hit Z-boy. "Zane!"

Mohawk leaned in. "Are you cops?"

Z-boy was offended. "Hell, no, bros. We're in distribution!" He smiled slyly.

Logan slowly turned to Z-boy. Panic swept across Z-boy's eyes. "I mean . . . we distribute surfboards . . ."

Logan whispered into Z-boy's ear. "What the fuck? Why don't you just invite them in for a cut?"

"Come on, man. They're surfers. It's okay."

"Come on, no secrets," said Mohawk. "You selling?" he grinned.

Logan acted innocent. "Selling?"

"You know . . ." He held his fingers up to his mouth and pretended to take a toke.

Logan shook his head. "No."

Z-boy jumped in. "Sorry, boys, no can do. We're on our way to Florida to see the big boys. I was just curious about surfers in Texas. We didn't know there were any."

The tattooed guy came over and talked to Mohawk in hushed tones. Logan didn't like it. "Z, I think we should split."

"Relax, it's cool. Can't you see they respect us now?"

Mohawk turned back to Z-boy. "You wanna see how Texans surf?"

Logan answered before Z-boy could. "Thanks, man, we'd love to, but we can't."

Z-boy did. "You got waves here?"

"Waves?" Brad said. "We don't need no friggin' waves! We make our own!"

Z-boy looked confused.

"Tankers!" Mohawk yelled. "We got oil, baby. Those super-tankers come cruising through the Gulf, leaving a two-to-three-foot wake that never breaks!"

"Get outta here!" Z-boy said, unconvinced.

Mohawk acted like he was surfing. "It's true, dude. I rode a wave for *one hour* once. I had to lie down; I couldn't take it anymore."

Z-boy nodded, unsure of what to make of them. "For real?"

Mohawk leaned in, close to Z-boy's face. Z-boy could see a large scar running across his shoulder and down his chest.

"See that? Once, I got too greedy. The bigger waves run right off the bow of the ship. We're talking four hundred thousand tons of brute strength." Mohawk smiled, flexing his muscled chest. "Got too close, sucked me right under and nearly ripped me to shreds."

Logan saw they were blocked in, with one guy on each side of the car. The engine was still running. He could make a break for it—

Brad reached in suddenly and grabbed the ignition key before Logan could do anything. "Don't get any ideas, boy. You in Texas now." He put the key in his shirt pocket.

Logan started to sweat. When he was in Santa Barbara one time, he almost got his ass kicked by some locals protecting their turf. He saved himself by sharing some homegrown that he had on him.

His business mind kicked in. "Look, Brad, maybe we can work something out here."

Mohawk nodded at the squirmy dude. "Why's he keep calling you Brad?"

Logan pointed to the name tag on the Brad's shirt. Mohawk laughed. "Yeah, *Brad*. Good one."

Brad looked at the name on his thrift-store shirt and giggled. "Shit, I thought it said Bad. As in I'm a Badass Mofo!"

Logan started fidgeting. "Z, give them some of your private reserve." He glared at Z-boy with venom in his eyes.

Z-boy wavered for a moment. "We . . . threw it away, remember?"

Logan gritted his teeth. "Come on. You and I both know that wasn't all of it."

Z-boy seemed lost. "But, you threw it away—"

"Zane!" Logan stared daggers.

Z-boy sighed. He undid his tie and unwrapped it from his neck. He avoided looking at Logan. Three joints were taped inside the fold on the backside of the tie.

"Unbelievable . . . ," Logan muttered to himself. "Give it to me."

Z-boy handed Logan the joints. Logan took them, letting his eyes linger on the guilty party. He then handed them to Brad. "Here. If I know my friend, this is grade-A weed. Guaranteed to fry your brain—"

A white light blinded Logan. His face felt numb. All he could hear was ringing in his ears. Then he tasted blood on his lip.

It took him a second to realize he'd been hit.

"What the fuck!!" yelled Z-boy.

"That's not what we want," said Brad. "You're a big-shot distributor? Well, distribute!"

Mohawk grabbed Z-boy's hand and twisted. "Shit, dude! That hurts!" he cried.

"That's the idea, big shot. Us Texans may not be as hip as you Cali boys, but we hit a lot harder. Now cough!"

Logan held his nose. His hand had blood on it. "What the fuck do you want?!"

"What do we want? Everything you got. What're you gonna do, call the cops?"

34

"JESUS," LOGAN NEEDED time to think his way out of this one. "We're in the middle of an off-ramp. You expect us to unload right here?" Blood dripped on his white shirt.

Brad looked around. So far, no one had come down this way. He opened the back door of the car and got in. "Pull up ahead."

He held the keys out to Logan the keys. Both his hands were holding his nose. "My nose . . ." is all he said.

Brad rolled his eyes and gave the keys to Z-boy. "You drive, surfer boy."

Z-boy was incensed. He took the keys and hissed, "Nobody hits my friend . . ."

Brad laughed. "I just did. Now move over and drive this heap under the bridge over there."

Logan could see Z-boy figuring the odds in his head. Finally,

Z-boy popped open the door and got out. Logan scooted over painfully. His nose throbbed.

Z-boy got in the driver's seat and just sat there.

"Well?" said Brad.

"Your car's in the way, Sherlock," Z-boy said.

Brad nodded at his Surf Nazi pal and signaled for him to move the car. Mohawk slowly walked back to the Jeep as well.

Brad leaned forward. "No funny business, okay? Just give us what we want and you'll be on your way."

"You're violating the code," Z-boy said.

"The code? What code is that?" he asked derisively.

"The surfer's code."

Logan saw Brad was getting pissed.

"There's no surfer code!" he yelled.

Z-boy closed his eyes. *"I will catch a wave every day, even in my mind. I will realize that all surfers are joined by one ocean. I will watch out for other surfers and honor the sport of kings."* Z-boy added, "Shaun Thomson."

"Who the fuck is Shaun Thomson?!" Brad shouted.

"Hello . . ." Z-boy seemed astounded. "Pipe Masters Champion 1975, '77 World Champion. Jeffrey's Bay?"

The dude was clueless. "Jesus, what century do you live in?"

Z-boy shook his head. "I knew it. Any good surfer knows the lineage of great surfers before him. *You're* the poser."

"Just shut up and drive. Pull up under the overpass."

Logan glanced at Z-boy out of the corner of his eye. Z-boy mouthed *Hold on*. Logan saw him put on his seat belt. Logan did as well.

Z-boy gunned it, peeling out around the Jeep, almost hitting Mohawk. Brad flew back and bumped his head on the ceiling. "What the hell're you doing?!" he yelled.

Z-boy yelled back, "Who the hell is Shaun Thomson? Who the hell is Shaun Thomson?! He's the king of the roundhouse cutback, you shitkicker!"

Z-boy let out his best banzai yell, and shot past the Jeep.

Logan held on. When Brad tried to regain his balance, his head popped up between the front seats. With the adrenaline rush coursing through Logan's veins, he elbowed the dude—POP!—square in the nose, sending him back into his seat.

"Goddamn! You broke my nose!" he yelped.

"Hurts, don't it?!" Logan yelled back.

Z-boy grinned like a madman. "Way to go, Logan. I say we dump this loser at full speed!"

Brad looked back. His friends were falling far behind.

"The Crown Victoria, in case you don't know, is the official car of choice for most police departments," Logan said. "What'll this baby do, Z-boy?"

"Full warp speed, captain!" Z-boy yelled gleefully. They were heading past ninety as they flew up the on-ramp.

The Texan started shaking. Without his friends, he was outnumbered. "Hey, man. Just let me get out! Just let me out!"

Logan gave him the evil eye. "Go ahead. Jump." They were back on the highway now.

Brad glanced down at the road flying by. "You're crazy," he mumbled.

Logan hissed, "We're crazy?! I got hit first!"

"I'm sorry, man!"

Z-boy yelled, "Push him out, Logan!"

"Don't do it," pleaded Brad.

Logan looked at the door.

"Do it, man!" Z-boy yelled. "Do it now!"

Logan started climbing into the backseat.

The dude cowered. "Don't!"

Logan stopped and glared at Brad, his face smeared with blood. Suddenly, Logan felt sorry for him.

Z-boy looked in the rearview mirror. "Shit. They're catching up."

They were hitting traffic again. "We have to ease up," said Logan.

Z-boy slowed it back down to seventy. Logan watched hopelessly as the Jeep made up lost ground and suddenly, they were right next to him, casting glares that meant they were dead meat.

Logan turned away. If he was going to die, he didn't want to see it coming.

"That big guy catches you, you're done," Brad said to Logan matter-of-factly. "That guy is one mean, ornery son of a bitch. Killed his dog and ate it, just 'cause it smelled funny."

Logan glanced at Z-boy. "I swear, if we get out of this, *I'm* gonna kill you."

Z-boy took a deep breath. Logan could see him thinking hard. "We get outta this, I'll kick my own ass. Hey, Texan!"

Brad looked up.

"I assume you want out of this mess too," Z-boy said.

Brad snorted, then glanced outside at the Jeep. "I might want to see them kick your butt more."

At that moment, Logan saw three things: A sign for a rest stop one mile ahead. An interstate patrol car sitting next to it with a speed gun. And Z-boy speeding *up*.

"Z, what're you doing?!" Logan yelled.

"Getting us out of this mess," Z-boy said calmly. He ratcheted up the speed to ninety, then watched his rearview mirror.

The interstate patrol pulled out, lights flashing.

The other guys panicked and slowed down immediately. Z-boy kept going.

"We got about a minute before I pull into this rest stop. Wipe your faces off with these." Z-boy grabbed a handful of napkins from the fast-food collection and tossed them to Logan and the Texan. "There's a couple extra jackets back there. Cover yourselves up and pretend to be sleeping."

Logan stared at Z-boy. If he hadn't admired Z's *chutzpah* so much at that very moment, Logan would be kicking his ass. He and Brad did as they were told.

Z-boy slowed up and drove calmly into the rest stop. Brad looked shocked when he noticed the Jeep kept going past the off-ramp.

Logan and the Texan pulled the extra jackets up to their ears and pretended to be asleep, facing away from Z-boy's window.

Z-boy stopped, straightened his tie and pulled out the Republican handbook from the pile of junk-food wrappers. "Let me do the talking."

"Don't fuck this up, Z-boy. I don't wanna go to jail," Logan said, dead serious.

Suddenly, everything was coming to a head. Logan's worst nightmares were about to come true. He closed his eyes and prayed to God for the first time in eight years.

Just get me out of this one, please, and I will be a better person. I'll never do anything bad or illegal again. I'll start going to church. Just don't let us get caught!

As he prayed, he thought of Emmie. Her voice, her tender kiss. And how, if he could just get out of this and be with her again, everything would be all right.

Logan heard the sound of the officer approaching as Z-boy rolled down the window.

"License and registration, please." It was a woman. Logan didn't know if that was a bad sign or not.

"Certainly, officer." Logan could hear Z-boy reaching into the glove compartment.

"California, huh? Long ways from home," she said without emotion.

"Yes, ma'am. Duty takes us all over." Z-boy sounded sincere.

A pause. "You realize you were speeding, Mr. . . . McDaniels?"

"Yes, ma'am. When you travel this long, the foot gets a bit heavy now and then. But I try to keep an even keel on things."

"What's your business out here, Mr. McDaniels?"

Here we go. Maybe I should make a break for it now.

"Passing through, ma'am. We're in the business of converting those who don't believe. 'Course, there's little to do here in Texas. That's why we did most of our work in California. Now we've been called to help out in Florida."

"Converting, huh?" There was another pause. "What's with them?"

Z-boy whispered. "We've been driving straight through. They're resting up for the final haul."

"And who is Art Bandini?"

Logan winced. He was ready to be cuffed.

"That would be the owner of this vehicle. He's moving to Orlando, so we're driving his car over. Saves us the airfare and all."

Logan could hear him take out the drive-away car receipt. "Here's our company I.D. too," Z-boy added.

Another pause. "Stay in your vehicle, please."

Logan heard her walk away. He opened one eye when he heard

another car pull up alongside of them. Another highway patrolman.

Logan whispered, "We're fucked."

Logan opened his other eye and saw Z-boy fiddling with the car keys.

"How far are we from the state line?" Z-boy asked.

Too far! Logan thought. "Maybe we could scatter, take off in separate directions."

"We're in the middle of the desert, jackoff. It's 105 degrees out there," hissed Brad.

"Yeah? And what's your brilliant plan?" Logan said.

"Maybe I tell them what you're packing?"

Logan stared him down. "Yeah? Maybe you'll go down as an accessory."

Z-boy cut them off. "Shut up, you guys. She's coming back."

Logan saw the other officer get out of his vehicle and walk behind them. *It was now or never.*

The woman officer stepped up to Z-boy's window. "Mr. McDaniels, you realize you were going ninety in a seventy-mile-an-hour zone?"

"Yes, ma'am."

"That's a pretty expensive ticket, do you know?"

"Yes, ma'am."

"And since you're out of state, we normally make the plaintiff pay in cash before we can release the vehicle."

Logan felt for the door handle underneath his jacket. He was ready to bolt.

"I understand."

There was a long pause, followed by some shuffling of paper. "Have a nice day then."

What? Have a nice day? Logan heard the officer walking back to her car. He opened his eyes. From the side-view mirror, he saw the two officers joking behind them. The one that had arrived late had two coffees in his hand.

Logan glanced at Z-boy, who was smiling. He held up a business card in his fingers. On it was a picture of the officer with this caption: Cheryl Johnson, County Coordinator, Texas Federation of Republican Women.

"Texas Republican women. With guns. Kinda sexy, huh?" Z-boy said.

Logan watched the officers share coffees and chat up the rest stop security. "And how did you pull that off?"

Z-boy waved his Young Republican I.D. card. "Must've handed her the wrong I.D. card . . ." He smiled. "Sometimes I can have a good idea too."

Logan shook his head. "Okay, Brad or whatever your name is. Out."

The Texan sneered, "We see you again, you won't be so lucky."

"Don't let the door hit you in the ass on the way out. You have a nice day then," added Z-boy.

"Bitch." Brad popped the door open. "I'm keeping the jacket." He slammed the door and scuttled quickly over to the men's room.

"I liked that jacket," Z-boy said, disappointed. "Ah, the hell with it."

There was a long awkward pause. Z-boy turned to Logan.

"Look, I'm—"

"Shut up. Just shut up."

Z-boy started up the car. "It won't happen ag—"

"Goddamn straight it won't. Get out. I'm driving."

"How's your nose? Is it broken?"

Logan grounded his teeth. Good thing he had more pain-killers.

Z-boy sighed and got out while Logan maneuvered himself painfully into the driver's seat. The passenger side door was locked. Z-boy stood there for a moment waiting for Logan to unlock it. Logan adjusted the steering wheel.

"Come on, man. Open the door!" Z-boy whispered. He looked back at the officers, then to Logan again. "I'm sorry, okay?!"

Logan took another painkiller, hoping it'd quell the pain in his ankle *and* his nose. He threw the pill container into his luggage in the backseat. He popped the lock and let him in. "I don't want to hear anything coming out of that mouth of yours, got it?" he huffed in Z-boy's face.

Z-boy nodded silently. Logan pulled back out onto the interstate.

He would not speak to Z-boy again for the next 400 miles.

35

LOGAN FOUND HIMSELF
driving through the empty roadways of Louisiana. The midnight
air covered the land with a heaviness that matched Logan's
mood. This was the Deep South—bugs hurtled themselves
against the windshield, their yellow carcasses strewn across the
glass. The trees hung sadly, draped heavily with Spanish moss
and the dampness of the swamps. The cicadas screamed so loudly
he could hear them even with the windows closed.

He thought about the promises he had made in his prayers—
to be a better person, to go to church again, to never do anything
bad. But the foulness of his mood squashed any hope that these
promises would come true anytime soon.

They hadn't said anything to each other for the last five hours.
But the anger kept building up until Logan couldn't take it
anymore.

"Why do you have to be a fuckup all the time?!" Logan shouted.

Z-boy had been sleeping. He wasn't anymore. "What?" he grumbled.

"You heard me. Why do I gotta pull your load all the time? I'm the only reason you're here on this trip, and all you can do is get in trouble! What's up with that?!"

"I also get us out of trouble, *Dick*!" Z-boy said, fully alert now.

"Yeah, well, maybe you can just shut your mouth for once in your life. You know, *act* like you might actually do something right!" Logan's face, flushed with anger, verged on tears.

"Fuck, man, I'm only human—"

"That's great, Z-boy. Is that some catchall excuse to fuck up forever? I'm only human? Well, I'm human too. You don't see me fucking up everything I touch!"

"Goddamn, a guy can't make a mistake—"

"A mistake? A mistake?! Your whole life's a mistake! You can't finish high school. Can't hold a job. Can't even keep your parents from kicking you out! And me, I gotta rescue poor Z-boy. And what's it get me? I help you study? You flunk out. I get you a job with my uncle? You don't want it. I offer to help you get on your feet again? You suck me into becoming a drug runner! Hold your hand across country, you almost get me killed!"

Z-boy spoke softly. "Well, it's great to know who your friends are and who has your back. I thought it all meant something, that we hung together because you actually liked me. But I guess it was all charity from the great Logan. No, you're just fucking perfect. In fact, your whole family is! Your dad's a fricking thief and your mom couldn't—"

"—Couldn't what?! She couldn't what??"

Z-boy turned stone cold. "Couldn't keep her son from being an asshole."

Logan hit the brakes. The car skidded to the shoulder of the road, bumping Z-boy's head against the dash.

"Ow, bitch! What the fuck?" Z-boy cried out.

Logan's face burned with anger. "Get out."

"What are you, fucking nuts? We're in the middle of nowhere! It's the middle of the night!"

Logan gritted his teeth as he calculated his next move. Then he reached back and grabbed Z-boy's bag. Logan pulled the key from the ignition, got out and hobbled around to the passenger side. When he dropped the bag in front of Z-boy's window, Z-boy locked the door.

"Open it!" Logan shouted.

"You're crazy! Why are you doing this?"

"Because next time, we're gonna end up dead or in jail, and I can't take that chance anymore. Now get out."

"No."

Logan made a fist. He was about to smash the window when he remembered he still had the key. He held it up for Z-boy to see.

"You're fucking evil, dude," Z-boy said.

Logan reached for his wallet. Pulled out $60. "Here's sixty bucks. There's a gas station back there. Call a cab, get to the airport, trade in your ticket and go home. I'm tired of this."

"Fuck, Logan! So it's all about the money? Dump your pal, take over and keep everything for yourself—"

"Look. When I get back, I'll give you your share. In fact, I'll give you *my* share too. I don't give a fuck! I won't tell Broza. And next time, you can do the job yourself, just like you wanted. Now, get out of the car."

Z-boy sighed and opened the door.

"Thank you. Now here's the cash—"

Next thing Logan knew, he was on the ground. Z-boy had charged him like a cornered bull, tackling him to the dirt. They went tumbling into the tall grass on the side of the road, grunting and clawing at each other. Z-boy broke free of Logan's grip, hitting him in the face, but Logan managed to push him off. He started scrambling back to the car, when Z-boy grabbed his cast—

"My ankle!" Logan shouted.

Z-boy didn't care. He scrambled onto Logan's back, pinning him to the ground. Z-boy looked around frantically, until he caught the glimmer of the key in the grass. He lunged for it, hitting Logan's ankle again on the way.

"Fuck, Z-boy! You trying to break it again!?"

Z-boy held up the key. "Serves you right, fuckwad! Now see how you like it!"

Z-boy ran over to the driver's side and jumped in. Logan scrambled upright, but as soon as he put pressure on the ankle, down he went again.

The engine roared to life.

"Zane!" Logan shouted.

Too late. The tires peeled out. Logan covered his head to protect himself from the shooting gravel.

Logan lay there covered in dust as he watched the car disappear into the darkness. Another car passed by, ignoring the late-night spectacle.

The cicadas started up again. He looked around. Nothing but blackness. Behind him about half a mile back was the faint glimmer of the gas station. He sighed and got up, wincing with pain every time he put weight on the ankle. He reached into his pocket for his painkillers, then remembered they were in the car. The car that Z-boy took.

Serves you right. He just wanted to get home and see Emmie again. He saw Z-boy's bag lying by the road. He picked it up and started to hobble slowly back to the gas station. He wondered what he'd do to Z-boy when he saw him next. Would they fight? Ignore each other? Make up? It all seemed unlikely.

It took a while for him to get to the station. But when Logan got within a hundred yards, he thought he saw a white Crown Victoria parked next to the air pump. As he limped closer, he saw Z-boy sitting in the driver's seat, waiting.

"Man . . . how'd he do that?" Logan mumbled to himself.

When their eyes met, Logan raised his arms. "Well?"

Z-boy just sat there. Logan realized Z-boy wasn't going to make the first move, so he started hobbling again.

I guess I deserve it, he thought.

Logan hobbled the rest of the way, both for effect and because his ankle hurt like hell. When he reached the car, he made his way to the passenger side. The door was locked.

Logan looked into the window. Z-boy gazed straight ahead.

"Can you open the do—"

"Can I help you?" Z-boy asked as if Logan were a bum begging for change.

Logan nodded, knowing he had it coming. "I'm sorry."

Z-boy tapped the steering wheel as he mulled it over.

"Please open the door, Z. I wasn't really going to leave you."

Z-boy waited a beat, then popped the lock.

Logan slumped into the passenger seat and sat there. "Now what?"

Z-boy started the car and pulled back out onto the interstate.

36

HOURS LATER, WITH nothing spoken between them, Logan noticed Z-boy starting to nod off. He watched Z-boy's eyes flutter, his head fall forward, then he'd straighten up.

"Z, you can barely keep your eyes open. Let me drive," Logan said.

Z-boy slapped himself in the face a few times to stay awake. "I got it."

"Come on. What're you gonna do, drive the whole way? Take a snooze and then you can drive again."

Z-boy glanced at Logan out of the corner of his eye.

"It's cool, man," Logan said. "Really."

Z-boy shrugged, then pulled slowly over to the side of the interstate.

When he came to a stop, Z-boy motioned to Logan to get out. "Go on."

Z-boy then slid over into the passenger seat. By the time Logan pulled back out onto the road, Z-boy was already asleep.

An hour passed uneventfully. Then Z-boy spoke.

In his sleep.

"You stay here," he said, his eyes half open.

"What?"

"Stay here, Logan. I'll be right back."

Z-boy looked right through him, his eyes a million miles away in another dimension. If they weren't talking, at least he could speak to Z-boy in his sleep. "Sure. I'm not going anywhere."

"Stay here. I'll take the money."

Logan raised an eyebrow at this. "What?"

"You just stay here. I'll take the money. Be right back."

This was interesting. "Okay, see ya."

Z-boy turned back to the front. He made like he was walking, but he wasn't going anywhere. "I'll be right back . . ." He was breathing heavily now, like climbing stairs. Then he stopped, looked around. Then sneered. "Fucker."

The hairs on Logan's neck stood up. He was going to say something but wanted to see where this was going.

Z-boy acted like he was taking something out of a bag. He was hiding something. He mumbled, "Now we'll see . . . leave me high and dry . . ." He was digging a hole.

Logan whispered, "What are you doing?"

"Oh, hey, Broza," Z-boy said.

Logan looked up, half expecting to see The King. Then Logan understood that he was Broza. "HeyZaneAdamsHowzitGoing?" he said in his best Brozanian.

"Yo brah, howzit?" Z-boy nodded.

"Are you . . . burying the money?"

Z-boy whispered back. "He'll never find it here."

Logan's throat tightened.

Z-boy had a devilish smile. "He didn't do anything for it."

They were on the outskirts of New Orleans. A strange fog settled across the road.

Logan decided to interrogate. "Hey, man, where's Logan?"

Z-boy waved him off. "He's not . . . here anymore."

"No? Where's he at?" Logan asked.

"Humph . . . He uh . . . I had to . . . humph . . . leave."

Logan cocked his head. "You left him? Why?"

"He, uh . . . dude bailed."

Logan saw a sign that said they were entering New Orleans. The fog was getting heavy now. He could barely see beyond the headlights. He eased off the gas.

"He was gonna keep all the money for himself," Z-Boy whispered.

That was it. Logan pulled the car over and stopped. "What the fuck are you saying?"

Z-boy hissed. "He wasn't gonna give it to you."

Logan couldn't believe what he was hearing. After everything he had done for Z-boy, now he was accusing him of stealing. "You're full of shit, man."

"No."

Logan studied Z-boy's face. His eyes fluttered and opened slightly, but he was definitely asleep.

Logan threw open the car door and hobbled out. His nose hurt, his ankle hurt. Now his chest hurt too.

Z-boy was quickly becoming a big negative. They had almost gotten caught twice, killed, detoured, towed, and humiliated. They only had another day to go, but look what had already happened.

He stood on the side of the interstate, the fog swirling slowly around him. When his eyes adjusted to the darkness, he saw an ancient cemetery covered in vines off to the side. Sure, New Orleans, cemetery, fog, double cross, why not?

Logan had had the same feeling at the end of their junior year. He had pushed hard to get good grades for his college applications, studying for his exit exams during the best swells of the spring. Z-boy flaked, surfing his way out of any chance to pass the test. At the last minute, Z-boy panicked and forced Logan, out of guilt, to help him study. But after two days of flash cards and making Z-boy focus, Logan had to cut and bail. He was losing too much time on Zane; he needed to get on with his own life.

Now, it felt like the same deal. Z-boy was making this much more difficult than it needed to be. This wasn't some lark. If they got caught, he would be fucked. And if he was fucked, it would surely be Z-boy's fault. Logan would be no better than his dad, just another surfer in prison.

"Goddamn it, Z-boy . . ." Logan kicked at the gravel by the side of the road. Then he got in the car and pulled back onto the highway. Z-boy slept, occasionally muttering something about cash and getting high.

Logan didn't know where he was going. He just followed the highway through the eeriness of this ancient city.

Then he saw a sign.

For the Louis Armstrong New Orleans Airport.

Logan followed the exit, not knowing what he was doing. The ravages of the last hurricane were still evident—abandoned houses, fallen trees and empty lots. It all seemed hopeless. The airport drew him in like a magnet, a way out. An escape.

He pulled into an almost-empty terminal parking structure at

3:30 in the morning. He parked next to the elevator and cut the engine. The fan ran high as Logan's mind raced.

He had a choice to make: he could head back to L.A., leaving Z-boy to finish up. Cut and run before his losses became irreversible.

Or . . .

What? Logan couldn't think straight. He was a doer at heart. Once he took on a task, he stuck with it till it was done. He stuck with high school, stuck with studying, and stuck with Z-boy when nobody else would.

He watched Z-boy sleeping. He didn't look like Z-boy anymore, with his short hair and suit. Maybe it wouldn't be so hard . . .

They were parked on the top level of the parking structure. He gazed up at the night sky. Because of the fog, he couldn't see the stars anymore.

He thought about calling Emmie. Maybe she could talk him through it. He took out his cell phone and started to dial. But what would he say? That he was a drug smuggler? That he had almost gotten caught and gone to prison? That he was really thinking of leaving his best friend behind?

He turned the phone off.

He wasn't a quitter. And he wasn't about to let anyone else screw with his future, best friend or not. This was serious business.

He couldn't mess around anymore.

He got out and opened the back door. Logan grabbed Z-boy's bag. He made sure Z-boy's plane ticket was in there. Zane could trade it in for another flight.

You're doing the right thing.

He put the bag on a bench next to the elevator. Then he walked over to Z-boy's side. *What if he woke up? No, Z-boy could sleep through almost anything.* He slept through the earthquake that had leveled parts of Interstate 10. *No, once he fell asleep, he was out for good.*

He softly popped the door open. Z-boy curled up against the seat, muttering. Logan leaned across and unbuckled his seat belt.

He whispered into Z-boy's ear. "Yo, brah, let's go in my house. I got some tasty weed for ya." Logan felt like an ass.

But Z-boy smiled. "Really? Broza, I knew you wouldn't bogart your product from an employee . . ."

Logan helped him up. Z-boy stood and looked around in a daze. "Sure is dark out . . ."

Logan guided him along. He padded slowly toward the bench. "Have a seat, brah."

He turned Z-boy around and laid him gently down on the bench. Z-boy grinned and muttered something about Doritos.

Logan stared at him for a moment. Z-boy seemed at peace, far from what was going on in Logan's head.

Logan ran back to the car. He tried to block out what was happening. *Z-boy will figure it out. He'll be okay.*

But he knew it would mean the end of their friendship.

He looked in the glove compartment and found a pen and a piece of paper. What was he going to say? *Sorry. Again.* There was nothing to say, nothing that would explain his actions, especially after what had happened earlier in the evening.

So he wrote the only thing he felt worth saying, the only thing left in his head after all the excuses were poured out.

I love you.

He folded the note and put it in Z-boy's hand.

37

LOGAN DROVE BACK onto the interstate. It seemed strange being alone in the car. The empty passenger seat stared back at him. What a prick he was.

Broza would agree with me on this. Logan knew Broza only used Z-boy to get to him. Now he had him.

But what would Emmie think? She'd be appalled, like he had tossed an abandoned puppy out the window of a moving car. If he was capable of that, what would he do to her? Could she ever forgive him?

Logan checked the map. Only 625 miles to go. With a couple of short stops, he could make it in under ten hours. No distractions now.

Just focus. Complete the drop-off, pick up the money, get back to L.A. Then figure things out. Of course, he'd give Z-boy his share. He wasn't that much of a jerk-off. But there would be hell to pay between them. In the end, Z-boy would see that he had been endangering both of them. It had been for his own good . . .

He imagined Z-boy waking up and being completely confused until the panic set in. What would he think? He'd probably think of a million scenarios before he got to the one where his best friend bailed on him. Maybe Z-boy would think someone got to Logan and stole the car and the drugs. He pictured Z-boy all alone, crying . . .

Mutherfucker! Logan pulled off the road. He slammed his fists against the steering wheel, letting out all his rage till his hands ached. He grabbed both sides of the wheel and pulled and pushed as if he were an exorcist casting out the demons. He shut his eyes tight until he saw red.

When he opened his eyes, the red was still there. It was blinking. And it was coming from behind him.

When he looked up, he had three surprises. One was obvious: there was a cop stopped behind him. The second surprise was that it was the Lincoln that had been following them from California.

The third surprise came when he saw three joints on the floor of the car. He quickly remembered they had come from Z-boy's tie.

He grabbed them, panicking. He thought of tossing the joints, but that would be too obvious.

Logan glanced in the rearview mirror and swallowed hard. The mystery man was getting out of the car.

Jesus Christ! I just wanted to make some cash, and now I gotta go to prison for it? He remembered something his mom used to say: *don't do the crime if you can't do the time.*

Fuck off, I am not doing time!

Logan then did the only thing he could think of: he ate the joints. Fast.

Eating a dry joint is no picnic. It's like eating a handful of dry oregano and some toilet paper. As he chewed ferociously, he looked around for a drink. He grabbed a Big Gulp. Empty. A bottle of Gatorade. Empty. *Fuck it!*

He chewed and chewed, swallowing as he could. It grated on his dry throat.

He saw the guy coming up fast.

Logan swallowed, gagging. A bit of bile came up his throat, but by an odd bit of luck, it helped the joints go down.

The man was at his window. He stared inside and tapped on the glass.

Logan cleared his throat as best he could. Then he rolled down the window a couple of inches.

"Thought it was you," he said calmly. "Where's your friend?"

Logan coughed a few times. "He stayed behind in New Orleans. Lot of room there for conversion, you know."

Logan saw the guy looking at his swollen nose and the drops of dried blood on his shirt.

"Jeez, what happened to you?" he asked.

Logan didn't have time to lie. "Met up with some surfers in Texas who didn't take kindly to what we were trying to do."

The stranger nodded. "Well, not everyone's on the up-and-up when you're traveling across this great country of ours. You never know what people are doing out here. I saw you pulled over here in the middle of the night in the bayou, thought I'd better check you out."

Logan thought fast. "No, I'm fine. I was getting a bit tired. Just pulled over for a minute."

Logan waited as the man considered this excuse. "I find stretching the legs is good for waking you up. I got my dog here who needs a bit of running."

He opened the door for Logan.

Logan hesitated.

"It's okay, I'm a cop. Detective Smith."

"Oh" was all Logan said as he scrambled his brains trying to figure out his options. He eyed the gas pedal.

Smith nodded. "Actually, I've transferred to Miami. Was gonna fly, but my dog don't take to airplanes. Come on out for a few minutes."

Logan looked up at Smith. His pale, ruddy skin and stiff stance made him seem more like a zombie than a cop. Logan had to make a quick decision. Something smelled fishy. Hell, it smelled like the Fisherman's Wharf, but what choice did he have.

He got out.

Sweat dripped down the back of Logan's neck. His ankle throbbed with a dull pain. Even in the middle of the night, the bayou was a hot and humid place. Maybe the joints were starting to make him paranoid.

"Are you allowed to use your lights like that when you're out of your jurisdiction?" Logan asked as he hobbled along.

"Why, you running from the law?"

Logan's jaw dropped and he started laughing uncontrollably. Smith considered him curiously, then started chuckling.

"That's right, I'm a murderer!" Logan confessed before he could think.

The detective smiled queerly, shaking his head. "Maybe you got a body in your trunk?"

Logan stopped laughing.

"Course if you're killing Democrats, I won't stop ya!" The guy snorted.

But before Logan could respond, Smith whistled toward his car. "Here, boy!"

The back window to his car was open. Out popped a German shepherd.

"Is that . . . a police dog?" Logan asked.

"K-9 unit. Best there is. He's mostly why they took me on in Miami. They need good drug-sniffin' dogs, with the ports and all."

The dog made a beeline straight to Logan.

It jumped up and put its paws on Logan's chest. It started sniffing Logan's mouth. Logan turned his head back and forth, trying to fight off the dog.

Smith stood back, amused. "I think he's taken a liking to you."

"I'm afraid of dogs." Logan squirmed, trying not to breathe on it.

"Down!" Smith suddenly barked. The dog sat. "Don't worry, he won't attack unless you try to run."

Logan nodded. "Got a busted ankle. Wouldn't make it far."

He looked at Logan's cast. "Doctor say it was okay to drive like that?"

Again, he was honest. "No. But I gotta drive. It's okay, it's my left foot."

While he was looking at the cast, the dog jumped up again onto Logan's chest and started barking. Logan freaked. The sight of a large barking German shepherd in his face set off alarms. Logan tried pushing him off, but the dog grabbed his sleeve and started tugging.

"Goddamn it, Bruce! DOWN!"

The dog dropped, but couldn't sit still. Logan trembled, but he didn't know what to do. Smith leaned in closely to Logan and sniffed.

"You been smoking something?"

Logan closed his eyes. Here was the great irony—he would go to jail and Z-boy would stay free. Logan's betrayal had actually saved his friend. He pictured Z-boy somehow believing this twisted logic, that it had been for his own good to be left behind. Maybe he would visit Logan in the pen.

He asked again. "I said—"

"Yes." Logan opened his eyes. "I just swallowed three joints."

The detective looked at him curiously.

"Now why in the hell would you go and do that?" he asked.

Logan heard the dog growling. His head started to spin; he felt like puking. Suddenly, it all came up. He fell to his knees and spewed out his guts. Smith just stood there, shaking his head. Logan heaved again. The dog moved around, confused. When there was nothing left in Logan's stomach, he just sat there, panting heavily.

"I panicked. My friend left three joints in the car. I saw your lights . . . I didn't want to go to jail—"

The dog stood two inches from Logan's face. Their eyes met. The dog was hungry.

"Got anything else in that car?" the detective asked.

Logan didn't answer. He was too tired. Too alone. And too far from home. He thought of his mom. This would break her heart for sure. She had fought so hard so that he wouldn't end up like his dad. Now he was a petty criminal just like him.

He thought of Emmie too. Would she wait for him?

"Mind if we have a look?" he asked.

Logan gave up. All he managed was a defeated "Whatever."

Smith gave the dog a series of hand gestures. The dog leaped into action. He headed for the car and started sniffing around its edges: under the bumpers, around the wheel houses. Logan watched Smith reach in the driver's side and pop the trunk.

The dog jumped into the trunk and had a go. Logan looked off into the darkness. He thought of running, but how far would he make it on a busted ankle? Logan looked the other way and saw the oncoming traffic. He could hurl himself into the interstate and end all of this. But he wouldn't get a chance to say good-bye to Emmie.

Then Z-boy came into his mind. He felt profoundly sorry for what he had done to his friend. And sitting there, watching his life go down the toilet, Logan was suddenly filled with the urge to see Z-boy again and apologize.

Fuck it. If they want to try and stop me, they're gonna have to take me down. And If I'm gonna go down, I'll take this bastard with me. I'll throw him and his dog into the oncoming lanes if they try to stop me. Especially that damn dog.

Logan dug his fists into the damp weeds around him. He pushed himself up. He wiped the spittle off his chin, standing up straight. He'd been beat up too many times this week.

Smith smirked at Logan's pathetic state.

I'll wipe that smirk off your face. The dog got out of the trunk and sat at attention. Logan thought the dog was smirking at him too.

Fine. You're next, pal.

"I'm going," Logan said. He started walking. But when Logan was just about past him, the detective reached out and grabbed his shoulder.

"I don't know what you're up to, kid. But Bruce gives you a pass, so we'll leave it at that. What you do on your own time is your business. But if this was my beat, I'd take you in."

Logan stared him down. "This ain't your beat. So, if you and *Bruce* will step aside, I gotta go pick up my friend."

Logan threw off the guy's hand, got in the car and fired up the engine. He looked behind him, saw no traffic and pulled out onto the interstate. He made an illegal U-turn over the grass divider and didn't care who saw it. Logan flipped off Detective Smith and his dog as they watched him pass.

All he could think of was how sweet motor oil and perfume smelled to him.

38

LOGAN PULLED INTO the airport parking structure expecting to find Z-boy gone. He had worked out the scenario in his head, how he'd go running through the terminal, find him waiting for the next plane to L.A. and beg his friend to forgive him.

Instead, he pulled out onto the top level and saw Z-boy just as he had left him: asleep on the bench. He couldn't believe it. It had been two hours since he had ditched him.

Logan parked the car. He was numb from the joints, but looking at his friend, a warm feeling passed through his heart. It felt good to see Z-boy again.

Logan got out and stood over Zane. He seemed peaceful. *Should I wake him or leave him be and just put him in the car liked nothing ever happened?*

The light of the coming day was starting to creep up. Logan stood there for a few minutes watching Z-boy breathe softly. He noticed his note lying on the ground under Z-boy. He picked it up, read it again. *I love you.* It was even truer now.

He tucked it safely in his pocket. Maybe he'd show it to Z when they were older and they'd share a good laugh.

Logan knelt down and whispered to Z-boy. "Come on, Z. Let's go for a ride."

Z-boy stirred . . . his eyes opened a slit. "Where to?"

Logan wasn't sure if he was awake or asleep. "I'll help you." He reached over and took his arm. He helped Z-boy up. They padded slowly over to the car. The door was open. He sat Z-boy down in the passenger seat, almost falling over his buddy as he plopped him down.

Logan stood there a moment, waiting to see if Z-boy was awake. Z-boy started snoring.

"I'm sorry," Logan whispered. "I'll never leave you again. I promise."

Z-boy didn't answer, but Logan didn't need an answer. A promise was a promise, no matter who heard it.

He ran over to grab Z-boy's bag. It was unzipped. Logan thought he had zipped it up tight. He looked inside—everything was there. *Had Z-boy woken up?*

He didn't want to know. Logan grabbed the bag and put it in the car. He saw the painkiller container lying on top of his luggage. He grabbed it and threw it over the edge of the parking structure. No more masking the pain. They'd face everything head-on. "Let's finish the job, amigo." He settled in, fired up the engine and pulled out into the coming dawn.

39

BY THE TIME Z-boy stirred, they had been driving for two hours. They were approaching Mobile, Alabama.

"What time is it?" Z-boy asked.

"Almost seven. Want to get some chow?" Logan asked.

"I had the weirdest dreams, man."

"It's been a weird night. Maybe you can take over. I'm about to pass out." Logan was feeling light-headed. He didn't know how much he should say.

"There was a cemetery."

Logan's heart pumped a little faster. "We passed through New Orleans."

"And then I was asleep on a bench or something in a parking lot. Freaky, huh?" Z-boy cracked his neck. "How close are we?"

"About five hundred miles. We should be there at the end of the day." Logan yawned.

"How 'bout some pancakes then? Let's have a real meal for

once." Z-boy rubbed his belly. "I could wolf down a few chocolate-chip flapjacks at the IHOP."

Logan smiled. "My treat, brah. Set your IHOP detectors on."

Logan pulled off at the first exit in Mobile. By some fluke, an IHOP was sitting right there. *It's a sign. Things will be all right from here on out.*

The pancakes, soaked in blueberry syrup, hit the spot. Logan felt good for once, wolfing down flapjacks with his buddy. It was like when they were kids and their parents used to take them to Denny's on Saturday mornings. Logan, Fin and Z-boy with their moms and dads, all chowing down on a hearty breakfast. All they had to worry about back then was whether or not they were missing any decent waves.

"When we're rich, we'll eat like this every morning. You think they have IHOPs in Mexico?" Z-boy asked.

"I doubt it," Logan said, but he felt magnanimous. "But I'll tell you what—I'll build you one. We'll start a franchise down there."

"Good way to launder the cash. I think Mexicans will like pancakes. They're like tortillas, only sweeter."

"You're ahead of your time, Z-boy."

"Z-boy's Casa de Pancake. Open only when the waves are flat, of course."

Logan sat back and patted his belly. "All we'll need is money."

Z-boy chewed on his pancake. "I been thinking. When we take over for Broza—"

He looked at Logan, waiting for him to interrupt.

Logan nodded. "Yeah?"

Z-boy swallowed. "I mean, when he retires, which'll be soon 'cause he did say he was close to his goal. When that happens and we take over, we'll have all that money and we could open a pan-cake house in Mexico for real. And surf the days away."

"Maybe." Logan smiled.

"Hey, man, no kiddin'. Look, we had a rough couple days, but we made it through okay, didn't we? We'll only learn from this, Lo. Soon, it'll be a breeze. In a year, we'll be pulling in more change than any of our bonehead friends who went off to college." Z-boy looked at Logan. "You know what I mean. Bill Gates didn't go to college."

"I think he did."

"Well, he didn't learn to be a billionaire there, that's for sure. He learned it in the streets. Broza's only been doing this like five years and see what he did. He was in the right place at the right time and he took advantage of it, that's all I'm saying. You want to go to college in a few years? Fine. You can pay for it yourself."

Logan smiled at his friend. Despite what they had been through already, he wanted to believe that dream. So what the hell . . .

"Now would this be an equal partnership?" Logan asked.

Z-boy grinned like a kid about to get his dessert. "Fifty-fifty, all the way."

"Course, we'd have to make a deal with Broza. He'll hand over the business in three years, say."

That got Z-boy thinking. "Three years. That should be about right. In fact, we'll give him a cut of all future earnings."

"Of *our* money?" Logan asked, pretending to be offended.

"Well, we'll call it a finder's fee."

"And what about Goldie and the boyz?"

"We'll keep them in the game. They'd probably kill us if we tried to weasel them out."

"And Broza's house?" Logan asked.

Z-boy's eyes lit up. "Got to keep the house. Dude, I'm moving downstairs as soon as possible. You can have the upstairs to yourself."

"Don't think so. I wanna stay by the beach."

Z-boy nodded. "Yeah, good idea. Then I could keep my board there. Crash overnight when the waves are cranking."

Logan got serious. "*If* we're going to do this, we've got to have a serious time limit. Like five years, then we're out. For real."

"Yeah, we'll work it out. Don't want to stay too long. We got to find that perfect wave, right?" He made his pancake into a wave. "The perfect tube, dude."

"I'm thinking bigger." Logan took an extra-large flapjack and made an even bigger wave. He took some whipped cream to make white water for his curl. "Sweet . . ." Logan chuckled. "Literally." He licked the cream off his finger.

Z-boy grabbed a wooden coffee stirrer, broke it in half and gently tucked it into the curl like it was a surfboard getting tubed. "Rip that sucker . . ."

Logan grabbed the other piece and placed it beside Z-boy's stick. "You and me, brah. Banzai!"

Z-boy and Logan sat there and admired their dream. *It sure would be nice.*

"Come on," Logan said. "Let's finish this job so we can start looking for this goddamn wave. I'm tired of being inland."

Z-boy held out his hand and Logan shook it, surfer-style. "I'm with you, brah, all the way."

40

THEY DROVE THE rest of the day listening to the only beach music they could find. *The Beach Boys Greatest Hits* CD beat out Kenny Loggins any day. Even if the Beach Boys sucked, at least they were singing about surfing. Logan caught up on his sleep.

The day passed uneventfully as they drove through Alabama and into the Florida Panhandle. They kept to the speed limit, stopping only for gas and supplies. When they switched, Z-boy would look at a map of Mexico he had printed out, trying to decide where they would settle once they reached their goal.

The time passed more slowly as they counted down to Orlando. The last four hours seemed to take forever in Logan's mind. They finally got off of Interstate 10, heading south on, of all things, the Ronald Reagan turnpike.

He started getting nervous again.

"We should call Randy," Logan said.

"Who's Randy?"

"Our contact, dweeb. The guy who's gonna pay us. Broza said to call ahead."

Logan glanced at his watch. It was 4 P.M.

"We should be there in about half an hour," Z-boy said.

They pulled off at the next exit and headed for a 7-Eleven. "You never been to Orlando, right?" Z-boy asked.

"Please. Why would I ever go to Orlando?"

"I'm just saying. Maybe after we do the drop-off, we could go to Disney World."

Logan turned and stared at Z-boy.

Z-boy broke out in a big grin. "Got ya, didn't I? I'm just yanking yer chain."

Logan laughed. "You know, if you'd have said Universal Studios, I might have gone for it."

Z-boy got serious. "Are you kidding me? We're doing the delivery, getting the cash, dropping off the car and heading straight to the airport. We don't have time for fun and games, mister!"

Logan held up his hands. "Relax, dude, chill. A little fun never hurt nobody. Work hard, party hard, that's my motto."

Z-boy shook his head. "I don't know why I bother. Sometimes I feel like leaving you behind." Z-boy looked at him out of the corner of his eye. "Course, I would never do that."

Logan's mouth hung open. Z-boy just smiled and hummed to himself.

He decided to change the topic when he saw a 7-Eleven up ahead. "Uh, let's call up here, Z."

Logan broke out the phone gizmo and jumped out of the car as soon as they stopped. He got out the card that had Randy's number on it, but it was one digit higher than the real number. So instead of 545, he punched in 434.

The phone asked for $1.75. He held the gizmo up to the phone and it delivered in spades. "I got to get me one of these," he said back to Z-boy.

Then he remembered the spiel. It rang and rang. On the tenth ring, someone picked up.

The voice was heavy with sleep. "Uh, yeah?"

"Yeah, is this Randy?"

"Mmph," said the voice.

"Randy?" he asked again.

"Yo, whassup?"

"This is, uh, Rick's Furniture," Logan said, trying to sound professional.

"Who?" asked Randy.

"Rick's Furniture. Uh, you know. We have a chair to deliver."

There was a long pause. Logan turned to Z-boy and shrugged.

"I didn't order no chair," Randy said in a haze.

Logan rolled his eyes. "This is Randy, right? Says here I got a delivery for you."

"Delivery, right," Randy said. Logan could almost see Randy trying to figure it out. "Whatever, man. Come on over."

Logan rolled his eyes. "You do know what we're delivering, right?"

Randy began coughing. "You just said a chair."

Logan made a fist. He had to take a chance. "It's a chair from your friend in California."

Randy hacked up a lung. "Oooohhhh. The chair, gotcha."

"Will somebody be home tomorrow?"

"Tomorrow?"

"Yeah, will somebody be—"

"Oh, got it. Yeah. Someone will be here *tomorrow* . . ."

Logan could almost hear him winking. He wrote down Randy's vague directions. If he got lost, he just had to ask where the police station was.

This last part worried Logan, but then again, nothing surprised him anymore.

41

AT THE CITY limit, Logan passed a sign that said WELCOME TO ORLANDO. YOU ARE WELCOME. DRUGS ARE NOT. He chose not to point it out to Z-boy.

After driving around for twenty minutes, Logan pulled up to the house. He had to double-check it to make sure he had the right address. The house was right *next door* to the police station.

"Are you sure this is right?" Z-boy asked.

"That's what it says," Logan said, checking each number and the street again.

"There's someone waving at you," Z-boy said, pointing to a bushy-haired guy wearing slaps and a Hawaiian shirt in the driveway.

"Whatever happened to keeping a low profile?" Logan asked himself.

Logan pulled the car into the driveway. Randy wandered over, puffing on a cigarette with a Bud Light in hand.

"Got my chair?" He grinned with a crooked smile.

"Yeah, you Randy?" Logan asked.

"Yup, in name and in spirit." He winked again and pushed the garage door opener. "Why don'tcha just pull her into the garage there . . ."

Inside sat two dudes playing video games on a small monitor on a workbench.

"Ease on in," he invited.

Logan pulled in and parked the car. He put his hand on Z-boy's arm before he got out. "Anything bad goes down, you save yourself first, right?"

"What and leave you behind?" Z-boy smiled. "Come on, man. If something happens, we could take these guys. They're just a bunch of stoners."

"And what are we?" Logan asked.

"Stoners with a hundred pounds of pot in their car." Z-boy popped open his door and jumped out. "Hey, boys, the mother lode has arrived!"

Randy closed the garage door. The two dudes continued to play their game. Whatever it was, it was loud. "Two minutes" is all they said.

Randy shook Logan's hand when he got out, chuckling at Logan's cast and bruised face. "Looks like you guys been partying hard. I hope the guy that ran into your face had the same results. Any trouble with Five-0?"

Logan leaned against the car. "Nothing we couldn't handle."

Randy nodded. "Well, we're glad to see you. I dig the suits, man. The last guy came dressed like an Amish dude . . . or maybe it was a Mormon."

Logan leaned in close to Randy and whispered. "Aren't you a little close to a police station to be doing this kind of thing?"

Randy chuckled. "You know what they say: keep your friends close and your enemies closer. They'd never look here because you'd have to be crazy to be doing what we do here."

Yep, we're crazy all right.

"Don't worry. We're good neighbors. They get no complaints. Cops got no reason to come over here," Randy said. "It's actually pretty funny."

"So what happens now?" Logan asked.

"The boys go to work. Take out the goods. We weigh them. You and me will go through the cash. The boys will put your car back together, and off you'll go, back to Cali."

"Actually, our flight leaves in the morning."

Randy got the attention of his boys and pointed to his watch. "Whatever. You guys wanna crash here tonight?"

The thought of spending the night next to a police station with all that pot and cash lying about gave Logan the willies. "Maybe we'll just crash at a motel."

"Your call, man. Just don't walk around with all that cash. I'm sure Broza don't want you to lose it."

"Oh, we won't. We're just gonna chill tonight. Get an early start in the morning."

Randy shrugged. "Try the Golden Egg down on Grover Street. Keys?"

Logan gave Randy the car keys and he tossed them to the other guys. "Come on, let's go find you some dinero. That means cash, dude."

Logan whispered to Z-boy as he passed. "You stay here and keep an eye on them. Make sure they don't scratch up the car."

"Got it, chief." Z-boy turned back to the video game. "Hey, can I try that?"

Logan followed Randy into the house. It was like a typical

surfer pad only they were two hours from the ocean. Some thrift-store furniture, a few surfboards, empty cereal boxes and cases of Mountain Dew sparsely inhabited the place. They headed to the kitchen. It was the only clean room in the house.

Randy opened the pantry door. There was a whole shelf of just coffee cans. "Coffee?"

"Um, no thanks. I don't really drink that stuff," Logan said.

"Oh, I think you'll like this." Randy counted the cans. He pulled out every fifth one. "Start opening."

Logan picked up a can and shook it. There was something else inside besides coffee.

Randy winked and popped the lid on one. Coffee grounds. He took a deep whiff. "Mmm. Mountain blend. Smells tasty."

He grinned, then turned the can over and poured the grounds into a bowl. Logan then saw that the top part of the can went down only an inch. It was a fake.

Randy pulled the second layer, revealing a huge wad of cash.

Logan couldn't help but smile. "Nice . . . but isn't all that coffee suspicious?" he asked.

"Nah. There's a Big Buy down the street." Randy opened a cupboard, revealing boxes of mac n' cheese and cases of cereal and beer. "Everyone buys bulk these days . . ."

Logan stared as Randy opened another can. "My boys rigged them up. Open the others."

Logan grabbed a can and started opening. Soon, they had a small mountain of cash next to a mound of coffee grounds. Logan had never seen so much money in one place before. It was a mighty vision—$140,000 in cold currency.

"Pretty, ain't it?" Randy said. "That's about how much Broza started his shop with."

"Yeah? Where'd he get this much?"

"Same way you got it now. Only when he returned to L.A., his boss had disappeared. No one else knew he had the money, and being the smart cat he is, he started his own operation. Now he's friggin' loaded."

"What happened to Broza's boss?"

"They say he went surfing in Baja and never showed at his hotel again. Probably the Mexicans got to him," Randy said. "Hey, go ahead and count that. I'll make sure the guys are getting started."

Logan watched Randy leave. Who were the Mexicans? he thought. Did Broza have something to do with that? He shook the thoughts out of his head and started counting. When he got to $20,000, he stopped and looked up at the pantry. *There must be twenty cans up there . . . They can't all be full of cash.* The thought of ripping these guys off crossed his mind. It was all just sitting there.

"The boys should be done in thirty minutes," Randy said as he came back in. "You stopped counting."

Logan nodded toward the cans. "Looks like you're doing pretty well for yourself. How long you been in this business?"

Randy sat at the table and cracked another brew. "Two years. It pretty much runs itself now. Overhead is low. Ever since the market dried up around here, everyone's been coming to me."

"Seems easy," Logan said.

"Let me tell you, anyone who says this is easy don't know shit," Randy said. "Yeah, it beats working at McDonald's, but no one ever talks about the pressure."

"Cops?" Logan asked.

Randy eyed him. "Let me ask you, who do you think runs the drug trade?"

Logan shrugged. "The Mexicans?"

Randy smiled. "Mafia. The Mexicans and the Cubans. Up to now, pot didn't pull in the numbers that smack and coke did. But lately, with operations like Broza's and legalized marijuana, the numbers have been damn good. In fact, dig this . . . Pot is now the number one cash crop in America. Shit even beats corn. Crazy, huh? So, of course, the Mafia is getting very interested. They go where the dough is. Because of them, our way of life may be dying out as we speak . . ."

Logan was dubious. "Really? The Mafia? Isn't that just some *Godfather* hype?"

Randy got serious. "They've been on our tails lately, scoping out our trade. I know Broza's been getting nervous they might do a smash n' grab and take our product and our cash. He didn't say anything to you?"

"No."

"It's hard to tell who they are. Sometimes, they look like Mafia. Sometimes they pose as cops."

The hairs on Logan's neck stood up. "There was this guy, who followed me from California. He said he was a cop."

Randy spit up his beer. "Did he follow you here?"

Logan thought hard. "I . . . I don't think so. I haven't seen him since Louisiana."

"How do you know he was a cop? Was he driving a squad car?" Randy asked.

"No. But that's what he said he was. Plus he had a siren . . . and a police dog," Logan answered. "He searched the car."

Randy leaned forward. "He searched *the car*? And?"

"And nothing. He didn't find anything."

Randy sat back, amazed. "Well, at least Broza knows how to pack."

The phone rang. Randy reached over and picked up. "Speak of the devil. Your boy was just telling me about his adventures." He nodded a few times, glancing at Logan. "Okay, you're the boss."

Randy hung up and stared at the phone.

"What'd he say?" Logan asked.

"He's such a jumpy guy. He said don't mess around. Get home in one piece. No celebrating tonight. He'll contact you when you get back. Now finish counting and put it back in the coffee cans. Then meet me in the garage." Randy got up and left.

Logan nodded and quickly counted through each pile. Soon, there were fourteen piles of ten grand each. Again, his thoughts drifted. This money would get his mom out of trouble. He could take it and disappear. Or . . .

"That's one pretty sight," Z-boy said as he sneaked up on Logan. He leaned over and examined it closely. Then he piled some of the cash together and lay his face in it, washing the bills over his head.

"What the hell are you doing?" Logan asked.

"Just enjoying the moment. I want to know what it feels like to have this much money. We may never see this much again."

"What are you talking about?" Logan said. "Soon, we'll have this much cash and it'll belong only to us."

Z-boy looked at the cash with a hint of melancholy. "You never know . . ."

Deep down, Logan felt the same uneasiness. "Let me try."

He laid his face on the cash as Z-boy rubbed the money all over his head.

"Merry Christmas . . . ," Z-boy said.

Logan watched the green tumble down over his eyes. If only Christmas could be like this every year . . .

42

LOGAN AND Z-BOY walked into the garage carrying shopping bags. Randy's guys had all one hundred pounds of pot laid out on the ground. Randy was weighing one of the bricks and gave a thumbs-up. "Looks good, guys. You did well. Money all there?"

"Yep. All counted. I borrowed a couple of shopping bags. You know, to make it look like we went to the store." Logan held up a bag for evidence.

Randy broke off a tiny bit of the corner of the brick and rolled it in his fingers. He inhaled it like a wine taster with a fine merlot. He smiled. "Oaxacan Green . . . good vintage, smooth, yet spicy, with a delicate hint of mint. Maybe you guys want to sample your wares?"

Z-boy and Logan glanced at each other. Z-boy jumped in. "Thanks, but we should take off."

Logan shrugged. "He's the boss. Another time, maybe."

Randy shook Logan's hand. "All right, amigos. We'll see you again next time?"

Logan just smiled. "That's quite possible."

The guys finished putting the panels to the car back together. One of them turned to Logan. "You should get this car washed before you return it. Always a nice touch."

Randy waved as they got into their car. "Remember, the Golden Egg motel on Grover Street. It's a decent place to crash."

"Got it."

Logan watched the boys cover the goods with a tarp as Randy opened the garage. Logan, Z-boy and the cash got in the car and pulled out. The boys quickly closed the garage door behind them.

Logan backed out of the driveway, careful not to hit one of the many police cars parked on the street.

As they drove away, Z-boy beamed. "We did it!"

"I guess we did."

"I can't believe we pulled it off! Wow . . ." Z-boy let it soak in.

"Hard part's over. Now we just gotta find the Golden Egg—"

"What Golden Egg?" Z-boy asked.

"Randy asked if we wanted to spend the night, but I said we'd feel better off in a motel, you know, one that's not near a police station. He recommended the Golden Egg motel. Unless you want to see if we can get a flight tonight."

"Nah. Motel sounds fine. I just want a nice bed to snooze in," Z-boy added.

"Sleep sounds good to me. Just a quiet night. Then we're off to the airport in the morning and on our way home."

"Home." Z-boy nodded longingly. "One of those guys said there's another swell coming toward L.A. this weekend. Should be some crankin' waves."

"Swells in the summer," Logan shook his head. "Must be global warming. Nothing surprises me anymore . . ."

"Sorry, brah. I'll hit the waves for ya. At least we're going home together," Z-boy said. "Thanks for not leaving me behind."

Logan swallowed hard. Z-boy looked away. Logan collected his thoughts. "I wouldn't leave you, Z. You're my brah." Logan meant it.

"I know it, Logan." Z-boy was quiet for a moment. "We've all done things we wished we hadn't, but the important thing is that we keep moving forward."

Logan smiled. "For a village idiot you sure can be a wise sage."

Z-boy didn't answer.

Logan looked at him seriously. "I'm sorry if I ever did you any wrong."

Z-boy considered this and grinned. "You could never do me wrong, brah. Even if you tried. You're too good at heart."

"No, I'm not."

Z-boy looked him straight in the eye. "You came on this trip with me, even though every ounce of your brain told you it was a bad idea. And you stuck with me."

"Barely."

Z-boy beamed. "Look at us, Logan. We're in Florida. Disguised as Republicans. With a hundred and forty thousand dollars hidden in coffee cans. How cool is that?"

Logan thought of how far he had come since graduation. Then he started laughing. "Man, if Principal Watson could see us now!"

Z-boy started laughing. "That douche bag. We have more cash in this car than he'll ever see!"

"What a loser!"

Z-boy snapped his fingers. "Hey, let's send him a postcard."

"Oh, that's mean," Logan said. "Let's do it!"

Z-boy acted like he was writing a postcard. "Dear Douche."

"No, no, have some respect. Dear *Mr.* Douche."

"Dear Mr. D. Wishing you were here with us in sunny Florida," Z-boy added.

"How 'bout, glad you aren't with us in sunny Florida?"

Z-boy pointed out a tattoo parlor. "Dude. It's not too late . . . you could get a *Mission Accomplished* tat!"

Logan laughed. "Yeah, my mom would really like that. No thanks."

Logan drove all the way to the Golden Egg motel feeling pretty good about himself. A great weight had been lifted off his shoulders. He liked being with Z-boy again. They joked around with each other as they drove through the foreign streets of this Mickey Mouse town. The streets were bright and sterile, tourists on their way to or from some expensive destination.

Logan felt like he was on vacation now, but deep down, all he wanted was to get back home again.

43

THE GOLDEN EGG was a Florida hold-over from the '50s. In a city that had been made over as a Disney resort town, the Golden Egg had no style or glitz. Even the pool was empty.

"Credit card?" said the motel clerk, knowing they didn't have one.

Logan and Z-boy exchanged glances. "Uh, cash," Logan said.

"Fine. How many hours?" he asked.

Logan was confused. "Um . . . for the night?"

The clerk shrugged. "Whatever. That'll be . . ."—he had to look it up—"ninety-four dollars." The clerk waited.

"For one night?" Logan asked.

The clerk smirked, revealing his yellowed teeth. "That's up to you. I didn't plan your vacation."

Logan counted their remaining cash. They only had $24. "Hold on. We'll be right back."

He pulled Z-boy back to the car. "We gotta dip into the funds."

"That's okay. Part of the overhead," Z-boy said.

Z-boy kept a lookout while Logan ducked into the backseat and counted out $80 from the stack of $10,000. He thought a moment, then grabbed an extra $40.

"I'll pay. You keep guard. We'll unload, then I'll deliver the car and grab a cab back," Logan said.

"Why do I gotta stay behind?"

Logan had no answer. "Okay, then you go."

Z-boy suddenly didn't want the responsibility. "No, you go. Maybe they have HBO."

Logan smiled. Same old Z-boy. "Okay. I'll pick up some chow on the way back."

It was almost 9 P.M. before they got everything into their room. Logan hid the money under the bed. The room wasn't much to speak of, but for two teenagers from Hermosa Beach on their own after three days on the road, it was heaven.

Logan called the car's owner, Mr. Bandini, and said that he was on his way. Mr. Bandini asked if he could come in the morning, but Logan said they had an early flight to catch. Z-boy channel-surfed while nibbling on the last of their food supply.

"Well, that's that," Logan said as he hung up. "I should be back in an hour or so. Remember, we gotta prep the cash for the flight."

"Man, we really have to wear those long johns?"

Logan made his way to the door. "Hey, better than wearing panty hose stuffed with cash."

"I don't know. Sounds sexy."

Logan opened the door and peered out. "Let's not go there. I'll see you in a bit."

"Yo, Lo. Maybe on your way back you can just grab something to eat at McD's. I'm starving," Z-boy said, staring at the TV.

"Okay. But don't leave the money alone. I'll be back soon," Logan said.

"But I'm hungry. Maybe I'll just pop over to 7-Eleven."

"Dude, don't go out. *And don't leave the money.* You can last an hour." Logan watched Z-boy carefully. "You hear me?"

"I hear you. Wait an hour, then scarf. You better bring something good."

"Sir, whatever Master desires, Master gets," Logan smiled. "I'll bring you the finest in Orlando cuisine."

"Just make sure it's thick and juicy and has the word *quarter-pounder* in it."

"With cheese." Logan waved, heading out the door.

"Hey," Z-boy said.

Logan stopped and looked back.

"We really did it, didn't we?" Z-boy asked.

"We sure did, Z-boy." Logan nodded at the familiar sight of Zane, crashed out on a bed watching TV. "We sure did."

44

LOGAN SAT IN the automatic car wash and watched the water slowly wash away three days of grime and memories. The mechanical drone and water spray emptied his brain of all the nastiness from the trip. He closed his eyes, breathing deeply until he came out the other end of the tunnel. After vacuuming and cleaning the seats, the car looked new again. The owner would never know what his vehicle had been through.

As he drove through the streets of Orlando, Logan felt grown up. He knew something of what his mom and dad must have gone through after they left the innocence of high school behind. He checked out the cars around him. He wondered how many people had broken the law, how many had secret lives. Probably more than a few.

Twenty minutes later, Logan pulled into Mr. Bandini's driveway. It was just your standard new development town house. The garage was open and still full of boxes from the recent move. Mr. Bandini was standing there in his purple bathrobe.

"Mr. Bandini, your car," Logan said as professionally as possible. "Still in one piece."

Bandini stared at Logan and his cast. "Where's the other one? The driver?"

"Oh, that was my partner. We co-drove the car here."

Bandini's eyes seemed to disapprove of Logan's broken foot and bruised face, but he took the keys and walked slowly around the car, inspecting every curve.

Logan continued. "She acted beautifully. No problems at all."

Bandini popped the trunk and peered inside. He felt a side panel over the rear wheel. "This panel is loose."

Logan walked over. He didn't care. Nobody had anything on him now. "Really?" He leaned in and tapped the panel with his fist till it popped into place. "There, good as new."

Bandini grumbled, then continued the inspection. Logan noticed a slight scratch that Bandini had missed. Maybe the police dog had done it.

Logan was growing impatient. "I'm supposed to collect the remainder of the fee. A check is fine."

He started up the car. It ran fine. Bandini seemed a bit leery, but he couldn't find anything else wrong with it. He reached in his pocket and pulled out a check. "I suppose you'll want a tip?"

Logan wasn't greedy. He was grateful for being free. "No, tipping isn't necessary."

Bandini took out his cell phone. "Need a cab?"

Logan nodded. "If you don't mind calling one, that'd be great."

"Wait here. I'll call. They should be here in twenty minutes." He turned and went into the house.

"I'll just sit here in the driveway then." He shouted back at the closed door. "Oh, and you're welcome."

A half hour later, a cab pulled up. This was also a first: taking a cab by himself. When he told the Cuban cabbie to go to the Golden Egg, the cabbie smiled, like he knew something Logan didn't. Logan didn't care. All he wanted was some grub and to lie in a soft bed for once. He didn't care if it was a hooker hangout or crack house or that there was an empty pool. He'd relax, watch some TV and maybe call Emmie.

Thoughts of Emmie made him relax. Everything turned out okay in the end, so he wouldn't have to lie to her anymore. He'd come clean and she'd understand. He could hardly wait.

Logan made the taxi stop at McDonald's. He felt the need to celebrate, so he bought an extra Big Mac and ordered dessert as well. They would pig out in style.

When they pulled up to the motel parking lot, the first thing Logan noticed was two men running to a van. He noticed them because they were wearing masks—Casper the Friendly Ghost and Spiderman—and carrying shopping bags. Like the ones in his room. The ones containing all the money.

Logan's eyes were temporarily blinded when the van's headlights hit the cab as it spun out into the street. It roared past them and disappeared around the corner.

When Logan's eyes adjusted, the parking lot was quiet again. Then he saw it. The door to their room was open.

His heart skipped a beat. "No . . . ," he said quietly.

"Typical Saturday night at this mutherhumping place!" said the cabbie.

"No . . ." Logan opened the cab door and looked more closely. The room light was out. All he could see was the bluish light coming from the TV.

"No . . ." He started walking toward his room.

"Hey, assman! I'm not waiting for them to come back and rob me too! You owe me fifteen dollars!" said the cabbie.

Logan kept walking. As he got nearer, he smelled something burning . . . Then he recognized the smell from the times he'd gone to a firing range with his dad when he was twelve. Gunpowder.

"Hey! Mutherhumper, I'm not going in there!"

Logan heard the cabbie put his car in gear and take off. The cabbie yelled "Assman!" at him, then disappeared.

It was quiet. When Logan walked up to the door, it was open just a few inches. He noticed there was a gaping burnt out hole where the peephole had once been.

45

WHEN HE OPENED the door, he saw Z-boy lying on the ground. His head was turned away from Logan. For a moment, he thought Z-boy had been sleepwalking, maybe trying to walk out the door, when he just fell down on the spot.

But then Logan noticed the blood.

He knelt down. There was a small trickle of blood on Z-boy's bleached blond hair.

"Zane?" he whispered. Z-boy didn't stir. Logan slowly leaned over to see his face. That's when he froze.

What used to be Z-boy's eye was now a clotted pool of dark brown blood. Logan must have stared at his face for a minute before his mind started turning.

He touched Z-boy's arm. It was slightly warm. There was blood on his SURF OR DIE tattoo. He felt for a pulse on his neck. Weak.

"Z?" he said again. "Can you hear me?"

Z-boy grunted. His finger twitched. Logan grabbed his hand. Z-boy squeezed back.

Logan's eyes filled with tears. "Z, what happened?"

Z-boy's one eye opened slightly and tried to focus, but it kept rolling back. His mouth moved, but no words came out.

Logan looked up at the blown-out peephole. There was a small smattering of blood on the door where Z-boy had peered through the peephole only to see the barrel of a gun.

"Z-boy, you have to hang on, you hear me? I'm gonna call an ambulance—"

"Where . . . were . . . you?" he whispered.

Logan's tears fell on Z-boy's face. "I had to clean the car, then wait for the cab to come. I got us some food—"

Z-boy struggled to look over by the bed. " . . . the . . . money . . . ?"

Logan's eyes shot up. Everything was overturned, the mattress, the desk. There was nothing left.

"Fuck the money. Don't you fuckin' leave me alone." Logan brushed the matted hair out of Z-boy's face. "Nothing matters now. Don't you—"

Z-boy smiled weakly. "Logan . . ."

Logan had to lean in to hear. "What?"

"Logan . . . ," he whimpered.

Logan held his hand tighter. "What, Z-boy?"

Z-boy took one last breath and became still. And just like that, Logan knew his friend was gone.

Logan started shaking violently. He tried to cry out for help, but no words came. He sat there, the anger building till he began to hit the floor with all his might. Tears tumbled from his eyes as his mind raced. *They had been set up. It had been Randy. No, it had to be Smith. He had followed their every move. He was Mafia. Or a corrupt cop. Or both.*

Then he looked down at Z-boy. *Did he know he was going to die? Did he suffer?* He had wondered the same thing about Fin. Now it was too much . . .

Logan held his friend for a long time. He had never hugged him in all the years they had known each other. But now he held him tight. Logan didn't care if they came after him. Logan rocked back and forth, whispering *I'm sorry* over and over. He felt ashamed for having left him here alone. *It should have been me.* He was the one who deserved to die.

46

AFTER AN HOUR, Logan knew he had to do something, call someone. He scrambled over to the phone, but remembered that Broza said to always use a pay phone. Nothing else was safe. He found one near the vending machines.

The first person he thought of was Broza.

He riffled through his wallet. He had written down the number. But his hand shook so much, he kept punching it in wrong. Finally, he got it right. He used the phone gizmo, but it followed with an odd ring.

"This line is no longer in service."

Logan slammed down the phone. He redialed slowly to make sure he got it right.

"This line is no longer in service."

Logan hung up. *What is going on? Did they get to Broza too? Did he bug out and hang us out to dry?* Logan called information. They confirmed that the line had been disconnected.

He looked at Randy's number. Randy had either set them up or they had gotten him too. He dialed. The phone rang and rang. Nobody picked up.

Logan took some deep breaths. Panic raced through his bones. He had to leave. He had to get to the airport and go home. He had to go somewhere, far away from here.

But then he thought of Z-boy. He remembered his promise never to leave him again. And he knew he wouldn't. He would have to ride this thing out with Z-boy or go down trying.

He dialed 911.

Logan sat quietly in a sterile, empty room when a Diet Coke–addicted investigator sauntered in reading a report. He stood in front of a mirror nodding his clean-shaven head as he flipped through a few pages.

"Logan, this still doesn't make sense to me. Two kids from California don't just pack up and drive across country to go to Disney World without telling their parents what they're doing. This isn't a TV show, son. This is real life, and you're in a heap of—"

"I just went to return the car—"

"I know you were involved with something. Why the fake names on the car delivery invoice and the hotel registration?" Logan had flushed the fake I.D.s, though he didn't have an answer for the investigator's question. All he knew was that there was nothing to tie him to Randy or Broza.

He stuck to his alibi. "Bandini and the cabbie will tell you—"

"Son, we already have their statements. But I tell you what . . . I do know that folks don't kill some kid for a couple of bucks and a Game Boy." He leaned in real close. "You're not the first one to do this, you know? You must've had something else in that room of real value, something—"

There was a knock at the door. The investigator made a face and opened the door a crack. Someone whispered something to him.

"Shit," was all he said. He glanced at Logan. "Looks like your pal is here."

The investigator turned and left the room. Logan's mind raced. *Broza? Randy?*

It was neither. A puffy red-faced man shuffled in, a large coffee in one hand, a worn leather satchel in the other. He considered Logan through his thick glasses, then motioned for him to get up and follow him.

"Who are you?" Logan asked.

"Donny. I'm the cleaner." He turned and walked out.

Logan followed, confused.

"What's going on?" Logan asked when he caught up to him in the hallway. Donny held his fingers to his lips and kept walking, huffing and puffing from one too many doughnuts.

When the sunlight hit him outside, Logan was blinded for a moment.

"Florida sun, ain't it great?" Donny kept walking.

"What's going on? Who are you?"

Donny finally stopped in front of an old white Mercedes. "You're lucky I'm still down here. Normally, I'd be back in Maine where I wouldn't be taking a bath every time I walk outside. But there's been a lot of activity lately."

"Did Broza send you?"

"Like I said, I'm the cleaner. I take care of messes, and seeing as you're in one, I was sent in to take care of things."

"Are you Broza's lawyer?"

Donny looked around. "My client has gone on vacation. He heard about what happened and sent me to straighten things out.

You are free to go." He unlocked the car door and threw in his satchel.

Logan stood there frozen. "What about Zane?"

Donny took a deep breath. "Yes, your friend. His parents have been notified by the police and are on their way here to collect the body. As for the investigation, there won't be much of one. That motel that you were staying in, the Golden Egg? It's known for drug trafficking and prostitution. Shit like this goes down all the time."

Logan started shaking. "But who did it? Who got Zane? Was it Randy?"

Donny looked into Logan's eyes for the first time. "Son, in my experience, trying to figure out who did it is not a question to pursue. *They* did it. That's all you need to know. Organized crime is going to go wherever the money is. And as soon as you start making real money, they'll show up, in one form or another. They got people everywhere. Police, insiders, people who aren't who they say they are. But trying to pin your friend's death on someone specific? You might as well try to figure out who shot Kennedy. *They* did it, that's all that matters, and there ain't shit you can do about it. Not now, not ever. Because you were on the wrong side of the law when this shit went down. So my advice? Let it go. Go home. Stay out of this business. You're still young. Grow older, kid."

Donny lit a cigarette he had stashed in his pocket. He gazed at Logan with tired eyes, then shook his head and reached into the pocket of his wrinkled suit. He pulled out an envelope with $200 and a plane ticket back to L.A. and gave it to Logan. He would yield no more information about Broza or Randy, but he had wrangled Logan's bag out from the evidence room. He offered him a ride to the airport.

Logan stood there, staring down at his ticket. All he could think of was Z-boy. After everything they had been through, all he had to show for it was his friend's death, $200 and a plane ticket.

Donny took him to the airport, but not for Logan's departure. Logan found out when Z-boy's parents were arriving and he waited for them, because he had promised not to leave his friend behind. It was a promise he would not break. He would take whatever blame they pushed on him, whatever hurt they felt. He wanted them to know what a good soul Z-boy was and that he had been Logan's best friend, despite the mess they had wound up in. He didn't want them to know what it was like in the end for Z-boy. Logan would keep that to himself forever. That was his burden.

All Logan wanted now was for them to hold on to the thought of their happy, lazy surfer son munching out on Doritos in front of the TV. It wasn't much, but it was enough.

47

A FEW DAYS later, Logan flew home with Z-boy's parents. They carried a small urn of Z-boy's ashes in their laps. He asked if he could hold the urn. They hesitated, but eventually, Z-boy's father relented and allowed Logan to hold his friend. When he did, he could almost hear Z-boy wisecracking about how Logan would make a better son for his parents anyways.

Logan wasn't looking forward to returning home. There would be lots of explaining to do to his mom and to Emmie. He had left a message for his mom saying he'd be a few more days, and to tell Emmie not to worry. But his voice betrayed him—there was plenty to worry about.

Z-boy's parents dropped him off in front of his house. He'd spent the rest of his money on hotels and food over the past few days. He had only $3 in his pocket—the total sum that was left from all that effort. Logan still wore his Republican suit since it was the only thing he had. When he opened the door, his mom was standing there.

They looked at each other for a long time, almost communicating telepathically. He sensed she knew everything already. Finally, he walked up to her and held her tightly. The tears that he had held back began to flow. His mom just hugged him tighter, never accusing him or questioning his judgment.

All Logan said was "I'll never let you down again."

His mom nodded. He hoped she knew that was the truth.

Logan showered and put on his own clothes. That helped a little. He stared into the mirror. He seemed older now, his sunny disposition hardened and strained. When he looked closely, he saw a few gray hairs poking through.

That night, he fell into a deep, deep sleep. He slept for fourteen hours. Those hours Logan spent dreaming of Z-boy wandering an isolated beach with him, searching for the perfect break. It was a beautiful day—no wind, glassy waves with perfect left angles.

"Looks like we finally found the right spot, brah," Z-boy said.

He watched Z-boy charge into the water, throwing his board ahead of him, then jumping on and sailing out into the waves. Logan would join him, but first he just wanted to sit back and watch his bud peel off one perfect set after another.

Something woke him up.

He heard a sound, then looked up to see a small acorn sail through the open window and land on his bed.

"Dude, I need to sleep!" he said automatically, still drowsy. Another acorn flew across his room and pegged him square on the head. "Bastard." He sat up and hobbled over to his window.

Each step brought him more awake. He slowly remembered

that Z-boy was dead. He stopped in his tracks. Maybe it had all been a dream, this whole thing. Maybe everything from Fin's death to the trip had all been some long-assed nightmare and now everything was as it was before.

He took a few more steps to the window and looked down.

Emmie.

He smiled weakly. Logan wasn't sure he was ready for her yet, but he waved her up since his mom was already at work. He sat down on the edge of his bed, trying to think of what to say.

Emmie walked in. Her face was pale and drawn, so Logan knew that she knew.

"Is it true? About Z-boy?" she asked, sitting next to him.

He took a deep breath. It hadn't been a dream. "Yeah," he whispered. He held his head in his hands. "I don't know what to say . . ."

She looked down, her hair covering her face. "You can tell me what happened."

He shook his head. "You might not like me afterward."

She took his hand. "I don't think that's possible."

"Oh, it's possible."

"Look, Logan. I know you were messed up in something you didn't want to tell me about. But I'm here, now. So tell me. I can take it."

Her eyes were so clear and full of trust. Opening up was suddenly easy for Logan. So for the next hour, he told her everything. She didn't say a word or ask a question, but she didn't back off either. Afterward, they held each other in silence for a long time.

Finally, Logan leaned over, searching for some sign of acceptance or forgiveness. Her blank stare told him nothing.

"The funny thing is," he whispered, "every time I was in trouble, I thought of you. I thought if I could just make it out of this alive, I could come back to you and it would be all right."

She gazed at him with her big blue eyes and nodded. "It's over now." She wrapped her arms around him and kissed him until all his doubts disappeared.

48

THE NEXT DAY, Logan borrowed his mom's car. He needed answers.

When he drove up to Broza's street, he passed the spot where the little black girl had shouted "Whitey's here!" She was gone.

He pulled up to Broza's house. From the outside, it looked the same. He walked up to the gate. The dog was gone.

He found the front door open so he walked in. But the inside seemed no different, so that didn't tell him anything.

"Broza?" he shouted.

There was no answer. Logan slowly hobbled over to the secret trapdoor. He stood there for a long moment, afraid to open it. He took a deep breath and reached down . . . It was unlocked. Logan pulled the door open and gazed into the dark void.

"It's empty," said a voice behind him.

Logan knew that voice without looking back: Goldie.

"He bugged out a few days after you guys took off," Goldie explained. "Some nasty shit must've gone down."

It was dark at the bottom of the stairs. "Do you know where he is?"

"Nope. But my bets are on Mexico. You white boys always head south of tha' border."

Logan shook his head. "He didn't say anything? Or leave a message?"

"I ain't his damn message service." Goldie picked at his teeth with a gold toothpick. "Mexicans came, though. But Broza was already gone, so we didn't stop 'em."

Logan leaned against the wall. He felt dizzy. "Fuck me."

Goldie nodded. "Heard about your boy." When Logan gave him a strange look, Goldie added, "I hear about everything. That's why I'm still here. But that was messed up."

"How come they didn't come after you?" Logan asked.

Goldie snorted. "Only ones to come in this neighborhood are cartel looking after their business, or white boys who don't know better. Cops and feds stay clear. Cartel, we get on just fine."

"So what now?" Logan asked softly.

Goldie answered. "So what now? You get the hell out of the ghetto and never come back. We'll give you a free ride out this time. But don't be showin' your white face around here no mo'."

Logan's face hardened. He got up and started to walk out.

Goldie put out his arm and whispered. "'Less of course, you wanna go into business for yourself, take up Broza's place. I'm sure he wouldn't mind." Goldie chuckled.

Logan stared into Goldie's mirrored glasses and saw himself.

He didn't look good. "No, thanks. I'm gonna stick with what I know."

"What's that?" Goldie smiled.

Logan had no answer. He shrugged, then limped back to his car and out of Compton forever.

49

LOGAN LOCKED HIMSELF

up in his room. He talked to no one except Emmie and his mom, but even they didn't know what to say to him.

He had to let everything out somehow, so he started writing. About when he and Z-boy first met. How they'd both shown up at Buddy's shop to check out boards to put on their Christmas wish lists. They both liked the same one. They started shoving each other until Buddy mediated and promised to make another one just like it. When they both got their boards, Buddy made them go surfing together and sent his son Fin with them too. The rest was history. They were eight years old.

Over the next few days, Logan wrote down everything he could remember about Z-boy, stopping only for food or sleep. When he finally finished, he almost felt normal again.

When Logan emerged from his room, the first thing he noticed was that his mom looked different. She was smiling. Sort of.

"What happened?" he asked.

"Court decided in your father's favor. They said since I've been the principal provider for the last four years and that your dad is 'mentally disabled,' I have to pay for his debt until he lands on his feet."

Logan frowned. "That . . . is *so* seriously messed up. How can they do that?"

"Kid, when you get older, you'll learn. You can't go home again, even if you live there."

Logan thought about it and realized she was right. "Yeah," he nodded. "I know." Logan looked at her and for the first time saw a glimpse of the woman she might have been before she met his dad. "But why are you smiling?"

"Yesterday, we came up with a potential settlement. I buy your dad out of his share of the house, plus some of *our* debts, for a lump sum. He declares bankruptcy, but the court keeps me from paying off the debt *he* built up when he became stupid in the head. Plus, there's still the real possibility of jail time for him."

"Wow," Logan said. He felt numb. "Where does that leave us?"

"It won't be easy," she said. "But we'll get to keep the house. *If* we can keep up with the payments."

Logan walked over to his mom and hugged her. "So we're not gonna be out in the streets?"

She held him tightly. "Not yet."

Logan squeezed her back.

"But I'll have to work even more to pay off your dad and the lawyer. It'll take a few years . . ."

Logan pulled back. "No. I'll find work. Honest work."

His mom nodded knowingly. "I know you'll do what's best, kid."

Logan paused. "What about the college fund?"

His mom sighed. "I'm sorry to say your college funds will be frozen until the case gets completely settled. There are a lot of details to this thing, and they tell me it may take three to six months to finalize the deal. The court may still use it as part of the bankruptcy settlement, or we may get all of it back. It's complicated."

Logan shrugged. "Maybe I need to take time off from school anyways, before I decide what to do with the rest of my life."

His mom nodded. "That sounds like a wise decision."

"Emmie's going to community college, so maybe, you know, for a couple years, I could go too . . ." Logan trailed off, embarrassed.

"I think she's good for you, Logan. If junior college is your choice for now, fine. As long as you're making that decision because it's right for *you*."

Logan smiled. "Thanks. I'm gonna think about it." He paused. "She surfs, you know."

His mom shrugged. "Well, nobody's perfect."

"No, they aren't," he added somberly.

"Oh, before I forget—" She turned to the kitchen counter and grabbed a piece of paper. "You have a couple messages here."

Logan glanced at the paper.

"You have an appointment on Tuesday to remove that cast of yours," his mom said.

"Finally." He looked down at his foot. He wouldn't miss it.

"And I got a call from a guy named . . . Broza, I think it was . . ."

Logan's heart skipped a beat. "What'd he say?"

"He said to go see Buddy." His mom frowned. "Buddy Hamilton? What business do you have with him?"

Logan tried to act calm. "That's all he said?"

"Yes. It was all very mysterious." She looked at him for answers. "Was he mixed up in your troubles?"

Logan nodded softly. "Yeah. But that's all over now."

Half of him didn't want to find out why Broza wanted him to go see Buddy. The paranoia he felt before crept back into his head. *What if this was a setup?* But the other half told him, *He might have the money Broza owes you.* He could use the cash. But why would Broza pay for a mission that had failed?

In the end, Logan couldn't help it. The week after he had his cast removed, he decided to ride his bike over to Buddy's. The doctor had recommended physical therapy, and that included bike riding. He took his time riding along the Strand, until he ended up in front of Buddy's house.

Buddy wasn't surprised to see him when he knocked on the front door. "Logan Tom, in the flesh. I've been waiting for you to show up."

Logan hesitated. Buddy frowned and then grabbed Logan's arm, pulling him into a bear hug. "I'm sorry about Z-boy. He was an original, that's for sure. Nutty, but original."

Logan held on for a moment. He never had this kind of moment with his dad. "I made it through the rapids," he said.

"I know you did, kid," Buddy replied sadly. "Now we're both in the same boat." He held on a minute longer, then let him go. "Come on, I have something for you."

Logan flinched. "Um, look, you don't owe me anything—"

"Shut up," he said warmly. "It's not from me."

Buddy put his arm around Logan's shoulder and led him inside to the garage at the back of the house. He opened the door. It was dark inside.

Logan stepped back.

"Relax, dude. Check it out." He flicked on the light. The Hummer was gone.

Logan scratched his head. "Where's the Hummer?"

Buddy chuckled. "Broza took it. He was going to go collect his other assets too, which are all under other people's names. I guess he was cashing out." Buddy hit the garage door opener.

They walked toward the driveway in the back alley. As the garage door opened, Logan saw Broza's old Ford Taurus sitting there in all its boring splendor.

"But he left *that* for you. Said you could use some wheels."

Logan shook his head and chuckled. "What a guy."

Buddy slapped his hand on the hood. "You know, Broza didn't make any dough from the last deal. And well, it pretty much put him outta business. But he thought you should get paid somehow, so here it is."

"It runs, I assume?" Logan asked.

"Sure, it runs. That's why it's America's rental car. It'll take you where you need to go."

Logan looked it over. It would do. "Do you know where Broza is?"

Buddy's face turned grim. "He's laying low. Broza buried stashes of cash all over California. I think he took a road trip to collect all his earnings, then head south to Mehico. He'll give me a call when he's settled."

Logan muttered, "At least someone is going to Mexico."

"Hey, you still going away to college?" Buddy asked.

Logan lowered his eyes. "Not right now. Gonna take some time off. You know, get my head straight."

Buddy nodded. "Well, look, after you take some time, come see me. I could use that head of yours to help me run the shop. I'm thinking of expanding."

"You mean a *job*?" Logan asked, letting the word settle in his mouth.

He smiled. "I like to think of it as a way of life, kid."

Logan nodded. Then he noticed Fin's board standing in the corner of the garage.

50

LOGAN WAS ITCHING to go surfing. When reports came in that the September swells were on their way, Logan needed only two things: Fin's board and Z-boy.

Buddy gave him Fin's board. Said he'd rather see it in the ocean than gathering dust in his garage. Logan said he'd try to make Fin proud.

Six weeks had passed before Logan got the courage to go see Z-boy's parents again. He had written them numerous e-mails, telling them how much Z-boy had meant to him, that he'd gone along with Z to try to protect him. After a few e-mails, they wrote back, and soon they had a reluctant correspondence.

Logan eventually asked about Z-boy's ashes, wanting to know if he might be able to scatter them in Z's favorite place—the ocean off of Pier Avenue. A week passed, then Logan received a call. They wanted to keep half of his ashes, but if he wanted, he could spread the other half in the Pacific.

Logan marked the occasion by finally getting a tattoo. He went to the tattoo parlor where Z-boy got his. He looked through their catalog of designs until he found one Z-boy would've liked. After a couple hours of pain, Logan stared at his raw shoulder in the mirror.

The tat showed a surfboard planted in the sand with Z-BOY written on the board as a logo. Underneath it said SURF AND LIVE.

Logan and Emmie stood on the cool sands, just north of the pier. They had been surfing this spot since they were in middle school together, but the waves had never been so perfect. Not as big as last time, but still, some powerful breakers were on display. The waves were firing and everyone was out there looking for that perfect ride.

"Does it hurt?" she asked, touching the tattoo.

"Still a little sensitive, but it's okay. Might sting in the water."

They watched the waves together.

"Think you can do this?" Emmie asked.

"I was gonna ask you the same thing," he answered, unsure. He could feel the pounding of the surf in the ground they were standing on. "If you mean my ankle, it's fine."

"No, I meant . . ." She looked down at the plastic bag holding Z-boy's ashes.

Logan nodded at the bag in his hands. "Seems weird . . . that he could fit into a baggie. He looks just like the sand."

Emmie held his arm. "He would have been dying to hit these waves." When she realized she had used the word *dying,* she grew flustered. "I mean, he would've wanted this."

Logan smiled at her mistake, then started laughing.

"It's not . . . funny," she protested, confused.

"Z-boy in a baggie. How perfect is that? He used to carry his weed in one of these, now *he's* in one!"

Emmie eyed him with concern.

"We should just roll him up and smoke him," he added as an afterthought.

"That's sick, Logan." Emmie chuckled.

Logan took a deep breath and exhaled. He could feel the mist from the white water on his throat. The taste of the ocean made him feel whole again. "You know, no matter what changes or how old we get or who moves away or who dies, this ocean will always be here. This sand and these waves, it's just like when we were growing up." He smiled thoughtfully. "No matter what goes down, I'll always feel happiest in the ocean."

Emmie nodded. "Then let's get happy."

They grabbed their boards and hit the water.

The surf was big and powerful. Getting out to where the waves broke was a battle against a mighty current. Logan had tucked the baggie into his wet suit. Having Z-boy so close to him felt like he was inside of Logan in a weird way. Logan thought he could hear Z-boy say, *Come on, man. Get your butt out there! We got waves to catch, brah! Today's the day!*

Emmie was quick and light. Every time the white water hit them, she dove underneath on her board and popped out the other side effortlessly. Logan felt sluggish. It had been a while, and his arms were already exhausted.

"Come on, we're almost there!" Emmie shouted through the crashing surf.

The waves were big, maybe ten- or twelve-foot breaks, but the angles were amazing. Logan watched some other surfers cranking off unreal rides—getting tubed in hollowed-out curls so big they could stand up straight. It seemed like the ocean was toying with him, saying, *What're you waiting for, brah?*

So far though, the surf seemed to be kicking his ass. For every ten feet he progressed, it felt like he fell back another twelve. Suddenly, a huge breaker exploded right in front of him, sending him tumbling off his board.

After five seconds of figuring out which way was up, he shot up out of the water and gasped for air. "Goddamn it, give me a break already." He looked for the next wave to bury him, but suddenly there was a lull. Emmie was ahead about twenty yards.

"You okay?" she mouthed, trying not to embarrass him in front of the other surfers. He waved her off, and reeled in his board. When he got back on, he powered ahead with all his might before the next set began. Finally, out of breath, he glided up next to her.

She smiled. "Hey there, sailor. New to these parts?"

He nodded, catching his breath. Only the very best guys were out there, mostly the younger members of The Hall or Buddy's surf team. He glanced over at the pier. A large crowd had gathered to watch the big waves.

"What am I doing out here?" he asked, remembering the last time.

"Surfing. That's what you do, Logan." Emmie sat up when she saw the next wave approaching. "You coming?"

Logan watched the wave rise up before him. "No, you catch this one. I'll get the next one."

She nodded, then swung her board around and paddled into the wave.

"I love you, Logan Tom."

Logan watched Emmie disappear down the face. He could hear her yelling gleefully as she caught a righteous angle.

He would tell her the same later.

Logan felt the current suddenly heading out to sea. A monster wave was coming. He reached into his suit and pulled out the baggie, clenching it in his teeth as he waited.

The wave roared up in front of him, exposing a perfect ride to his left as he swung his board around. He couldn't believe his luck. And he was the only one in position to get it.

Logan paddled hard. The ocean floor dropped out and then, it was like he was flying, skimming down the face faster than he'd ever been on a board. The wave unfolded effortlessly before his eyes. The big lip of the curl started to form a tube around him.

Let it rip, brah! he heard Z-boy shout. Logan tore open the baggie. The ashes flew out, swirling around him as he sailed through the giant hollowed-out barrel.

And for that moment, a few seconds by his watch, but an eternity for Logan Tom, everything that had happened to him over the last three months seemed to fall away. Maybe the wave would crush him, or maybe he'd be in for the ride of his life. For now, it didn't matter. Logan Tom had finally found the perfect wave.

ACKNOWLEDGMENTS

—To everyone in my writers groups: Teddie Aggeles, Nina Wright, M. K. Buhler, Rebecca Gall, Sue LaNeve, Mickey Davis, Karen Bachman, Molli Nickell, Nancy Cavenaugh and others, who not only asked for more when this tale began as a short story, but saw it all the way through to the end, and literally forced me to send it out when I was thinking of shelving it. Always listen to your writers group.

—To my agent, Edward Necarsulmer IV, who spoke to me before I was ready to talk to agents and convinced me to show him this book before I thought it was done. He never doubted or wavered in his loyalty to this story. Plus, anybody who likes Dylan is okay by me . . .

—To my editor, Stacey Barney, who despite being a scrappy

Brooklyn gal far from the shores of Southern California, got this story better than anyone else. I learned—you can't always judge a book by its cover. She's a good person to have in your corner.

—To the SCBWI and the many author and illustrator friends I have made through it, including everyone in the Class of 2K7, my debut authors group. You've journeyed with me into the big, scary world of publishing and made it more fun that it should've been. And a special nod to Carrie Jones, who even though she had never read my work, convinced Edward N. that I was somehow really good and worth getting into business with.

—To L. P. for being such a free spirit and truly unique person. Thanks for sharing your memories. And for the two Matts, who took the surf-mule journey to live a life without rules, but didn't make it back.

—To my bud Doug Ertman, for his never-ending support and friendship. We started a screenplay many, many years ago about muling that never came to fruition, and somehow that notion was reborn as a young adult novel. Go figure. Thanks for your blessings.

—To Mom and Dad, Oma and Opa, my brothers, my lifelong pal Steven Lovy, and most important, my wife, Maggie, and our daughter, Zola, who never questioned my leaving a high-paying executive position for living the life of a writer. Even if they had their doubts, they always thought what I did was great and still do. Thanks, Maggie, for understanding and keeping us alive.

—And finally, to young men everywhere who dare to read.

ABOUT THE AUTHOR

G. Neri is an ALA Notable author who writes teen fiction for boys. He spent most of his life in Manhattan Beach, Santa Cruz, and Venice, California, where he was always happiest in the ocean (especially if there were good waves). He now lives with his wife and daughter somewhere on the Gulf Coast of Florida, where the water is warm and the sand white, but where there is a noticeable lack of wave action. To compensate, he surfs the web and can usually be found at www.gneri.com. *Surf Mules* is his first novel.